CRIMSON CROSS

A CHARLIE STONE
CRIME NOVEL

Crimson Cross: A Charlie Stone Crime Novel

www.trevortwohig.com
tjtwohig1@yahoo.co.uk

ISBN: 9798677047329

This novel is dedicated to the memory of Jim Woodward

Alan and Norm Forever x

PROLOGUE

'The thing is, I love the fact that she is there for me and doesn't mind me going out with...' Carl said.

'...The boys? She doesn't mind because she is out with her girls and enjoying herself!'

'Leave it out mate she is loyal to me. Isn't she?'

'Well, I don't know. You need to make it clear tonight though. if you want Sam to be with you, tell her.'

'Here, Jonno. Come down here. It will be a bit quicker this way...' Carl said.

'Whatever mate, I'm freezing...'

'My ex used to live around here, that's her dad's garage...'

'What the hell is that!?'

'Jesus!'

'Is that what I think it is!? Quick, call an ambulance!'

++++++++++++++++++++++++++++++++

1

'Dad, this is boring!' my six-year-old daughter, Maddie said, as she hopped out of the wooden chair and onto my lap.

'I know, darling. I know,' I replied, recalling her journey here which involved: two separate police escorts, a change of vehicle in an NCP car park and a helicopter.

You've probably always wondered why police helicopters are out and about?

Well, the truth is, it is sometimes to catch criminals or save you from the bad guys, and at other times it's to cover up police mess, total mess. This time it was my mess.

'Let's go out and ride the bikes, Dad,' Maddie grumbled as I moved her from my lap, placing her in the middle of the makeshift sofa.

'You know we can't leave the house. What about the toys in your room?' I asked, losing patience.

'It is not my room!' she replied, pumping her fists and exiting towards the bedroom, she so swiftly maligned.

Tara looked at me from across the room, and sensing my mood, moved into the kitchen. I was like a grizzly bear, aggressive and frustrated. I knew it was rubbing off on my fiancé and daughter, but what could I do?

Since Mr Green's death and his wife Jennifer Green's subsequent escape, we went into hiding.

The phone rang, and I jumped up to get it, desperate for a way out of this incarceration.

'Hello?'

'Charlie, it's Darren. How you holding up?' It was DCI Jackson, the new boss for East Kent.

'Darren, you need to get me out of here. Honestly, I'm tearing at the walls mate…'

'Calm down, Charlie! You are going to be there for a good few weeks yet, I'm afraid.'

'Weeks? Are you kidding me? What the hell is going on?' my voice raised and Tara's eyes bore into me from the kitchen worktop where she was standing. I tried to quell my anger.

'It's not safe yet. We still don't have any leads on Jennifer Green's whereabouts. It's most likely she is overseas, somewhere in Europe, but she hasn't reared her head yet.'

'What about Gibson?' I asked.

'The supposedly dead and buried Nikki Gibson, who you mysteriously saw open a car door for Green in Folkestone? That Nikki Gibson?' Darren replied.

I moved around the frayed green sofa and turned my back to the kitchen. I spoke in a low voice so Tara and Maddie couldn't hear. Police protection was liveable, but certainly not roomy.

'Listen, Darren. Don't take the piss here, mate. I know you're my new boss and everything, but I know what I saw. Gibson is alive; she is still working for Green. I know it,' I whispered into the receiver. There was a pause.

'For what it's worth, Charlie, I believe you. But all I'm saying is, officially, Gibson is dead. As far as the CPS and the rest of homicide are concerned, she is as dead as our old friend Mr Green,' Darren said.

I winced at this flippant comment. Darren Jackson was an excellent DCI, another DFL'er who had done well in a London nick, Hackney to be precise, one of the worst boroughs for homicide and gun crime in London. But despite his cocky, cockney wit, he wasn't there during the Amy Green case. He didn't see Mr Green's body hanging high above the seafront. He didn't hear the children's screams. Maddie's screams.

'And Mr Green?' I asked.

'Well, he was dead before they strung him up…'

'…let me guess, asphyxiation?'

'Bingo, Charlie. How did you know?'

'Call it an educated guess. Darren, while these killers are out there, no-one is safe. This sick stuff is going to go on; I need to…'

'… Charlie, listen to me!' Darren raised his voice. 'You said it yourself. It's not safe. We can't crack the case if something happens to you. What if, heaven forbid, something happens to Tara or…'

'…Yes, OK, I get it. But weeks? Come on! I need to be out of here before that! I'm useless in here.' I said, the frustration seeping out of me.

'Try and stay calm. Spend time with your family, rest up, Charlie. I'll give you a call in a few days. OK?'

'Fine, boss.'

The line went dead and I placed the receiver down.

Tara and Maddie were standing in the doorway to the kitchen, looking expectantly at me.

'What did he say?' Tara asked as she dried a plastic ladle in her hand with a red dishcloth.

'Do you want the truth?' I asked them, knowing the response already.

'Of course, Dad, you must always tell the truth! That's what you always say to us!' Maddie waggled her finger at me, and we all smiled.

'The truth is… we could be here a little while longer, a couple of weeks or so…'

Tara turned away, disappointed. Before Maddie had time to register, I ran at her, picked her up and carried her upside down to the makeshift sofa. She started giggling as I tickled under her arms and on her tummy. Wriggling like a worm, she was a mess of bright clothes and flesh. Now howling and snorting, the way only little kids do, when they are genuinely in the moment, truly happy.

Tara turned and smiled, joining us on the sofa. 'See, it won't be that bad! We'll have some proper family time,' I said. I was putting a brave face on it. I knew this time away from the job would hurt me more than my family. In any case, Maddie went back to her Mum tomorrow, so thankfully she could return to some semblance of normality. I looked through the net curtain at the Dover sky; cloudy and dark. 'So, who fancies getting out on the bikes if we can?' I said, changing my mind from earlier.

'Yes, Dad!' Maddie said, jumping up and down and pushing directly on my bladder. Tara didn't look as keen.

'OK, let me see what I can do.'

I went over to the CB radio that was sitting on the sideboard in the living room.

'DS Stone to DC Bullen, you reading?' there was no response, just the sound of white noise. My trusty DCs were in an unmarked car that was opposite the flat in central Dover that we were currently staying in. Well, at least they were supposed to be.

'Karl? Jimmy? Get off your phones. It's Charlie. Do you copy?' Silence, once more.

'Is everything all right?' Tara asked.

'Dad?' Maddie said, moving towards me.

'Karl!? Jim!?' I shouted, looking through the

window, my heart started to race. I felt a little panicked. Our whereabouts were supposedly secret.

If anything happened to these guys, then my family was vulnerable; it was as simple as that. 'DC Bullen!?' I replied for a final time. There was a rustling on the line.

'DC Bullen here, hi Charlie,' Karl sounded out of breath.

'What on earth is going on?' I demanded.

'Well, erm… we were just getting some lunch, to be honest…' Jimmy replied sheepishly.

'Oh great, well I hope it was something nice?' I said and waited like a disappointed mother for a response.

'Erm, yeah, KFC actually…we got you guys some too…?' the voice came from the receiver. I couldn't quite believe what I was hearing. I know surveillance can be quite dull, but it would be nice to know I had some back up when I needed it.

'Not for me. KFC is really bad for you, and they are really mean to the chickens,' Maddie said as she put her shoes on. I smiled at her proudly.

'No, we're fine thanks, boys,' I said a little disappointed. Some greasy take away would probably cheer me up in the short term, but Maddie was right.

'So, lads, now you have had your lunch, any chance of us getting out for a bit, maybe on the bikes?' I asked. Technically, these two numbskulls would be our 'protection' if and when we left the safety of the house.
'All quiet out here, boss. I think you'll be fine.'
'Yes!' Maddie said, with a fist pump. 'Come on Dad, let's get out of here!'

2

Despite the all-clear from Karl and Jimmy, I was anxious and nervous about being away from the safe house. Tara stayed in; she wasn't into sport at all. No matter how much I tried to convince her to do some exercise, it was to no avail.

It worked though, she got to chill at home and I got to have some time with Maddie before she goes back tomorrow.

The sun was shining through the clouds and we decided to go to the park which was situated at the end of this long straight road filled with terraced houses. We were in a flat block at the far end, generally reserved for prostitutes and drug addicts. The Kent Police kept a relatively sanitised two-bedroom flat at all times, which was our current home.

There was excellent visibility at either end, which made life easier for Karl and Jimmy. They decided to follow us on foot. Maddie found it amusing to speed away on her bike, making the guys run after her. I had to admit I found it pretty funny too.

We got to the park and I marvelled at how quickly Maddie had picked up how to cycle. She was so much quicker than she used to be. She knew how to use the gears correctly and could turn entirely without having to put her feet on the floor. I was very proud of her.

'Dad, can we have a rest, yeah?' She did, however, get tired quickly. We got off our bikes and laid them on the grass. Maddie sat down and took off her helmet. I followed her lead as the boys sat down twenty yards away from us.

'Why do we have to stay here again, Dad?' Maddie asked, playing with a daisy she had picked from the ground.

'We need to be safe. Remember the bad people who tried to hurt me last year?'

'Yeah…but can't you catch them?'

'I will catch them, honey, we just need to stay out of the way for a while. But after that, I'm going to make sure I get them, OK?'

'OK. They're not going to hurt you again are they, Dad?' Maddie asked and for the first time, her face looked at mine.

'Not this time, darling. I promise. I'll catch them; then we can go home, back to Folkestone. To our old house. All right?' Maddie sighed. 'Yes, Dad. I'd like that.'

I could sense she was deflating. Her youthful brain could not contend with the criminals and killers of this world. Maddie just wanted her life back to normal. Or as normal as it could be being the daughter of Charlie Stone; the poor kid.

'Right, the last one to the playground buys the ice creams!' I shouted and ran for my bike. A smile spread across Maddie's face as she ran to hers.

I let her win and after we went on the swings. I took her to the ice cream truck and bought us both a 99 with a flake. Maddie sat and I watched the sugary mess drip all around her face and down her top. I didn't care though. Even in the darkest times, life could be beautiful.

3

We got back on the bikes and headed home just before dusk.

Tara was on the sofa watching Tipping Point. Ben Shephard's friendly face was beaming back at me from the screen. He looked happy and free; I was jealous.

'How was your cycle?' Tara asked.

'Good! We had ice cream,' Maddie confessed, giggling, knowing I'd be in trouble for forgetting to bring one back.

'Daddy, you know I love ice cream!' Tara looked at me, smiling, joking. I looked at Maddie. She hid her cheeky face behind a cushion before running off like a guilty party into her bedroom.

'Everything OK here?' I asked, knowing that nothing really could happen, but making polite conversation.

'Yeah, but you've received a package,' Tara said.

'Righto, what a special delivery from Harrods is it?' I laughed.

'No seriously, Charlie. You have a delivery. I found it on the doorstep. I heard some noise out the front and thought you guys had come back. I went to check and there it was, sitting on the step.'

'What? And you brought it inside? Where is it? It could be anything!' I said, perplexed that Tara would not only open the door but also bring a strange package in the house.

'I haven't opened it, Charlie. Relax!' she said. 'Let's face it if someone wanted us to be, you know…' she put her finger to her throat and moved it side to side, 'then that probably would have happened by now, wouldn't it?'

I mulled it over and avoided the argument. Tara was right. If the package was a bomb, why would whoever left it have made sure Tara heard them drop it off?

'Fair point. Where is it?' I asked.

'I left it on the kitchen side.'

I got up immediately and went to check it out. I looked at the package. It was about two inches thick, just over A4 size and covered in brown paper. The name Charlie Stone had been written in thick black ink on the front.

It was solid and when I turned it over carefully, it was wrapped perfectly, like an envelope and tied together with string. I sensed Tara was standing next to me. She was intrigued, as was I, at what might be inside.

I tore the package open and revealed a red, velvet cover. Embossed on the front were the words, 'Original Sin.' The initials TW were written at the bottom.

I opened the cover to reveal a message, handwritten inside:

Dear Charlie,

As you know, I left teaching to become a writer. Well, here it is, my first book. Hopefully, it will help you.

Best,

Troy.

Troy Wood, the English teacher, framed for the murder of Amy Green. I thought back to last year and the turmoil he went through. Fingered for a crime that he didn't commit, forced to live in fear and terror, his family threatened.

I was pleased for him, glad he had managed to get his life back on track and that he had a future. But right now, I had no interest in reading his memoirs. I had bigger fish to fry, catching Jennifer Green and her associates. Sadly, I didn't have time for works of fiction.

4

It was 8.23 pm on a Friday night. Tara was pottering around, straightening hair with Maddie. I could hear giggles and quiet 'girl' chat from the bedroom. They seemed able to handle the situation far better than me.

I was restless, anxious.

What was Troy Wood doing? I wondered. Why was the book hand delivered and who by? It wasn't a DHL or FedEx job; there was no postage. So how did he know where we were? I thought it best not to pass this on to Darren. I liked the guy, and he was somewhat laid back, but he was also wholly straight and didn't like cutting corners. As much as he was becoming a pal, he would be scared, and he would uproot us again to somewhere even more remote and desperate. And what's worse than being uprooted? Being uprooted twice.

I could smell something fruity, light and uplifting and in wandered Maddie; seven years old, going on seventeen. Her hair was straight, and she was wearing some of Tara's expensive perfume.

She smiled as she walked towards me and I smiled back.

No matter how frustrated I was, I had my

family with me. Anger subsided.

'What ya watching, Dad?'

I looked at the screen for the first time this evening.

'Oh nothing,' I handed her the remote.

She sat down next to me and snuggled into my chest. She changed the channel, and I kissed her forehead.

Tara's footsteps followed from the bedroom. She serenely surveyed the scene, before rubbing my head affectionately.

She poured us a large 'team squash' in the adjoining open-plan kitchen, before settling down in the comfy chair just to our right.

She had Troy's book on the arm of her chair. She perused it and paused. I watched her from the corner of my eye.

I knew her and Troy were friends before all of last year's drama. I knew she liked him. I mean, he was a likeable guy. In a short time, I had become reasonably good pals with him, meeting for coffee and texting to make sure his life was going well.

He had been immersed in this book and it was finally here. The last thing I needed was reminding of the horrors of the Amy Green case. I am glad he got out of a job he hated through that book, but it was too raw for me. There it was, the stab in the gut; guilt, shame.

I'm sorry, Polly. I should have protected you. Another kind soul doomed, thanks to Charlie Stone.

'Dad, are you OK?' Maddie asked, clearly sensing my anxiety.

'Of course, sweetheart.' I replied. I wasn't.

I looked over at Tara. The book was on her lap, open.

5

'Sleep tight, my angel.' I heard Tara say as she pulled Maddie's bedroom door shut.

My mood dropped.

I loved the evening when Maddie was around: the TV, the dinner, the team drinks. It was innocent and kept my mind in a safer place.

Tara came to the doorway.

'Do you need anything, handsome?

I didn't feel handsome or useful or good in any way. I was trapped in this hovel and legally, I needed to stay. The safety of my family depended on it.

'No, thanks,' I replied.

Tara gauged the mood.

'I'm going to go to bed and read.'

'Sure.' I replied.

Troy's book, no doubt. She would much rather be reading about him than spending time with me. Still, I looked down at myself. I was a mess. I couldn't blame her.

I picked myself up from the sofa and went to the kitchen.

I took out a bottle of Russian Standard vodka from the fridge and poured myself a large glass, straight.

I took a large gulp and refilled it, then headed

back to the sofa and the endless TV. At least the drink stopped the voices in my head for a while.

+++++++++++++++++++++++++++++++++

I woke to the sounds of shuffling outside of the front door.

I checked my wrist, no watch. I moved to grab my phone and felt the dull ache in my skull. I knocked the empty bottle of vodka over while grabbing the phone, which caused an almighty clunk on the floor, but mercifully it did not smash.

5.46 am. I was pleased. I usually was awake around 3.30 am like a light, alone with my thoughts and unable to get back to sleep.

The shuffling got louder and turned into scratching.

I got up quietly and went to check on Tara and Maddie; both were sound asleep. I crept to the side of the front door feeling for heat and potential fire, but it wasn't that.

The sound came again, and this time was more muffled. It sounded like rats.

I felt for the door handle and slowly moved it down. I knew with every movement the door creaked, so I pulled it open as quickly as I could and the unsteady frame of my old friend Dave

Woodward fell like a sack of potatoes into the doorway.

I checked the pavement outside the flat for anything else suspicious. All seemed calm, so I shut the door as Dave slowly got to his feet.

'Charlie! I found you...' his big, joker-like grin spread maniacally across his face as he pulled me in for a hug.

I embraced him; it was lovely to see him.

'Good to see you mate, but keep it down...' I pointed towards the bedrooms.

Dave nodded and made his way to the kitchen. He poured him and me a glass of water.

'Take it, Charlie; you stink of booze,' he said.

'I was thinking of having a drink to take the edge off my hangover...'

Dave shot me a warning glance; I took the water.

'So, to what do I owe this pleasure...?' I asked.

'Well, I have been trying to find you, but they did a good job of hiding you,' he said.

'Not that good though...you and Troy Wood have been able to find me.'

Dave grabbed what looked like a very technical walkie-talkie and waved it at me. I pretended to know what that meant, but he was always far more technically minded than me.

'Cool... you know it's like... before 6 am?'

'No, I didn't, I've been working and that's why

I needed to speak to you. I have some information that might be of interest.'

My ears pricked, Dave rifled through his bag. 'Some bad news, Charlie. You need to take a look.'

Sounded about right: darkness, violence and bad news equal Charlie Stone.

Dave removed some A4 photographs from his man bag.

'Jesus...' the pictures were shocking. What looked like a teenager… or at least what was left of him.

'A young boy from Hawkinge, found last night by some lads heading to the pub,' Dave said.

'Hawkinge?'

'Yep, believe it or not.'

'The state of him... '

'Yes, pretty gruesome. The force over there are extremely unsettled. I thought you might want to... you know, take a look,' Dave said furtively.

'Yeah but you know I can't leave here. It's not safe.'

Dave shot me a sideways glance.

'Well, we could always sneak you out...' he said.

'Yeah...' I smiled, the thought of getting back to work. 'We could, give me a minute.'

'See, Charlie, there are benefits to being an early riser!' Dave smiled at me, filling up his glass with tap water.

I went into the bedroom and got back into bed. Tara turned over and harrumphed in her sleep. 'Hun..?' I touched her arm. It was warm and soft, and I realised in my melancholy what I had been missing.

'Why are you waking me up?' she said grumpily.

'I'm not, stay asleep...'

'...What time is it...?'

'Don't worry, sweet. It's just I need to go out with Dave for a bit...'

'Dave? Wh...? Are we allowed to go home?'

'Well...err... soon hopefully... I love you, stay here and I'll be back later, OK?'

'But, Charlie… it's not safe...'

'It will be fine. Don't worry.'

I kissed her on the top of her head and fortunately she stopped questioning me and went back to sleep.

Next was Maddie's room. She was out for the count, so I left her.

Dave was at the front door.

'Ready?'

6

'The first problem is getting past the boys,' I said.

'Leave Karl and Jimmy to me. When you get an opportunity, jump out and head to the car. I parked it around the corner.'

'What car?'

'You'll know when you see it,' he said, smiling. Dave burst out of the door in a mock-rage. Through the glass panel, I saw him engage Jimmy and Karl, who were diligently standing guard.

'Hi, Dave. How are you? Long-time no see…' Karl started.

'No time for pleasantries lads…. he's not in the property. You are supposed to be looking after him, where is he!?'

'We've been here the whole time! How did he…?'

'I think he's at the garage on Sydney Street. If you get him back in the next four minutes, I'll keep this under my hat.'

The DCs started the car and sped off, clearly panicked. Dave, although retired, was a legend in East Kent. He had worked with both Karl and Jimmy and been DCI to both of them.

I nipped around the corner, Dave, not far

behind.

Then I noticed Dave's car, sticking out like a sore thumb in the early morning Dover gloom. I wasn't sure what it was, but it was big, bold, American and… lime green.

'New toy?' I said, moving around to the passenger side.

'Dodge Charger, 1969. Get a load of this.'

Dave got into the driver's seat and turned the key in the ignition.

There was a loud, throaty roar as he put his foot to the silver metal of the pedal. I shut the door and looked impressed, although cars were never really my thing.

'Let me guess; you are responsible for this paint job?' I asked.

'Of course,' he said, smiling.

'Oh, well, that's good. At least we won't stand out.'

He pulled out and headed along the coast and back inland.

7

The A20 from Dover back into Kent is a beautiful stretch.

As the sea falls away to your left, rolling hills appear across the vista and for a moment, East Kent becomes something quite magnificent.

The majesty of England's green and pleasant land was short-lived, as in only a few miles Dave was taking the slip road and we were climbing the hill to Hawkinge.

The road turns into a dual carriageway and a lad in a fiesta tries to overtake, Dave gently puts his foot down and the Dodge growls into life and leaves the car far behind.

At the top of Spitfire Way, there were two roundabouts before the left turn towards the private hospital.

The body would usually be moved down to Folkestone or Ashford, but Jackson understandably wanted this kept quiet.

Crimes of this nature are not familiar, let alone in a village such as this.

Dave parked up, leaving a bit of distance between the building and the car.

'I'll check if it's clear, Charlie.'

In the eyes of the police force, I needed to stay in the safe house. Being out risked my job.

Dave ambled to the door and disappeared inside.

I checked my phone. I had a voice note from Tara and Maddie telling me to be safe.

If they were angry at me for leaving, they didn't show it. A wave of gratitude passed through me.

Dave came to the entrance and signalled me in. Through the main door of the building was another smaller door to the right. Inside was a table with the body covered in a beige sheet. There was a doctor in a white coat standing over the table.

'Doctor Randall, this is…'

'…I know who this is. Charlie Stone, your reputation precedes you,' the doctor held out his hand. I shook it.

'Charlie needs to see this, given the... you know...'

'Yes, I understand. OK...' the doctor pulled back the sheet and revealed a heavily brutalised male torso. His legs were missing.

'As you can see, a lot of the body is missing. The legs, the bottom jaw is missing too. It would appear this has been torn or ripped off in some way.'

'How...?' I asked feeling a bit nauseous about what was in front of me. I had to remember that this was, in fact, somebody's son.

'Difficult to say really. Maybe a machine of some description. There doesn't seem to be any high impact, which was my first thought. This mutilation has been done slowly, over time…' the Doctor stated.

'Look at the eyes, Charlie,' Dave muttered under his breath.

The whites were discoloured, black in fact.

'The boy's bottom half...?' I asked tentatively.

The doctor shrugged, 'No idea. As I said, it looks like some form of repeated pulling has caused this.'

'And that is what's caused the death?' I asked.

'Difficult to say at this stage, but what is clear is that this is a case of extreme torture. I have never seen anything like this. This poor boy may well have died from sheer pain.'

Silence fell across the room.

'We have to find who did this, Charlie, before it happens again.' Dave said.

There was movement at the door and in bustled DCI Jackson and DC's Jimmy and Karl.

'Here you are, Jesus, we've been looking all over for you!' DCI Jackson said.

'Sorry, err... I can explain...' I muttered, feeling very much like I was in serious trouble again.

'No time for that. Since the infamous Charlie Stone has made it from Dover to Hawkinge in a luminous Dodge Charger, I guess we're OK, aren't we? You might as well be back at work at the station. Anyway, guess who's popped her head back up? That's right, Jennifer Green. She certainly doesn't seem bothered about you – no offence. DS Stone, you're back on duty. Get your things together and report to my office as soon as possible,' Jackson said, matter of factly. I couldn't hide my elation.

'Oh, and bring your mate too,' Jackson continued.

As the DCI left, Dave looked at me and raised an eyebrow.

I smiled - we were back.

8

I went back home to see the girls and explained to them the situation. I took a quick shower and grabbed my badge, then made my way to the nick.

Homicide in East Kent had now moved to Ashford, but it was no problem, only ten minutes extra for me in the car.

The payoff was that the station was newer and shinier and most importantly, the coffee was better!

I made my way to the second floor and knocked on Jackson's door. He nodded at me as I entered; Dave was already there waiting. He flashed up some photographs on his computer screen and I inspected them.

'Do these ring any bells with you? We pulled them from CCTV on Pelham Gardens,' he said slowly.

'Where the Greens live?'

Dave showed me a pixelated video of a mid-sized woman jumping out of a Land Rover and entering the Green house.

'Jennifer Green…?'

'Difficult to say, but likely. Who else would have access to the house? We have been watching it for months and no-one has been in and out. It was left empty. This is the first movement there since the case,' Dave said.

'No, that's her. So, what happened?'

Dave fast-forwarded the video of Pelham Gardens. Three minutes and thirty-four seconds later she leaves, locks the house, gets back into the Land Rover's passenger side and drives off.

'Hmmm… not much to go on. Green's not driving though…'

'No, so who is?'

'Good question. Did you track it?' I asked.

'Yes! Headed to Heathrow.'

'Going abroad?'

'Flight 753 – headed for Copenhagen.' DCI Jackson stated.

9

'I guess our first port of call is the alley where the body was found, after that who knows,' I said.

'Yes, get up there and see what you can find. Be sensitive though; we don't want this getting out,' Jackson said.

'What about the guys who found the body?' I asked.

'They've been offered counselling and signed an NDA, so they don't spread this. The last thing we need is a community running around terrified.'

I went to gather my car keys and wallet. 'And erm, about…me?' Dave muttered. He was technically retired and was no longer in the employ of the Kent Police.

Jackson, who was already making his way out of the office, stopped. 'Well, you had better go with him, eh? On an agency basis, daily rate.' Dave's eyebrows raised, and a small smile appeared on his face.

'Well go on then!' Jackson shouted.

+++++++++++++++++++++++++++++++

The alleyway was in the centre of town in a

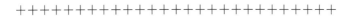

highly residential area.

We took my car, Dave left the Dodge at the station, but we decided to park a road away. The less attention, the better.

We walked towards the site where the body was, thanks to Dave's coordinates. The coppers who took the initial call had cleared the area; no police sign, tape or anything.

'Here,' Dave stopped. There was a pile of leaves and some old branches that had fallen. I knelt and moved the leaves gently; we searched the entire ground area and found nothing of note, not even a drop of blood left. Very strange. I looked up and noticed something shiny hanging in the tree. I jumped up and caught it, surprised the forensics team had missed it. I suppose they were so busy with the clean-up operation and, given the short time frames Jackson had given them, I was amazed they had done such a great job with the rest of the site. It was a necklace, hanging from it a gold cross with a bright red rose in the middle.

'What do you make of this then?' I asked Dave. 'No idea, but it's a start. Leave it with me and I will get forensics to look at it.'

'How comes the SOCO didn't find that then?' I asked.

Dave shrugged. 'Short-staffed I think, so they only have an amount of time to spend at each crime.'

'Even for something like this, Dave? A grisly murder?'

'Well, either that or it was too high up. Perhaps it was a pint-size SOCO who was called out?' Dave was smiling at himself.

'Well, either way, we best get it checked out.' I had a look into the garden that backed onto this alley. It was quiet with nothing to report. I wanted to knock on the front door of the house and see if they heard anything, but the Chief's words rang loudly in my ears about keeping a low profile.

'Shall we head back then?' I asked.

Dave stood in the alleyway, thinking loudly.

'Where were those lads from, who found the body?' he asked.

'Just down the road, one was… Lancaster Drive. Unsure about the others…'

'And where were they headed?' Dave asked.

'Out for "Friday night drinks," Chief said.'

'So, they couldn't have been going to 'The Dragonfly' as why would they walk this way? The 'Fly is south of Lancaster Drive…where else could they be going?' he pondered.

'The only place people go out for drinks around here is the Hockey Club, up on Horseshoes Lane.'

Dave nodded, 'fancy a drink on the way back

down?'

On any given weekend in Hawkinge, the hockey club was well known for debauchery and revelry.

It was chock full of revellers on a Friday night, often had bands or DJs and sold cheap drinks. Given that Hawkinge was on a large hill, a lot of the residents would choose a night out here rather than have to head into Folkestone, where cabs could get expensive.

The time was now 4.32 pm on a Monday, so the club had only just opened, as such we were the only two people in there.

Dave went to the bar and ordered a couple of cokes, and then we sat down outside.

To our left, there was a large hockey pitch. There were a few youngsters who were hitting the ball to one another gently. To our right, more lads were making their way onto the ground.

Dave gulped his coke before motioning to one of the boys to come over.

He did slowly, looking tentatively at Dave.

'Have you got training, young man?' Dave said, somewhat awkwardly.

'Yes. Under-thirteens on Mondays and Saturday,' the boy said.

'I work down at the school and was wondering when there is other training. Any ideas?' Dave continued unconvincingly.

'Adults are on Wednesdays and matches on Saturday I think,' the boy looked over to his pals, desperate to get over there.

'Anyone on Friday nights?' I jumped in.

'Yeah two older groups, I think under-eighteens but not sure…' the boy began running over to the pitch. 'Coach will be here in ten minutes; he will be able to help you.'

'Thanks, young man!' Dave called after him.

'Under-eighteens on a Friday, eh? Could that boy in the alley have been heading up here, do you think?' Dave asked.

I thought about it. It was tenuous. It was the right age bracket, but we were really grasping for connections in this case.

'Possibly, but who knows? We need to get the forensic report and autopsy back. When's it due?' I asked.

'I'll call now and chase it,' Dave said, getting up and heading back towards the clubhouse.

I phoned Tara.

'Hey, Charlie!' she chirped.

'How are my beautiful girls?'

I heard Maddie shout 'hello!' in the background.

'We're good, missing you. When are you going

to be home?' Tara asked.

'Within the next hour, hopefully. Everything OK?'

'Yeah, we moved all of our stuff back to the flat. Maddie was super-helpful. Everything's back to normal. It's just that… oh, it's nothing…' Tara said, sounding a little uneasy.

'What's up sweet...?'

'No, it's just…that book of Troy's. It's not what I expected. It's creepy,' she said.

'Well how about I take my girls out for dinner tonight, my treat? Get out of the house?' I suggested.

'That sounds awesome, but you can't be late. If you are not back in an hour, I'll put something on here.'

She was used to me being late due to work, but I didn't want to let her down tonight. I never wanted to let them down, but time had a habit of slipping like smoke through your fingers in this line of work.

'Get your glad rags on; I'll be back.'

As I said goodbye and put my phone back in my pocket, I noticed a man with a large sports bag entering the clubhouse.

I moved towards him to get a better view, but he was still unclear through the glass.

Dave was still on the phone, and the man with the bag was talking to someone at the bar. As he turned away and made his way to the changing rooms, I noticed his dog collar. He was a priest.

Dave came back outside. I nodded at him and he smiled.

Maybe the gold cross at the crime scene had something to do with this coach, perhaps not. But I was relieved that we finally had our first lead.

11

I got back to the station and dropped Dave off, before heading along the motorway back to Folkestone.

The days of the Dover hovel done, I was made-up to be returning to the creature comforts of home.

I opened the door and walked up the inside staircase to the hallway of our second-floor flat. There was a warm, orange glow from the main front room, drawing me in; home.

I breathed in and smiled, grateful at the feminine touch that Tara had added to the flat... to my life.

Before I knew it, a Tasmanian devil of energy had flown around the corner and into my arms; beautiful Maddie.

'Daddy! We missed you!' she gave me a massive hug and a kiss on the cheek. I was lucky; typically, it was a fist bump.

'I missed you too, sweet,' I replied, overjoyed to be home.

'Yes, yes, Daddy, we missed you massively! However, where are you taking us for dinner?' Tara said, coming into the hallway from the living room, beaming.

She loved our family and me, but she also loved

food.

'Right get ready then. ETD is five minutes,' I said, heading for the shower.

+++++++++++++++++++++++++++++++++

We went around the corner to the Bay Tree Hotel and Restaurant, the only four-star hotel in the town.

For all of Folkestone's regeneration, this fact brought the reality of coastal life home. The town is still in the grips of extreme poverty; nearly a third of residents live below the poverty line.

It's a summer town. Visit on a cold, February evening, and it feels very different. Here we were on a mild November evening, and the streets were quiet.

The sound of the sea washing the coastline provided the soundtrack, as we walked into the magnificent Bay Tree bar. It was incredibly designed, trees growing inside the fixtures and the attracting gold-orange glow that seemed to permeate around the room.

We took our table and I told Tara and Maddie to order whatever they wanted; knowing they would anyway. I felt terrible about how I'd been over the past weeks; caged in and angry. Despite my drinking and general awful mood, it dawned on me how much I had missed them today. The home was certainly where my heart was now; Tara was making the puzzle complete. I made a pact to myself that I would endeavour to be around much more. I loved the job, it was my vocation, but I needed to make my family my vocation. I couldn't make the same mistakes my father did and neglect them.

After the meal, I drove home and we put Maddie to bed.

She was happy, and when I went back to check on her five minutes later, she was fast asleep.

Tara and I also went to bed early. It was around 9.30 pm, and after the time we'd had, we were both exhausted.

It was an incredible feeling… our own bed with fresh bedding. We cuddled, kissed and despite the flashes and pangs of desire, our collective fatigue was too much to handle, so we decided to turn in.

Tara was asleep before I had even turned the light off.

12

I woke up in Tara's arms.

My phone was buzzing incessantly. I tried to ignore it, but I didn't have a voicemail and whoever was on the other end really wanted to speak to me.

I wriggled free and checked the time, at 6.37 am. A night of good sleep for the first time in weeks.

I checked the phone, DCI Jackson was calling. I wasn't due in until later today.

'Hi, boss, what's up?' I asked.

'Charlie! Good news, you're going on holiday,' he said.

'…Wh…What?' I uttered only half wake; Tara stirred next to me.

'Things are hotting up with the Gibson/Green Case. I need you to go to Denmark and chase up some big leads for me.'

'Denmark…?' So much for me staying closer to home.

'Yes, Copenhagen to be exact. Can you get into the station as soon as you can? I'll text you the flight details, but you're heading out from Gatwick mid-afternoon.'

'Sure,' I said and put the phone down. I had a weird mix of feelings. Sad to be leaving the family, but also pleased to be back involved. It was difficult to describe to someone who hadn't been in the force. Being on the job was like a burning inside that just felt right. Time seemed to speed up to the point you didn't even notice it passing by.

'Hey…' Tara said through a muffled yawn.

I came to her side of the bed and kissed her.

I thought it best to bring her a milky cup of tea and two biscuits before breaking it to her that I was on a plane this afternoon.

It wasn't that she didn't want me to work; she just worried about me. Also, the whole family set up must be a shock to her.

A year ago, she was single and going out with her girlfriends in Folkestone.

Now, she is a homemaker with a step-daughter and a slow cooker.

I made the tea and brought it back through to her. She sat up in bed and smiled, sensing something was up.

'Tara, the boss just phoned me. He needs me to go away for a day or two,' I said tentatively.

'OK… I am happy you are back at work, Charlie. It's what you wanted. I'll miss you, of course, so get yourself back soon. Where are you going anyway?'

'I need to chase something in Copenhagen; it might help finish off the Green Case…'

'…Copenhagen? Really?' she said, looking confused.

'Yeah, I know it's not ideal but…'

'… No, it's just in Troy's book, he has just gone to Denmark, to a weird place near Copenhagen too…' she said, trying to piece things together. '…What did it say in the book…?'

'I've wanted to tell you. It's weird, Charlie. Not like you'd expect. There is lots about his childhood and weird religious stuff.'

'Religious?' I asked.

'Yeah, like odd branches of Christianity, you know? A bit kind of cultish…' she trailed off.

'This is important, Tara. It could be connected,' I reached for my phone and googled gold cross rose in middle. I showed Tara the picture.

'Any mention of something like this?'

She nodded slowly, 'Yes! Oh my God! It's like a symbol of this sect that Troy was involved in, let me show you.'

Tara reached for the sizeable velvet-covered book and took a moment to find the section she wanted.

'Here, listen… "the crimson cross is the symbol of the sect. It depicted the beauty and innocence of the natural world, juxtaposed with the power and durability of the movement…."'

'What movement is he on about?' I asked.

'I don't know really… it's been a bit vague. All

it says is how Troy was taken to this Church just outside of Copenhagen and he was meeting some people; the symbol of that cross was outside. That's as far as I've got.'

'Wow… well, keep reading and keep me updated. I need to get in the shower, Darren wants me in ASAP.'

Tara hugged me and smiled. I knew she was sad not to see me but also wanted me to be happy. Solving this case after all of these months that had passed would go a long way to doing that.

13

'Charlie, come in and take a seat.'
I was back in Jackson's office, and after a good night's sleep, I was feeling fresh and ready to go. I'd only been to Copenhagen once when I was younger, so despite the nature of the work, I was looking forward to getting away.
'Let's talk about the body in Hawkinge. Where the body was left, a gold cross was found. Initial forensics have given us nothing, but the cross may have some relevance,' Jackson stated.
'It must have been left there for a reason, it was hanging in the tree,' I added.
'Yes, agreed. The cross is associated with a strain of Christianity that dates back to medieval times…' Jackson continued. 'The crimson cross or 'cramoisi croix,' if you're that way inclined.'
'Yes, I looked into this a bit myself. It's interesting as it can be a symbol for several different things. Like, the cross is representative of Christ and his suffering, but the metal it is made of represents the power of the order or sect behind it.'
'Sect… yes, that is what we hear too,' Jackson interjected. 'Look here.'
Darren fired up the large, flat-screen in his

office.

On it was a black and white photograph of a small, yet ornate church in the middle of a field. 'This is a church on the outskirts of Copenhagen. Look closer…'

Darren zoomed in to reveal the crimson Cross on the side of the old church building, exactly how Tara had described it in Troy's book.

'That's where you want me to go?' I asked.

'Yes, for now…' Jackson started, 'as you know, Green was last spotted in Copenhagen, so I want you to work with the Politi out there to see if you can find her. Get her, and we can find out what the hell is going on here.'

'Wait… do you think the two are related? Green and the crimson Cross?'

'Seems plausible. How often are there murders in Hawkinge? Brutal ones? Of children?' Jackson stated.

'Well, yeah I mean what, the kid was sixteen or seventeen, right? Does seem odd. Maybe Green is letting us know she is still around and at large,' I surmised.

'Quite possibly. Anyway, get your arse in gear, Charlie. You have a flight to catch.'

'Just one thing boss, what do you know about the Hawkinge Hockey Club?'

'Very little. I'm guessing they play hockey there?' he said dryly.

I gave him a wry smile and left the office.

++++++++++++++++++++++++++++++

I got into the car and my first thought was to ring Dave.

'Morning, international traveller!' he said with joviality to his voice that was very welcome, considering the sinister nature of this case.

'Oh, so you have heard then? I'm on my way to the airport now. Any luck with that hockey club?' I asked, as I put the call on to Bluetooth and pulled away.

'Bits and pieces. Some interesting allegations against the guy who runs the bar. But leave it with me, I want to check out a few more leads and see where it takes us,' he said.

'Well… I guess I'll see you in a couple of days,' I said.

'Don't miss me too much, Charlie. I would come with, but the boss wouldn't let me. Wants me to work on the cross and question the victim's parents.'

'Do we even know who the lad was?' I asked.

'Not yet, forensics are back later today.'

'OK, keep me updated.'

14

The flight touched down at Kastrup at 4.40 pm. I managed to sleep on the plane, if only for half an hour, but it had left me feeling woozy and a bit unsettled.

Jackson had sent me details of where I would be staying, so I headed straight for the taxi rank and onwards to my hotel, near the city centre. By the time I arrived, checked in and showered, I felt much fresher.

I checked my phone and I had no work messages, so I sent a brief voice note to Tara, telling her I had arrived safely, then I headed out into the city to enjoy the last of the daylight. Despite the autumnal skies, Copenhagen was as charming as I remember.

I travelled to Tivoli, a colourful Christmas market, surrounded by towering, regal walls. There were white Christmas lights, orange lanterns, chestnuts warming over open fires. It was a magnificent scene, and quite refreshing, no 'hard sell' or overpricing like Winter Haven in London. Just families and couples, wandering around… enjoying.

I sat and had a hot chocolate with a shot of Bailey's in it, to further accentuate the Christmas spirit obviously!

However, the cup wasn't as warm as I'd hoped, and I drank it a little too fast, which made me feel quite tipsy by the time I hit the dregs. Usually, it would take more than that for me to be affected, but I think the flight and the ambience had gone to my head. For once in a long time, I felt at ease; happy being out of control.

I smiled to myself, tempted for another, but thought it wise to get back on my feet and moving again.

There were a handful of touristy bars outside Tivoli, so I decided to take a walk further north and headed into the backstreets.

The time was coming up for 6 pm and the light had almost completely diminished. Workers had finished for the day – as they tend to do on the dot in Denmark. The bars were rapidly filling with drinkers.

I settled on a place, with a green and gold sign called the 'Battling Irons.'

I walked down a few steps and into the gloomy half-light of the nightspot. The bar was busy and loud, which is just what I wanted for now, while I waited out the night. Tomorrow I was meeting up with Arik from the Politi and visiting the church, but now it was about getting my bearings without getting myself into any trouble.

I bought a large glass of beer and sat down at the only spare table there was.

I had a text message from Dave, 'call me when you get this.'

Rather than fight my way and lose my table, I got my headphones from my pocket and plugged them into the phone before calling his number.

'Dave! How's it back in Blighty?' I asked, surprised by the good humour in my voice.

'Cold, grey… you know, the usual. The forensics have arrived on the boy in the alley,' he said.

'Good stuff….' I got out my trusty claret and blue pen that always travels with me, home or away, and a small book. It was a green, faux leather one; my journal. Although I have so many half-filled booklets, I tend to grab the one nearest to hand.

'So, the boy's name is Bryan Rattle. Sixteen years old, would have turned seventeen in January. We've informed the family, he was on the missing persons list since last Thursday.'

'That rules out him heading to hockey practice. Any previous?'

'Nothing at all. Seemed like a good boy. 93% attendance at school, no issues there or with the police.'

'What school was he at?'

'Hang on a minute… the one in Appleton, just been taken over… was called Valley Park…'
'Oh …uh… Frederic Schools?'
'Yep, that's it, good student by all accounts. Got accepted into their sixth form to do Media, Creative Arts and Photography.'
'I see… So, the forensics?'
'Yeah, I hope you're not having dinner…'
'Go on; I am sure I've heard worse…'
'Well… they found vast quantities of pure ethanol in the stomach and traces of barbiturates. So, I guess in some ways that's good as he was anaesthetised.'
'I guess… the lower half?'
'This is where it gets a little… weird… It seems that the pelvic area was serrated over time and some form of device separated the torso and abdomen…'
'Like a torture device?'
'Yes, there wasn't a straight cut; it was as if the…' Dave steeled himself, 'he was…ripped apart…'
'Jesus… it's like something out of the dark ages…'
'Funny, you should say that… I think it was…'
I felt quite unwell. The thought of my large Danish beer became somewhat unpalatable.
'His jaw…' Dave continued, 'was again ripped or pulled off probably by some form of

machine. All very depressing…'

'But why…? I mean, why this kid?'

'Well, what we've got so far is the cross, which links him to the church in Denmark. And we know that Green is over there somewhere.'

'Are we sure about that?'

'No recorded flights anywhere else. She hasn't left the country; Danish Politi are monitoring the borders.'

'OK… the cross though, I mean its loose isn't it? All churches have crosses, don't they…?' I said, beginning to feel deflated that we were chasing things blindly.

'No, this one is specific. If you look at the pictures closely, it's the same cross. On the database we have, there are no other matches that we know of yet. It's too much of a coincidence for this to be a dead-end.'

'Cheers, Dave. I'll see you when I'm back.'

'Not if I see you first,' he said, hanging up. The bar had become busier during my phone call. I realise I hadn't touched my beer. I got up and left, pushing through increasingly drunk Danes.

Outside the air was crisp and refreshing; the dark night had set in over the Danish capital. The back streets had become filled with revellers. One man stumbled across the street and into me, I stopped and smiled; he abused me in Danish. At least I thought he did; his tone indeed suggested he wasn't happy.

Slightly rattled, I found another underground bar.

Again, it was dark and busy. People were talking loudly and drinking heavily.

I grabbed a bottle of beer, not wanting to drink, but knowing it was a little early to be heading back.

There were no seats, so I stood and checked my phone, wanting to re-read Jackson's brief for this trip.

Tomorrow I would meet Arik Larsen, of the Danish Politi and be briefed on their intelligence thus far. Then the plan was for Larsen and me to head to the church and investigate it. In the afternoon and evening, I was going to trace Green's footsteps, or at least what we knew of where she'd been in the city.

There was a sharp thud in my back and I dropped my mobile phone.

I picked it up and turned angrily.

The man in front of me was about five foot eight and stocky with brown, spiky hair.

'What you doing, Englishman? You must watch…' I waited for the final word of that sentence which frustratingly didn't come.

His eyes were a glassy brown and I could see he was with two other men who had now taken an interest.

'I haven't moved buddy. I was standing here,' I said calmly.

'No, you watch it, asshole. Who do you think you are?' The man's accent was strong, and there was a distinctive smell of spirits on his breath. I was amazed at how drunk he was, given that the evening had only just commenced.

His friends jeered. Part of me felt compelled to challenge him, but I was out of my depth in Denmark, and sober. I knew this wasn't worth it.

'OK, sorry,' I said and turned my back to re-open my phone.

The shove came again.

I turned and pushed the small, swaying Dane, into his pals. They were less drunk than him and moved sideways, as their friend landed in a heap on the floor.

The friends didn't know what to do. I couldn't contain my laughter as the drunk man tried to get to his feet; he was like a woodlouse on his back, flailing impossibly.

Rather than stay and see how it played out, I finished my beer and left to a volley of Danish abuse. My heart was pounding, and the blood was pumping, I felt it was time to get back to the safety of the hotel, so I jumped into a cab.

Copenhagen had done me no favours this evening; it was a stark reminder of why I very rarely went out at night anymore.

15

The hotel was called 'The Cabinn.'

It was small, but perfect for what I needed. I was staying for just two nights, theoretically. There was a twenty-four-hour bar, and when I returned, I ordered myself a double scotch.

There was a couple on a table in the corner, but that was it. So, I grabbed a seat at the bar and took a swig of my drink.

It went down far too quickly; the fiery liquid hit the pit of my stomach and brought my senses to life briefly.

 I finished it and ordered another which I took to my room, knowing that if I stayed, I was bound to have more.

The room was small and compact and that was fine. I changed and jumped into bed without brushing my teeth or washing. While the cat's away...

I checked in with Tara, who was also in bed. It was 10.30 pm, and she was usually asleep by now, but she had waited up to talk with me. After our chat, my head hit the pillow, and I was gone.

When I woke up, the sun was already coming through the paper-thin curtains.

The time was 6.36 am. I turned on the TV and

watched the moving images and a dialogue I couldn't understand.

The Cabinn had a gym, so I decided to grab a glass of water, brush my teeth and head down there. It wasn't often I had the time for it. After a half-hour run on the treadmill, I came back and showered, put on my clothes: smart chinos, a long sleeve polo shirt and a sports jacket. I didn't need to be in a suit, but I also didn't want to feel too casual for the meeting with Arik.

Jackson had ordered me a car for the trip which was waiting in reception. I picked up the key and headed out.

The car was a perfectly acceptable VW Passat, dark blue. It had a sat-nav system, so once I had entered the Danish address for the police station (which took longer than it should have done), I was off and into the city streets.

The station was seven kilometres away, and the journey was very straightforward. Apart from the different road signs and driving on the right, the route was simple.

I drove to the back gate, and a miserable policeman in a booth nodded and grunted at me.

You catch more flies with honey, I thought to myself, so I smiled a big grin and told him my name. He asked for my passport, which I gave him and he signalled me onwards and into the car park.

Arik Larsen was waiting for me at reception as I entered the building.

I went towards the receptionist, but Arik waved his hand nonchalantly, leaving both myself and the girl bemused.

'Walk with me,' he said in a deep, monosyllabic tone, as he made his way up the corridor.

He was dressed in a blue suit and was surprisingly tanned for a Danish man. He had brown hair and stood at around six foot, heavily built.

'So, Charlie Stone. How are you?' he asked, smiling in my direction, without making eye contact.

'Good thanks, Arik. It has been a…'

'…Can I ask, what primarily is the purpose of you being here?' He interrupted.

I could sense the mood and this guy was not happy with me. I guess he put it down to the Brits interfering. This case wasn't like that though. Kids were being mutilated, and it shouldn't be about borders and countries.

I resisted the temptation to say 'there is something rotten in the state of Denmark,' for fear it would incite violence, or indeed go right over dear Arik's head.

'A teenager in England has been murdered…' I

began.

'… Yes, I am aware…'

'… And there may be some links with a church near here…'

'…See, this is where I get confused, Mr… Stone…'

'D.S. Stone, if you will…'

'Yes… I don't understand the connection?'

Arik seemed confused, but I could tell he was bluffing me. He was trying far too hard to convince me, but his eyes skirted upwards and to the right as he spoke. He knew full well; he just didn't want to help.

I stopped him in the corridor.

'Listen… I know my boss has briefed you. There is a significance between the crimson cross, or cramoisi croix, at that church and Bryan Rattle, the murdered boy. I found the same cross at the scene, but of course, you know this, don't you, Arik?' I said, staring into his eyes.

'I just think it is… a bit of a loose connection, if I may…'

'It is, but currently, that's all we have to go on. Can you tell me where this church is please, and I'll be on my way?' I said firmly.

Arik smiled.

'Of course. Wait one moment.'

Arik disappeared into an office, leaving me in

the corridor. He returned with a slip of paper and a scribbled address.

'This is the church, but please don't upset any of the local people. It is a small conurbation, good people. We don't want them spooked, D.S. Stone.' Arik said.

'OK, Arik. I will tread carefully, as long as this 'conurbation' has nothing to hide...'

Arik fixed me with a steely glare as I took the paper from him and left the building.

16

I had made my mind up... driving in Denmark
was far less stressful than back home.
I took motorway Twenty out of Copenhagen
and met up with the Four that brought me into
the small village of Risby, where the church was
supposedly located.
I followed the sat-nav through the small town.
Everything looked the same; the buildings were
low level, the roads were straight and nondescript, even the hedges were cut to the same
length.
The directions continued out of Risby and onto
a one-lane backroad. The buildings fell away,
and the grass became browner, and the scenery
sparser. One-point-three kilometres to go to the
church.
As I approached the blue dot on the screen, I
presumed Arik must have given me a false
address as there was nothing in sight, just
empty fields and lowlands. The plan was for
him to come with me as back up, but he had no
intention of helping us with this case.
I halted the car and got my bearings. I went
into my backpack that was on the passenger
seat and grabbed my binoculars.
I stepped out of the car and looked around.

Nothing. I looked closer, just to the North-west of where I was, I could see a tiny white building which blended into the melange of light grass and grey sky.

I took the car off the road and towards the white building.

As I got nearer, it became clear that it was a small white church; more like an outside toilet than a place of worship.

I brought the car to a halt about twenty metres away and stepped out, approaching slowly.

The crimson cross was affixed to the side of the church and was around three feet in size. It was bright gold, made of some form of heavy metal, potentially brass. The red rose was wooden and jutted out from the smoothness.

The church was closed: no signs of service, no information board, nothing.

I went to the front door and noticed a rusty padlock on it. I took one more look around to confirm the area was wholly deserted then went back to the car. In the boot, there was a heavy metal car jack which I used to remove the old padlock forcibly. After around five full strength hits, the lock dropped off, and the doors creaked ajar. I opened them tentatively.

Inside was a plain and simple room. There were worn brown benches and a small wooden altar at the front. There were three pews on either side, space for potentially twenty people, maximum, but there was nothing of note. I checked under them, around the altar… no clues, nothing of any importance.

I moved out of the church and circled it once more for anything of interest, or something to take back to my DCI, but I was left fruitless. Jaded, I went back to the car and sat to collect my thoughts in the driver's seat. I looked out into the ashen and despondent vista, only to see some form of movement in the distance.

I brought the binoculars up, and there were people, scurrying around, one was looking directly at me. The scurrying continued back to a black car that was further down the road. All four people I could see got back into the vehicle and started driving away.

I waited for a moment before starting the car.

17

I moved the vehicle forward but stayed far enough away to remain revealed from their sight. I rang Jackson and put the call onto speakerphone.

'Charlie, how's it going?' Jackson's voice sounded curt and he was a little breathless.

'Interesting. So, the contact, Larsen, was very evasive. Like he had something to hide, you know?'

'Perhaps he is just protective, a lot of these guys can be when you come into their station…'

'I know what you mean, boss, but it wasn't like that. He was just rude, didn't want me to meet anyone and said he knew nothing about the case…?'

'He was briefed though…?'

'Yes, I know, which is why I'm surprised he lied about it.'

'Weird. Did he get you to the church?' Jackson asked.

'He gave me the address. I'm there now. The church…seems empty. It's tiny and I tore the place apart, there's nothing there… I mean it's in the middle of nowhere, the whole area is deserted.'

'Jesus!'

'…But, when I left, a group of men were in the distance. As soon as they saw me, they got in their car and left, so I thought I might tail them. Are you OK with that?'

'Follow them, Charlie, but don't get caught. We don't know if these people are connected with the murder, they could be dangerous.'

'I'm going to get after them, but they've been spooked, so they are heading away from the church. Whatever they have been doing or were going to do, it won't happen today,' I said.

'OK, well let me know. If you need more time out there, no problem. We are running on fumes here, Charlie. I got the Chief Super on my back. It's only a matter of time before the press sniffs this out and then we have a whole new world of trouble.'

'Well, you deal with that, let me see what I can find out.'

I put the phone down, acutely aware that I was about to re-enter the road from the dirt track to the church.

The black car was around twenty-five metres ahead of me. I deliberately kept my distance until it was right at the periphery of my vision. Remember the training, Stone.

I managed to get the plate number by using the binoculars. It quickly became apparent that these guys knew that I was following them; no indication and speeding away at certain junctions.

I decided to forget the chase. It was futile anyway. As much as I loved the trusty Passat, if that Mercedes 5.0 V8 wanted to lose someone, it would.

I turned off at the next junction and headed back towards Copenhagen.

18

Back at the hotel, I called Dave and asked him to run the plate.

He needed a few hours before he got a result, but I thought there would be a better chance of success than asking Arik.

I lay on the bed with free time on my hands. It was a strange feeling; is this how normal feels? I felt like reading a book, something I hadn't done since I started the job.

I picked up the phone and rang Tara.

'Hey, hun. How's it going?' she asked.

'Yeah, good,' I replied.

'What did you find at the church?'

It wasn't always ideal to have your other half knowing about a case, especially one as potentially dangerous as this one, but Tara was involved due to the Amy Green murder. Plus, she was bright, motivated and wanted to help me to make our life together more comfortable.

'The church was just… I don't know. Like a red herring. It was deserted and small, very small.'

'Really? In the book, like I know the book isn't the case, but there are some odd similarities.'

'What, so Troy goes to the church in Denmark… in his novel?'

'Yeah, he gets taken to Denmark, Copenhagen,

and he visits a church…'

'…Wait, where is the church, in relation to the city…?'

'He says a similar thing, it's out in the suburbs surrounded by fields and stuff, but how he describes it is different…'

'Yeah…?'

Part of me realised it's stupid to be following leads from a work of fiction, but we didn't have much to go on in this case, and I wanted to find whoever was behind the murder of Bryan Rattle.

'…But it's different, Charlie. Like he says… it's big: brick-built and with candles.'

'Well, it's not the same church then…'

There was a pause on the phone.

'Perhaps a different church, but also in Copenhagen?' Tara suggested.

'The problem is, there will be a lot of churches in Copenhagen. Wait… did you say there was a cross on the outside of it?'

'I think so… let me check,' I could hear Tara leafing through the dense pages of Troy's tome. 'Yeah, here it is…'

'I must say, I can't remember much of these early years, but I do remember the bright gold cross, with the red flower in the centre. It was such a vivid image and I had never seen the cross of Jesus represented like this. It stood out against the white wood.'

'Fits the description,' I said. 'White wood, gold cross.'

'He goes on… *my memory becomes blurry at this point, but the gold and red continue inside. There were hanging incense burners, golden tables, altars, triangles, images a sensory overload…*' Tara stopped.

'Hmmm, it's a different place.'

'Damn. So, no leads then?' Tara asked.

'Well, not as such. I saw some guys in a black Mercedes come towards the church and then leave when they saw me. Dave's trying to get some more information for me. T, going back to that passage… read the bit when he's outside again…'

'Hang on… *and I had never seen the cross of Jesus represented like this. It stood out against the white wood… my memory becomes blurry at this point, but the gold and red continue inside. There were hanging incense burners, golden tables, altars, triangles, images, a sensory…*'

'Wait, so it doesn't actually describe him going into the church, does it?' I ask.

'No not as su…'

'…. He says he sees it, and then it goes blurry… then he's in the church. But he might not even be in the church. It could be somewhere else.'

'But isn't it like a deserted place, you said?'

'Yeah…it is. It is deserted on land, but what if the place these guys are trying to keep hidden is underground?'

'Oh…like the cells in the Green case…?'

'Exactly…lots of similarities… his memory is blurry, Troy says that. What if he's drugged, to hide the whereabouts?'

'Sounds plausible. You need to be careful, Charlie; this whole thing gives me the creeps,' Tara said, I could tell she was anxious.

'Honey, relax. Don't worry, I will be careful, and I'll see you very soon…'

'You're back tomorrow, right?'

'Hopefully, but I may need to stay one more night, to get what we need.'

There was silence.

'Right, fine, I'll see you when I see you.'

Tara said goodbye and put the phone down. I knew she was only worried about me and disappointed I wouldn't be back sooner.

I was excited; I felt we might have a breakthrough.

By the time I had gone downstairs and ordered a drink and some dinner, Dave had got back with an address for the plates.

The black Mercedes was registered to an affluent address in the suburbs of Copenhagen. I wanted to go back to the church and see if I could find something that lent itself to the church Troy describes in his book, Original Sin. It made no sense for there to be a solitary church out there; something else had to be going on.

I also wanted to pick up a tracker for the black Mercedes, so after my club sandwich, (washed down with an Apple Fanta… the joys of being in Europe), I drove to the police station. The time was 6.57 pm on the car clock.

I got to the desk and asked the receptionist for Arik.

The receptionist sniggered, 'Unfortunately you have just missed Detective Larsen. He leaves at 5 pm every day.'

'I see…'

'Wait there though… Mr….'

'Detective Stone,' I produced my badge. The receptionist smiled and nodded while picking up the phone.

Within a couple of minutes, a lady appeared who looked busy and flustered. She had short brown hair and was stocky, about five foot two. 'Hello, Detective Stone. Detective Larsen has left for the day. May I assist?'

She ushered me up to the hub of the station, where there were a handful of officers working at desks.

'Well yes, I mean, are you aware of the case that I'm investigating?'

'Yes, sounds pretty gruesome...' she shot me a worried glance.

'Well, indeed. Leads are short in number, but I think I have one,' I said.

'Excellent, that's good. I am Detective Jensen, Rita Jensen,' she held out her hand and I shook it.

She also gave me a card with her number on it for future reference.

'What I was hoping for, Rita, is a digital tracker for a vehicle,' I knew this would be difficult but, Rita seemed nice and I was hoping that I could sweet talk her into lending it to me.

'I see, you know there are protocols with handing out equipment such as this...'

'Oh, of course, I understand. It's just that I haven't had much assistance from Detective Larsen up to this point and so haven't had access to a lot of the information I need. I'm kind of in the dark, really.'

Rita looked around and indicated a side office. I followed and shut the door behind us.

'Detective…. you won't get much help from Larsen, the man is…. well…' she smirked, before maintaining her professionalism, 'he won't help you.'

'I don't understand though… why wouldn't he want to assist with the case?'

'No… there are lots you won't understand… some strange things are happening in Denmark,' I wanted to use my rotten in Denmark quote again, but as Rita was opening up about the case, I thought it best to keep my counsel.

'Listen, Detective, you seem like a nice man. Take this…' she reached into a drawer and pulled out the tracking device I wanted. She took out her keys and unlocked a filing cabinet. She rifled around and pulled out a small handgun in a black leather holster.

'Take this… the tracking device you want… it's for a car, right?' she asked.

I placed the gun carefully in my man bag, not asking any questions. I mean, how dangerous could an empty weapon be?

'Yep.'

'Black Mercedes?'

'Err, yes. How did you know?'

'There are some dark forces at work here, Detective.' Rita said prophetically. She carried on furrowing through the filing cabinet and pulled out a carton of 9mm bullets. I took them and asked no questions. 'You need to be careful. Good luck.' I thanked Rita for her understanding. I knew she was risking her badge to help me. Her veiled words worried me, but I knew if I pushed her for more information, I wouldn't get far. She had given me enough.

20

The night was quiet and the roads clear, as I took the short motorway journey to the home of the black Mercedes.

It took me to an affluent neighbourhood called Fredriksburg. The apartment buildings were low lying and modern, and the greenery was lush.

The car sat on the driveway of an attractive, modern house; clearly, the owner of the car was well off.

There was a moving camera guarding the front of the house and lights boomed brightly from the large bay window. This wasn't going to be easy at all.

The tracker was a modern device that sent information directly to my phone. I set it up quickly and turned it on. There were shadows across the bay window as I crept slowly towards the Mercedes. I wanted to get this done as soon as possible, but securing the tracker effectively and so it wouldn't be found, was not an easy job.

I managed to creep towards the rear driver's side wheel and knelt down. I checked the bay window... nothing.

The black leather gloves did not make it easy to

slide the small device under the wheel arch.
There was a crevice in these Mercedes which it
should slip into; it was just finding it.
Suddenly, the driveway became darker. The bay
window lights were turned off.
I rushed to find the nook to secure the device,
but it was also essential to keep my movements
light so as not the set off the car alarm.
The front door opened, and Danish voices
grew louder as the door slammed behind them.
I found the crevice and dropped the tracker in
it. A man came around to the side of the car, so
I rolled into the hedging to the right and
waited.
My heart pounded, *surely, I had been spotted?* I
thought to myself. I kept my body flat on the
floor and watched as a figure with shiny black
shoes opened the driver's door and got in. He
waited a moment before shutting it, and I
wondered where the gun that Rita had given me
had gone.
After silence that felt like forever, the door
slammed, and the engine started.
I breathed again, as the car pulled away, into the
night.

My temptation was to follow the car, but I

wanted to put some space between myself and what happened this afternoon at the church. They may well have spotted my car, so I thought it best to let some time pass before I tailed them again. Besides, the tracker would tell me if they were going anywhere of interest.

I knew I had to get back to the church and see if I could find anything else of importance. I set the sat-nav to the co-ordinates and wondered if the Mercedes would be going there too... no such luck. They headed into the city, from what my limited knowledge of Copenhagen told me. As I left the suburbs, it dawned on me how isolated the church was. It was very, very dark, so I kept the lights on until I reached the side of the church and saw the glinting crimson cross.

I turned the engine off and pulled out a torch from the glovebox, continuing on foot. I listened for any sounds, but other than those of small crickets and birds, there was nothing. The lock hadn't been fixed and the door still open, so I checked around the church again.

I tried to reframe the building and think of something that I might have missed; it was to no avail. I went back outside and looked at the side of the building again, but I found nothing of any note.

Turning off my torch, I was ready to give up

again and get back on the road when I noticed the gold cross seemed to light up in the darkness of the Scandinavian night. The petals on the rose lit up bright crimson. Through the blur of what I was witnessing, the flowers seemed to move, but I shook myself back to reality and common sense.

I checked there was no-one around me, just the glow of the cross and the throbbing of the rose.

I reached towards the cross with my hand and moved it clockwise. It turned. I kept rotating it until there was a metallic clunk underneath my feet. The grass beneath my feet seemed to separate slightly and what looked like two doors appeared in the ground.

It suddenly dawned on me that the crimson cross wasn't a symbol of an occult sect; it was a doorway to it.

21

I pulled at the doors, which opened easily and led to a dark staircase leading down.
I saw the roman numeral 'VII' on a gold plaque to the left as I entered.
Easing my way down the stairwell and into a dark corridor, I kept my torchlight aimed at the enveloping darkness before me. The passage was bricked on either side, and there were candelabras, unlit, lining the sides of the walls.
I checked I had Rita's gun with me, and my phone, before taking a deep breath and moving forward. I could see nothing ahead. My tiny flashlight was gobbled up by the gloom. I slowly continued down the corridor, my footsteps echoing on the cold, stone floor.
To my left and right, there were a series of doors appearing. They were dark wood with gold fittings and round door latches. I tried them, but without success, all locked.
I pressed on, nervously. I seemed to walk for a few minutes until the flashlight flicked off, leaving me in total darkness. I shook the torch back into action and breathed again.
At the end of the corridor was a doorway that led to a large stone staircase heading below. I followed it, watching my step as the footing

wasn't secure, the stone crumbling away in places. I couldn't quite gauge how old this place was. Despite the style, some of the brickwork seemed relatively modern; however, these stairs must have dated back centuries.

I continued down, down into the unknown, the belly of a beast I had yet to encounter fully.

I was desperate for a light switch, or a way to light the candles that continued down the wide, open stairwell. My only respite was this place was locked and hidden; therefore, I had to be on my own. Surely?

I reached the bottom of the stairs, and a large room opened up. The floor was now dark wood, and I could see the gold candle holders around the room again. I searched further and found some coloured cables that ran along the top of the wall. They disappeared above a door which I opened, revealing a small room.

I breathed a sigh of relief, the power supply.

I flipped the switch, and the lights buzzed on which created a dark, ethereal glow to the room which was far more significant than I previously imagined. It was more like a hall.

There were gold plaques under the candles that had Latin script written on them. Throughout the long room, which just seemed to go on and on, were a variety of different machines, many I had never seen before.

These were torture devices, mostly from the middle ages, some I had seen before and others I had not. I recognised an Iron Maiden, for instance. There was also an iron chair, that was covered in spikes. It looked more at home in Game of Thrones than in this warm, orange light.

As I explored, there were several hand-held devices, too often made of metal. There was one device which was made entirely of thick wood. It had a large circular frame, that was attached to the floor by a wooden pole. I walked towards it, and the wheel spun slowly. A breaking wheel… victims were tied to it and then repeatedly beaten.

The room smelt musty, dry and old. What I found bizarre was with all these unknown mechanisms and tables there was no sign of human interaction, no blood; the place was pristine.

I carried on walking through the long room and eventually found a side room. I pushed the heavy door open and went in. The room was lighter, and there was a plain wooden table, large enough for a body, to my left. Above it was a series of manacles and chains.

On the wall, in large black letters, read: 'Ludibriums.'

I knew it was Latin and had some meaning, but

was unsure what it was. The heavy door slowly closed behind me.

My phone buzzed in my pocket, I checked it… it was telling me I had no reception…. But the tracker was flashing. I opened the app, and the GPS was searching, what it did do was show me the movements of it in the last five minutes, and with high speed, the dot on the tracker was moving towards my current location.

The men in the black Mercedes were coming.

22

I knew I had to get out before they arrived, so I grabbed the heavy door and pulled…it didn't budge. I pulled so hard that the handle came clean off.

I was trapped inside. Even if I shot off the lock, there was no way I could pull that door back as it was so sturdy.

The light was gloomy, but with the flashlight, I inspected the walls to see if there was anything that could lead me outside; nothing.

My heart was pounding, and I was sweating profusely now. I pulled out the gun; double-checked it was loaded, with the safety off. I waited in the room as quietly as possible, seeing if I could hear something, anything.

Nothing.

A minute passed, still no noise.

I waited again and thought of Tara, beautiful Tara, my saviour; how I loved her.

I pulled out the phone and wrote a message, 'I will always love you xx.' I sent it, knowing there was no reception, but it didn't matter.

I put the phone away, silence once again.

Then in the gloom far away, there was a clunk, and the lights all around me went out.

I was in total darkness.

Panic set in, but also adrenaline. I had to find a way out, but it was pointless, the door wouldn't budge.

I heard voices getting nearer. The gun pulsated in my hand; I wasn't used to using firearms. Dave always taught me that the unknown was usually a lot worse in your imagination. The paedophile you were hunting was often a physically weak, middle-aged loner. The killer often a geeky outcast. It was only in the movies you faced terrifying villains.

Except, I couldn't get the vision of Bryan Rattle out of my head. I was concerned about who could have done that, and I needed to make sure that they couldn't do it again.

I was prepared for a showdown as voices got even nearer, they must have been in the long room now as there was a glowing orange light coming from outside.

Suddenly, the voices stopped, and I wondered what to do. Did they even know I was in here? I waited; silence.

A bead of sweat dropped from my brow and onto my hand that was clasping the gun.

Sound came… a hissing from beyond the door. Two of my worst fears… snakes and spiders…it couldn't be...

A grey smoke filtered into the room from underneath the door. Well, I guess they knew I was here. At least it wasn't snakes, I thought, as I began to feel light-headed and dizzy.

+++++++++++++++++++++++++++++++++

'Dad, let's feed the ducks!'
'They're not ducks, son…they're geese,' my dad said, looking somewhat agitated.
We were by a lake in Eastbourne. A day trip or weekend away, I couldn't be sure. I was around seven, my Dad bordering on fifty.
My mother and sister were by the playground; we often split like that.
'Go on, Dad. Mum's got some bread,' I said eagerly.
'No way, son. They're vicious little…' Dad trailed off, reaching into his pocket for a mint.
'Polo?' he asked me.
'Yes please,' I said, taking one from the open packet. Suddenly I noticed two geese, pick up pace towards the edge of the lake.
They got out and flapped their mighty wings dry. We were dealing with Canada Geese here, who although not huge, would make a formidable opponent for any man, woman or duck.
Dad rapidly put the Polo's away. The geese moved nearer.
'No, no, no…' he said, backing against the wall, as they surrounded him, moving closer. Here he was, my father. A man who in the eye of a son was omnipotent,

afraid of nothing… now cowering at the threat of two
geese, on the hunt for fresher breath.
I felt Dad's panic, but I couldn't help but giggle. I was
out of the firing line; they weren't stupid these guys...
they knew who was holding.
Dad backed away from the wall and made a run for it.
The geese followed in quick pursuit, Dad's leather
jacket and chinos, like a middle-aged Fonzie, became a
blur to the soundtrack of the squawking, feathered
aggressors.
I was now in fits of hysterical laughter, as were my
Mum and sister who had caught sight of this.
Dad eventually made it out of the park and away from
his pursuers. This was not before he took out the polos
and threw them, to ward off his predators.
As he told me afterwards, the moral of the story was…
never feed the geese.

++++++++++++++++++++++++++++++++

'Charlie! Wake up!'
A voice I recognised…
'Come on,' I felt slaps to the face as I tried to
regain consciousness, but my head wasn't
having any of it.
'Charlie… mate… we need to go!'
Then there was a crash, and I was very wet but
slightly more conscious. I shook myself dry.
I was on a wooden table, lying down. My top

half was bare, but I was still wearing my jeans, thankfully.

There was blood on my chest and right arm. As I inspected my body further, I noticed I had many gashes and deep cuts, but I felt OK.

My vision focused, and Dave was in front of me, holding an empty cup.

'What the...?'

'No time... here put this on,' he said, throwing me my t-shirt.

We were still in the underground building, but I was sure it was a different room to the one where I was trapped.

'Charlie, we need to go… now!' Dave said with urgency.

'OK…'

He helped me to my feet, and I steadied myself.

'You good?'

I nodded as he watched me hobble to the door.

In the corridor outside, there were two bodies on the floor. Both had on long black robes, one of them appeared to be bleeding, both were unconscious. Dave skipped over them as if they weren't there, so I presumed he had taken them down to get to me.

We continued down another dank passage with minimal light before we appeared back in the long room again.

Dave signalled me to stop and be quiet as there were murmurings in the gloom up ahead. He had a gun cocked and loaded. I checked for mine, but it had gone.

I moved up with him at his command; however, I slipped on the cold floor and crumpled to the ground. The noise alerted the men up ahead, Dave raised the gun and shot twice; both men fell to the floor.

We kept on running, this time up the staircase and back along the corridor towards the main entrance of the underground chamber. As we got to the top of the stairs, we looked around to ensure no-one was lurking.

The coast was clear, so we hot-footed it to the car which was still exactly where I left it. I was steadier on my feet now, so I was able to check my pocket, and the keys were not there. I looked over at Dave, who thankfully had them in his hand.

'You can't drive, Charlie.' Dave said as we got to the car.

We swapped sides. Once I got into the car, I collapsed into the passenger seat.

23

*I loved my Dad, but he was a prowler and growler.
What I mean is, when he was in a lousy mood… you
knew about it. I mean, the whole house and probably
the street knew. He had a terrific temper, although that
is undoubtedly oxymoronic as there was never anything
terrific happening when he lost it.
One day, we were all sitting down for lunch and Dad
was upset about something.
I can't remember exactly what it was, again I was only
young, maybe eight or nine this time, but he was cross.
Silently cross, waiting for someone to cross him.
We all sat down at the dinner table in trepidation. He
was grumbling about what a mess the place was.
We had a new glass bottle of Heinz ketchup on the
table which was notoriously hard to get the ketchup out
upon first usage.
I tried, to no avail, then my sister did with no luck.
Mum went next and couldn't do it.
Harrumphing as he did, my father then took the bottle
and slammed it down on the table. It appeared that
Mum hadn't entirely sealed the lid back on and it flew
off, spreading Heinz tomato ketchup all over the table,
curtains and ceiling.
There was silence.
I couldn't help myself, so I started giggling.
My dad, caught between rage and ecstasy, laughed too.*

For once, we all laughed.

++++++++++++++++++++++++++++++++

I felt light on my face, a beautiful transition
from the gloom of the underground lair.
Sunlight was streaming onto my face. I tried to
open my eyes, but the bright light infiltrating
them was too much to bear.
I caught a glimpse of Dave and was delighted
to see him.
'Hello, sleepyhead,' he said.
I rolled over and forced my eyes awake,
checking the alarm next to the bed. 11.40 am.
'Jeez…'
'You needed it, mate. Get yourself packed;
we're going home today. I'll meet you
downstairs when you're done. I need a coffee,'
Dave said, leaving the hotel room.
I got into the shower and noticed I had cuts
and abrasions all over my upper body. Some
were deep and looked infected. I tried to gouge
out the infection as best I could but really
needed a professional to look at it.
My body felt achy and tired, probably an after
effect of whatever gas they had used to knock
me out.
I got dressed and went downstairs. I didn't have
the stomach for coffee, so just ordered

sparkling water with ice and lime.

'So, what the hell happened?' I asked as Dave took a slurp of his black coffee.

'When we found out that you had a lead on the black Mercedes, Jackson got itchy feet about leaving you out there. We then got a phone call from your good mate, Arik Larsen, who was absolutely fuming.'

'With me? Why?'

'He said you were getting involved in things that were out of your jurisdiction, tracking civilians, putting pressure on other detectives…'

'Wait… wh...?'

'Jackson knew he was full of it, so sent me over to give you a hand. Well you know me, Charlie, I much prefer the surprise entrance…'

'So, how did you know where I was…?'

'I went to the station and that…. Rita… told me a few things and that you had been to see her. Lovely lady…' Dave said, smiling.

'Oh, wow...OK, she is certainly more in your age bracket pal…'

'Well, that's what she thought. I have her number now…'

'Yeah, purely for professional reasons I'm sure. Wait… but Rita didn't know where I was…?'

'Clever boy, she didn't. But I could track your phone, well up to a point, before you completely lost signal. Then about fifteen minutes after that, maybe twenty, a text left your phone, so I had an idea where you were. They must have taken it from you and moved it to a place where you got signal…'

'That is lucky…'

'Very. When I got there, those men dressed in black had you manacled to a table. They were taking it in turns to beat you, hence your wounds. I was tempted to have a go myself if I am honest…'

I laughed, and it hurt. 'They drugged me, right?'

'Yep and used gas to knock you out. It's all very odd and creepy. We need to find out what the hell is going on here.' Dave said.

'Did you get an idea of who those guys are… and what was that place all about…?' I asked.

'Your guess is as good as mine, Charlie…' Dave said back. I mean, what was I expecting? Him to save my life and solve the case for me at the same time?

'Well, it's clear that this is some kind of occult sect of the church, right? I mean lots of gold… the cross symbol… use of gas…'

'…Incidentally, that was laughing gas…'

'What like NOS?'

'Yes, but obviously higher doses and designed to knock you out rather than give you a temporary high… easy to get hold of, difficult to trace…'

'Well, it would explain the dreams, I guess…'

'What?'

'Oh, don't worry, mate. Anyway, this is some cult. Two things of real importance, the number seven I saw written in roman numerals…' I said.

'Seven…has lots of mythical and symbolic meanings….'

'Yeah, or could just be the number of the church… as in this is number seven of… God knows how many around the world…?'

'Bloody hell, Charlie. I never even thought of that,' Dave said, draining the dregs of his cup. 'The other thing?'

'Ludibriums… a Latin word, I think.'

'*Ludibriums…?*' Dave reached for his phone.

'Yes, meaning a 'plaything' or something of scorn or derision…'

'Really… an interesting juxtaposition…' I said.

'So, what happens now?'

'Left in the capable hands of Rita Germann. The Politi have been there overnight with forensics. She said she would be in touch. My hope is they get what they need and then burn the place down.' Dave said.

'Absolutely. What about the…erm…bodies...?' I asked tentatively. I had worked with Dave for many, many years, and I would be lying if I said that I hadn't seen death in the line of duty. However, Dave was semi-retired, and I was wondering if he was OK about everything.

'I told her about that. It was in the line of duty. You were drugged and tied topless to a bench when I found you. I also walked past five medieval torture devices on the way through. I couldn't take prisoners.'

I looked out of the window and smiled. You didn't need lots of mates, just a few good ones who would follow you to Denmark and save your arse when you're fighting international crime.

'Cheers mate,' I said. 'Hey, you haven't got my phone, have you?'

'Aah… lost… and currently off. I would let that one go to be honest, Charlie,' he said.

'Let's have yours then,' I asked cheekily.

'Fine, don't spend hours on the phone to Tara though. I'm not made of money!' He smiled at me. 'Anyway, phone her in the car; I want to get to the airport.'

'Good shout, I have had about enough of Denmark. I thought this was supposed to be the happiest place on earth?' I asked.

'Probably is, when you are not chasing criminals,' Dave returned.

'True. A bit cold though, don't you think?'

'Get in the car, Charlie!'

PART 2

24

We landed back in Blighty on Wednesday evening, and I spent Thursday with Tara, resting. We did raise ourselves to walk into town and pick up a new phone for me, but apart from that, I was indoors keeping my head down.

By 9.45 am on Friday I was back with Dave, Jackson, Karl and Jimmy at Ashford Police Station.

'Charlie Stone! Good to have you back in one piece! What a bloody ordeal eh…?' Jackson said, half asking a question.

'Yeah, I mean, it wasn't great, but hopefully, once we get the information back from the Politi, we will have some further leads.'

'Yeah, great work you two, we are getting somewhere in this case. Lots to fill you in on, get a coffee and take a seat.'

I used the coffee jug at the side of Jackson's office and sat down.

'So, I have had an update from our new contact in the Politi, Rita Germann. There were four men found in the hule; two are in hospital, two are no longer with us, all have been ID'd.'

I looked at Dave; he looked perplexed.

'Sorry, boss… *hule?* What on earth is that…?' I asked.

'Hule – Hoo – la, like hula, you know the Hawaiian dancers… its Danish for 'lair'… that's what they are calling it. Everyone likes to do the hule… except maybe you eh, Charlie?' Jackson laughed to himself.

'Bit too soon boss…' Dave said.

'Sorry mate…'

I shook my head; god love him. At least he was in a good mood.

'…Anyway, they are all connected via a Gentleman's club in the centre of Copenhagen known as 'The Boiler Room.' We don't know much about this yet, but ultimately it seems like a private club where old men go to do… what old men like to do.'

'Nice…' Karl said.

'Not really. Very seedy and avoided by the Politi as these men are generally quite powerful people in the Danish community – businessmen, bankers, media outlet owners, the type of people who will cause a lot of trouble if you make a mess for them…'

'…Which we have…' I added in.

'Yes, so we await further confirmation of what the Politi wants to do on this. Two courses of action really: more arrests and try and snub it out or wait until there is some form of retaliation. Those were the words of Germann.'

'Retaliation? As in further deaths?' Jackson nodded.

'Ultimately though, the hule will be closed down, shut up and gone. So as far as that's concerned, good work,' Jackson added; Dave and I remained unmoved.

'In other news, I am certain that Jennifer Green and that lapdog of hers, Gibson, are in on this too. Why else would she be going to Copenhagen? Seen in a five-star hotel? Shifting out before the doo-doo hits the fan,' Jackson added.

'Shifted out? Where's she gone?' I asked.

'Well, unknown currently. But it appears since she caught wind of us tailing her, she has continued her journey on foot… or you know, by car… we had confirmation that she crossed into Germany a couple of days ago.'

'Why didn't we know this when she *actually* crossed?' Dave asked.

'Not all of those with badges have the same commitment as you gentlemen. The Danes aren't that fussed. As far as they are concerned, Green is our problem.' Jackson stated.

'Well, that's a bit rich given we have just busted a torture cult for them! The cheek of it!' Dave said exasperated.

Jackson paused, 'Remind me never to put you in charge of International Relations… anyway, fear not, we have some of the best Polizei trying to locate her for us. The minute I hear anything, we may need another overseas trip. For now, have a few days off. I will be in touch.'

'Boss, what about the hockey club? There has to be something doing there, surely?' I asked. Jackson handed the floor to Dave.

'There is something not quite right about the bloke who runs that place. Do I think he's involved in something as sinister as this? No…but…'

'…Maybe worth another look, though?' I asked him. Dave looked at me and nodded.

'Listen, I can see what's happening here, and no! If I found out you have bothered anyone up there, you will have me to deal with! Charlie, you go and have a nice weekend with that lovely girlfriend of yours and you, Dave, go and do whatever it is you do to relax.'

'Yes, boss,' we both said in unison.

'Good. I will be in touch.'

25

I only had an hour or so until I needed to collect Maddie. The pick-up point was just a half an hour away now at Maidstone services, somewhere far more convenient for Tara and I.

I decided to head up there early, get a coffee and collect my thoughts, as I wasn't entirely sure what the next steps to take were. I made notes in my journal as it always helped me to navigate the murky waters of my mind. As far as the Politi were concerned, this was a closed case. They would forward us the bare details of the men involved, and that was it.

For me, this case had just started. What we had found was one of possibly seven of these hules or chambers or whatever we want to call them. Green was one hundred percent involved too. I didn't know how, but she had to be. I just knew: the gruesome nature, the covert operations and the age of the victims all suggested it.

Finally, the boy Rattle. We were no closer to finding who his killers were. We had the link, and this Lubidriums sect had to be involved to some degree, but still nothing concrete.

I had decided to check out the Hockey Club in

Hawkinge again, but Jackson needed not to find out. I made the note in my journal before finishing my coffee and returning to reality.

Jo arrived thirteen minutes late.

These days we tended not to talk unless it was absolutely necessary. The split was acrimonious, and she went through the courts to try and stop me seeing Maddie as much as possible, but through the courts I ended up seeing Maddie more; so Jo was frosty, to say the least.

Maddie ran up to me and gave me a big hug; seeing her made my heart melt and my fears fade away.

Tomorrow was Saturday, or when Maddie was down, 'Daddy Saturday' as we called it. I vowed to make sure we did something fun together.

We drove back to Folkestone and Maddie talked the whole way, telling me all about her friends at school, the cake sale she helped with on Thursday and how her tag rugby event had gone. I adored her and the peace she brought me through simplicity. In the eyes of this seven-year-old, the world was pure and beautiful.

We got back, and Tara had made Maddie's favourite, Mac and Cheese. I wasn't quite sure when Macaroni Cheese got rebranded, but even the old favourites eventually fall victim to commercial targeting.

We sat at the table and ate dinner before

settling down on the sofa for a film. We watched the Lego Movie 2, and halfway through I made a chocolate pick n' mix… a hand me down from my father. Chopped up Mars Bar, Maltesers, Revels, Munchies and whatever other bits you fancied in there.

At around 9.30 pm, we all began to feel a little tired, so we went to bed.

Tara had bought the paper so we could do the crossword while Maddie read her book on the edge of the bed.

'Dad, can I sleep in here?' Maddie asked.

'Wh- why…?' I asked, a bit bemused.

'Well, it's not fair. You have T to sleep with, but I have to sleep on my own…' she said, pulling her best sad face to yank on the heartstrings.

'But that's not true,' Tara interjected. 'You have Maxxy, Gav the Gorilla and all the other toys in your room.'

Maddie harrumphed, 'it's not the same.'

'Plus, you don't want to sleep in here… daddy farts all night!' Tara exclaimed.

'And T snores all night too,' I added.

'Yeah, Mummy lets me sleep with her in her bed, and she snores,' Maddie exclaimed.

'You sleep in Mummy's bed?' I asked, shooting a glance at Tara.

'Only when I'm scared,' she added.

'Did you sleep in Mummy's bed last night?'
Maddie nodded.

'Oh well, if you're scared…' Tara added, giving Maddie a little hug.

'I don't sleep there when *Josh* is staying over…' Maddie continued.

I sighed. What fresh hell is this now?

'Who's Josh? Mummy's new boyfriend?' I asked.

'Mummy's friend. He sometimes stays…'

Hearing enough, I went to the bathroom to brush my teeth and left Tara to deal with this latest breaking news. Despite there being fifty percent shared responsibility, Jo never felt the need to tell me anything, even if she had a new stranger, or as good as, staying under the same roof as my daughter.

I guess she wanted to keep her men quiet, as she knew I would check them out.

I heard Tara put Maddie to bed in her room, and I went back and laid down.

Tara came back in, looked at me and stroked my hair.

'So, she's at it again,' Tara said.

'New year, new bloke it seems sometimes,' I said.

I stopped myself from being judgmental. I had no right, but what frustrated me was the message it sent to Maddie. Still, I had to keep reminding myself; she could do what she wants. I just needed to make sure that my daughter was safe and looked after.

I rolled over and went to kiss Tara.

'Don't you get over-amorous, Detective Stone…' she purred. 'We have a big day tomorrow.'

I nodded, pretending I remembered what we were doing.

'Alton Towers, Charlie! You're up at 6 am, to collect Iris, Maddie's friend!'

'Of course, of course! I remembered,' I said, smiling at her.

26

The morning of a trip away was always chaos: the preparation of child-friendly meals, half-zipped bags, clothes strewn everywhere, me wandering around trying to be helpful and failing massively.

I went and got the car cleaned and filled it up with petrol. I grabbed three bags of car sweets, an 'i' newspaper and two bottles of water: one still, one sparkling. I was the only one in the house that liked sparkling water, but I wasn't going to be denied, given that we had at least a three-hour journey ahead of us.

I checked the journey on Google Maps, and it was actually over four hours with the roadworks on the M20 and M1. *The things you do for family.*

I came back in the house and announced I would pick up Iris now, which sped up the process, and I expected the gang to be ready in ten minutes.

To my shock, we were on the road in fifteen. This was very quick by family Stone standards. The sun was shining, so I hoped we would get as clear a run as possible.

Tara sat next to me in the passenger seat and leafed through the paper. She wasn't the most exceptional reader, nor indeed the best passenger, but she let me drive the first part of the journey.

Once she was bored, she reached behind her seat and grabbed Troy's book.

'Oh, I forgot about that, how's it going?' I asked.

'It's excellent… a complete page-turner,' Tara replied.

'What's happening in it now?'

'Well, after his Copenhagen stint, he has come home, back to England. I think he's about fourteen now. He keeps talking about Hamburg, so I guess the next part of the story will be set there…'

'Hamburg, eh? *A city of sin*…you might learn a few things about your old boyfriend!'

Tara tutted, 'Don't be silly, Troy was just a friend. Anyway, Hamburg has its nice parts too, I've heard…'

'Well, no plans to go there anytime soon, so hopefully the whole Copenhagen thing was just a crazy coincidence,' I replied.

'I guess…was a bit odd though, eh?'

'Very,' I agreed. I stopped talking and let Tara read on.

When the roads were clear, I enjoyed a long drive. Maddie and her friend were playing in the back, Tara was engrossed in her book, so I turned up the radio and put my foot down.

+++++++++++++++++++++++++++++++++

We arrived at the theme park just after midday. The kids were excited, and I was too if I'm honest. I had been toying with the idea of leaving my phone in the car while we were in the park, but I chose to take it with me. That said, I planned not to check it unless I really had to.

'Dad, can we head to the Smiler first?' Maddie asked.

'Yeah sure, no problem,' We walked around to the ride with Iris and Maddie skipping ahead. The queues were busy as it was a Saturday and one of the most popular rides.

As we got around the corner, I saw 'Oblivion' and remember going on it as a kid. The wait was only ten minutes, so I convinced the kids to go on it with me. It was very short, but the basic premise was holding you over a dark chasm, before flinging you at high speed down it. *A bit like adulthood,* I thought to myself. *Poor Maddie had it all to come.*

I loved the ride; it was one minute and fifteen seconds of pure escapism. Maddie loved it too, but Iris felt a bit sick afterwards.

The girls queued up for 'Smiler.' Tara and I

were taking it in turns on the rides, so I hung back and got myself a coffee.

Reluctantly I checked my phone and Dave had called. I had time, so I rang him straight back.

'Hey, Charlie. Where are you? It sounds noisy…'

'Hi, mate. Alton Towers with the family. What you up to?'

'Not a lot. Doing a bit of work on the Dodge. I've been thinking though. Maybe we need to get in and have a closer look at the Hockey Club guy, *Dave Miller*…' Dave said.

'Yes, the same thought crossed my mind. You can track a straight line from Bryan Rattle's house to the club. His body was found directly on that line. Could be a coincidence, but maybe not.'

'Indeed. When are you back?'

'Sunday evening. Maddie has got school on Monday.'

'OK, we should go and have a little look then? Or Sunday night, maybe?'

'Perhaps we should,' I confirmed.

'Have you heard anything about the parents? Have we questioned them yet?' Dave asked.

'Last I heard, the mother was in shock and had been admitted to a psychiatric hospital. Dad was nowhere to be seen. I think he went for a night out and never came back,' I told him.

'Grief?'

'Possibly. Chief wanted us to leave well alone for a bit, you know, not push too hard.'

'Yeah, sure. We have to speak to the parents at some stage though,' Dave said, I think this case was affecting him more than I gave him credit for.

'Totally. Let's have a look at it this week when I'm back,' I said.

Screams of joy cut through our conversation, as I watched the 'Smiler' speed over my head in a whirl of crazy hair, wide arms and broad smiles.

'Well, I'll let you get on mate. Catch you tomorrow,' Dave said.

'Here Dave, have you heard about this book by Troy Wood… *Original Sin?*' I asked.

'Err…nope…'

'It's beautiful, velvet bound, crimson red, lovely finishing…big heavy thing it is….'

'Right, what are you saying, Charlie, you want to buy me a gift?'

'I think maybe if we can get a copy, it might help,' I said tentatively.

'Help? What do you mean, pal?'

'Well, I mean…' *what did I mean?* 'Oh, don't worry about it.'

'Cool, see you.' Dave said, putting the phone down.

++++++++++++++++++++++++++++++++

The day zoomed past at high pace, in a flurry of excitement and Slush Puppies.

The girls went on about seven rides in the end and were exhausted by the time we were done. Tara had booked a Holiday Inn four miles away, so we drove back, ate in the local pub and relaxed.

It was 7.40 pm, and I was ready to hit the hay. I supped on a bottle of beer while the girls did the colouring given to them by the pub staff. I got up and headed to the toilet, yawning slowly, in a dream-like state.

I shivered and felt the strange, warm, intoxicating feeling I felt when I was gassed in Copenhagen. I steadied myself, took a deep breath and went into the men's toilets.

I stood at the urinal and waited.

The door opened behind me and in walked a small, scruffy-looking man, who I didn't recognise from being in the pub. It wasn't that I had to check out every person who was in there, but when you do my line of work, I got into the habit of gauging a room before I sat down.

This guy, I did not see.

He looked up at me and smiled. His teeth were

yellow and crooked, and he looked greasy and unkempt.

He kept looking at me, smiling.

'All right, mate?' I asked.

The man leaned across to me and whispered, 'Ludibriums.'

'You what, mate?' I said, as he did his flies up and went to leave.

I was still going, so I pushed trying to finish while trying not to urinate all over the floor. 'What did you say?'

He looked at me from the entrance to the washroom, 'Ludibriums… It's happened again.'

I finished off and then ran out of the toilet after him.

'Where did he go?' I asked T, a bit panicked.

'What… wh… who, Charlie?'

'That guy, who came in the toilet after me?'

'I didn't see anyone go in…'

'What?'

I ran around the bar to see if he was anywhere else in the pub, but he wasn't. I went outside and looked across the car park. Nothing. Not even a light on in any car.

He had disappeared.

27

We went back to the hotel and the girls got ready for bed. They were very excitable, wanting to stay up late and watch TV. It was 8.45 pm and we let the girls watch fifteen minutes, before putting them to bed; it had been a long day.

They were in an adjoining room in the hotel, so I showered, brushed my teeth and got myself ready for bed while they played in their room. Tara told the girls to turn off the lights and go to sleep, which I think in the end they were grateful for. The plan was to head back to Alton Towers briefly tomorrow morning to go on one or two more rides and then come back home.

When all was quiet, I pulled Tara closer to me.

'Hey, that book you are reading…. Does it ever mention…*ludibriums?*'

'Ludibri- what? No, why?' Tara responded.

'Oh, no reason… just curious.'

'Where have you heard it?'

'It came up in Copenhagen and I thought I'd ask.'

'Go to sleep, Charlie… try and relax,' Tara said, turning over, making a small spoon.

If only I could, but my head was whirring.

++++++++++++++++++++++++++++++++

The noise from next door was growing, no matter how much I pretended it wasn't. The kids sounded like they were jumping up and down on the bed. I looked at Tara, who was stirring but still asleep.

I got up and went through, despite every fibre of my being wanting to stay in bed.

'Morning, Daddy!' Maddie shouted.

'Morning, sweetheart. How did you guys sleep?' I wrestled Maddie to the bed and tickled her senseless.

'Good, thanks,' Iris replied.

I checked my watch… 7.33 am. Not bad I thought to myself, I must have got at least five hours, once I was finally able to settle.

'OK, shall we get ready and do the last few rides?'

There was a resounding yes from the girls, so I told them to get changed and brush their teeth while I went through and woke Tara.

She was snoring, so I let her be, instead grabbing the large copy of Troy's book by the side of her bed.

I flicked through the pages trying to find the word I was looking for, but it was to no avail. I read a few passages and it was a lot to do with

Troy's childhood and how he'd been dragged around Europe.

I felt for the guy, sounds like he didn't have it easy. Hopefully, his book would give him the life he wanted now, but I wasn't so sure. From what I had heard, it wasn't so easy making good money from writing fiction novels. Still… I guess he enjoyed it.

Tara was awake now and smelt of mornings: soft, feminine, warm. She snuggled in and I suggested she got in the shower as the girls would want to leave soon.

Tara nodded and reticently went towards the bathroom.

The girls came bounding in, and by the time Troy's book had hit the floor, I had two hyperactive young ladies on top of me, and I was fully immersed in the second tickle fight of the morning!

+++++++++++++++++++++++++++++++

The theme park was like a ghost town. It was just before 10 am and most of the rides hadn't opened, but we were in and walking around. 'The Wicker Man' had a one-hundred-and twenty-minute queue yesterday, so that was where we started. This time it was only half an hour, but even so, I was surprised at the hullabaloo around this ride. It was an old wooden rollercoaster, with no loops or upside-down sections; yet, it was the most popular ride on the park.

Was it because it was new and the one that had been advertised the most? Or was it because the public had gotten bored with the new shiny rides and wanted something authentic?

I guessed it was the first reason, but hoped the second. Either way, I enjoyed my time in the park. It was awesome seeing Maddie so excited. Plus, it was time away, like being in a fun bubble, where reality couldn't get to me.

The 'Wicker Man' was great fun. Then it was onto '13,' a spookfest in the dark with thrills aplenty. There is one part where the ride reaches its climax and Iris cried. That wasn't great, but apart from that, the weekend seemed a huge success.

I waited outside the ride 'Hex,' as it was Tara's turn to take the children on the ride.

I sat and watched as the park got busier. I looked and noted potential people of note… dangers, threats. Will there ever be a time when I don't do this? Retirement? Even then I'll still have the guard up, no doubt.

I felt the gentle pull, the pull away from what was right and wholesome. Apart from the thing that saved me, I was always brought back down, back towards darkness.

I texted Dave, 'I should be back by five.'

He sent back the smiley face. I couldn't be a civilian for too long; this peace wasn't for me. I was a bit part, a visitor, a guest in my own life. The girls came rushing over from the ride, all smiles and butterflies.

'I guess we should think about heading home,' I said abruptly.

Maddie looked sad but nodded. Tara was happy to sleep in the car, so with reticence, we agreed to leave.

+++++++++++++++++++++++++++++++++

I drove most of the way. Even Bruce 'The Boss' Springsteen couldn't keep my spirits light, so I flicked it onto the radio.

The kids were quiet in the back; Tara was dozing.

The phone rang via the Bluetooth; Jackson.

I gulped and picked it up.

'Hey, boss. Can I call you back? Now's not a good time…' I said quickly, knowing that what he might have to tell me was not for little ears through the speakerphone.

'Sure, but make it snappy please, Charlie.' The line went dead.

'Right, pitstop…. five minutes until the next

services,' I announced.

The girls grumbled, and Tara woke up.

I pulled into the services, 'everybody out!'

'Kids, come on…. toilet!' Tara announced.

I was alone in the car, so-called Jackson back.

'Boss, what can I do for you?' I asked, trying to remain upbeat.

'Two things, Charlie, both bad,' he said.

'Righto…'

'First thing, there has been another murder…'

'What, really…? Where?'

'Ashford, near the fields by the outlet…'

'Chrissake, really... when?' I asked.

'It happened yesterday… a girl called Laura Unsworth…'

'Yesterday!? Why didn't you tell me then?'

'You needed a break, to see the family… anyway, the work starts now, forensics have been done. Same style and modus operandi as the first killing.'

'What do you mean?'

'Well… severed body… brutalised in several ways… left in a public place. The girl was drugged before the murder, young…seventeen… was going to work in the new Haribo Store at the outlet over there.'

'I take it the parents know?'

'I've sent Karl and Jimmy to talk to them and see if there are any leads. I'll let you know if they bring anything back. I need you in tomorrow morning, first thing, to look this over.'

'OK. What was the second bit of bad news?'

'You are going to Hamburg. We have good intel this time that Jennifer Green is there. Apparently, she has a residence and has been going in and out of Hamburg quite frequently. I want you to find her and bring her in, Charlie.'

Hamburg? That's weird…

'Right,' I took a deep breath… that familiar mixture of exhilaration and trepidation, my good old friend.

The girls came back to the car with two packets of Pringles and a bag of Starburst.

Tara was holding two cups of coffee too.

'I have just got to nip inside,' I said, as Tara got back in the car.

'What have you been doing?'

I looked at her furtively, 'I will explain later.'

28

Tara drove the rest of the way home, so I got a bit of rest.

I explained with the music up so that Maddie didn't hear what Darren Jackson had said; Tara fell silent.

I thought it best to leave it and not push it. The kids dozed in the back, and I thought about my plan of attack. Jackson had already started texting through information about the Hamburg mission. Places Green has been spotted, a local church that had been visited and the area where they propose her home is; I was on a flight tomorrow.

'I think I should come,' Tara stated.

'What?'

'I'm going to come… to Hamburg,' she reiterated.

'Really. This is work though. You can't…you know…'

'Look, I think I can help you in this case. There is something strange going on, with this book of Troy's… odd connections and stuff. The more heads together, the more likely we will be to solve it,' she said pragmatically.

'But what about the flat and you know, things here?' I grasped.

'Listen, Charlie. It will be what? A few days? The flat will be fine. We haven't got Maddie next weekend either,' she asserted.

I thought about what she was saying. It went against protocol, but what Jackson didn't know… besides, there was no law against her coming along and having a city break while I was there.

'Sure, why not?' I said, Tara smiled.

'You know that Dave is probably going to be there?' I said.

'Separate room for him, I'll pay if I have to!'

We dropped Maddie off, who by the time we got to Maidstone Services was zombie-like after the excitement of the weekend. It was then up to Hawkinge for Iris and then back to the flat. By the time we got there, I noticed Dave's Dodge parked over the road.

Tara smiled, 'off you go then! I'll get us packed for tomorrow.'

I kissed her goodbye and jumped into Dave's car. I think I was the only person who could have a couple of relaxing days off and come back feeling exhausted.

'All good, my man?' he said, leaning over to hug me as I got in.

'Yeah tired, but like a different type of tired, you know? Lots of walking around with the kids and so on, but it was fun. What have you been up to?'

'Oh, this and that. Put a new exhaust pipe on the Dodge. Made a bird table. Found out there is more to this Hockey Club than we first thought.'

'I see. Would you care to elaborate?'

Dave waved a CB radio at me. 'It's amazing what you can listen into with these old things… but I could have sworn I heard this Miller guy talking to people in all sorts of places… Ashford… Folkestone… Copenhagen…'

'Really?'

'Hamburg…'

'Oh wow, so he's like…involved then?'

'Only one way to find out…'

We drove slowly up to Hawkinge and stopped at The Dragonfly pub in the centre.

We had a diet coke each, grabbed a bite to eat, and caught up, but primarily bided time until any punters had long gone from the Hockey club. As it was Sunday, it was likely they shut earlier.

Once it was past 10 pm, we drove the further few minutes up the road to the hockey club. It was dark and locked up. Dave passed me gloves and a balaclava. After checking no-one was in the vicinity, we crept into the grounds of the sports club.

The front doors were locked and bolted; an

alarm was flashing.

Dave went towards the back of the building and managed to jimmy the lock on the back door, which was far more straightforward to break than the elaborate front door mechanism.

'Charlie, the alarm is on a sensor, so you need to make sure we don't go across its activation points. Look…'

Dave shone a light into the dark of the empty bar. You could see that several red beams were bearing down from the alarm system but, if you were careful, there was a route through without setting them off.

'Can't we just use a codebreaker?' I asked.

'Well, yes… but if anyone notices the alarm is off, it might alert them quicker,' he rebutted.

'Good point. Fear not, care and sensitivity are my middle names.'

'Yeah, right. You haven't had any beers, have you? I know what you're like.'

'Very funny. I've been driving, and as you well know I barely touch the stuff anymore,' I said.

'Right, well lead on then, twinkle toes.'

I walked gently through the open space of the central area and crept around behind the bar. There was an opening to a kitchenette which Dave signalled me through.

'Where am I headed then, mate?' I asked.

'Your guess is as good as mine. But there must

be a cellar here somewhere.'

Into the kitchenette and I noticed that there was a hatch in the floor. The alarm system also didn't seem to work in this section, which was handy.

There was a large sign written in big black letters, 'IF THERE IS A DELIVERY CALL DAVID.'

I pointed it out to Dave, 'Here. I guess someone wants to know when the delivery guys need to access the cellar.'

'We're on the right track…' Dave suggested.

I tugged at the hatch door, but it was locked.

'Hmm… who locks the cellar door in a pub that already has alarms, locks and so on?' I asked.

'Someone with something to hide. Out the way, Charlie, let me see if I can pick it…'

Dave pulled out a large set of keys and spent a few minutes getting the right one to open the door. I looked out of the window; the night was clear and I could clearly see the black shapes of sea on the moon. It reminded me that at some stage I should buy a telescope so Maddie could explore the night sky, she would love it.

In my peripheral vision, I noticed a moving shape, so I ducked down and pushed Dave to the floor.

'Bloody hell!'

'Ssssh!' I replied, poking my head back up slowly to see out of the window. Walking across the tarmac and towards the football pitches adjacent was a young lady walking a large Alsatian. As far as I could tell, she hadn't noticed us.

'Sorry, dog walker… can't be too careful, pal!' I said, as Dave shook his head.

Eventually, the old hatch door opened creakily. I went to turn on the light, but Dave put his hand on mine.

'Don't…. it'll be too bright,' he said, flicking on his flashlight. A deafening reminder that he was the master, and me, still very much the apprentice.

There were some rickety wooden stairs which Dave started traversing. I checked one more time out of the window and around the perimeter. It was clear, so I followed.

Dave turned to me and intimated to close the hatch. As soon as it was entirely shut he found the switch for the lights.

The first room that we were in seemed like a standard pub cellar. The air was cold, and there were several beer kegs, bottles and snacks in the place. There was another wooden door towards the back of the cellar. It had a large red sign on it saying, 'DO NOT ENTER.'

We searched the cellar first. There was nothing

of note, except everything you expected to find in a pub cellar. The smell of stale beer put me off the thought of drinking.

I analysed the mechanisms and the plastic tubes and chillers. They certainly put a lot into making it taste decent. Looking at the pork scratchings and the cheese and onion crisps, my favourite, made me peckish though.

'Nothing in here. Have you found anything?' Dave asked.

'Nope, not unless you're hungry.'

Dave signalled me to try the door at the back of the cellar. I slowly took the handle and turned it to the right. Locked again. Dave fiddled briefly with it, and then the door creaked open. The room was dark, with no windows, but there was another light switch.

There was a desk in the corner and a large leather seat behind it. The bookshelf on the far wall housed many folders and old books. Some were about religious sects, the occult, forms of satanism; I shivered.

Dave leafed through a folder, and when he did, some photographs fell out. I went to pick them up… they were all of young girls and boys…mostly girls, teenagers.

Some were profile photos from social media sites; others were surveillance photos of them in the community; a couple were school photos.

'Well, he gave us both the creeps when we met him,' Dave said.

I grabbed another folder. The same thing, photos of people, this time young and old. Dave was taking them from me and placing them in his backpack. We took about five before making the decision that we had been here long enough. Given that Miller was using the club as a front for whatever sordid online stuff he was doing, realistically he could come back at any time.

The locked doors and hatches showed that he was careful and would go to great lengths to protect himself. As much as we had enough to arrest him, ideally we didn't want to be caught having broken in without a search warrant.

As we went to make our exit, we both heard a small knock coming from the floor. We stayed stock still and silent. The pause seemed to last an age.

I held my breath, not wanting to alert whoever, whatever was beyond the walls. Perhaps I imagined it, I thought... then there it was again. I looked at Dave who shrugged nervously, his eyes widening.

'It's coming from the floor!' I said.

29

I listened intently while getting onto my hands and knees. It happened again.

I knocked back.

'Charlie! It could be Miller! It could be anyone setting a trap!' Dave hissed.

The thud came again. Then there was another beneath my feet and another to the left of the room.

'Dave, there's someone down there... *people* down there...'

I searched the floor as did Dave for some form of opening or hatch. Had they been cemented into the floor?

'We should call this in, mate. We can get a cement digger and go right through this,' I said.

'Yeah but if there are people alive down there, a cement digger many not be the best answer.'

'Have you got any better ideas?' I said, losing patience, worrying about the lives that could be at stake.

'Charlie, it could be anything!'

'They are responding, Dave. Come on. You know what that means...'

'OK, OK. If there is not an entrance in here, there has to be one somewhere else.

Check *everywhere!*

We rechecked the basement and cellar area. Dave had called it in, in case we needed back-up, yet our search was proving fruitless.

Think, Charlie, think! What did I learn from Copenhagen?

I went to the front door. I could hear the sirens cutting through the cold, dark night. I looked out, racking my brain for clues.

Then there it was, across the way…

I ran forward as Jackson and the squad cars pulled up outside the hockey club.

'Charlie, where are you going?' Jackson shouted, getting out of his BMW X5.

I kept on going to the building over the road: Horseshoes Lane Church. Why did I not think of this earlier?

I scaled the outside of the building for signs of the crimson cross; it had to be here somewhere in the darkness. I went to the back of the church where the old graveyard was, Dave followed behind.

'What on earth are you up to?' he asked. He didn't know yet about how to enter the chambers.

I continued to search, and there it was, a large, gold cross with the red rose in the centre, glinting in the lights of the police cars; The crimson cross.

'Here, give me a bunk up pal,' I asked. Dave clasped his hands together and took my weight as I thrust myself up towards the glinting symbol. I reached up at full stretch and tried to grab it, missing it altogether.

'I think one too many takeaways on that weekend away, Charlie… hurry up will you!' Dave exclaimed.

'Give me a little push up again…' I said. He grunted and up I went. I clutched the red rose and twisted it as fast as I could. Karl and Jimmy, who were now watching next to us, looked utterly bemused.

The familiar clunking sounds started from the deep. There was a rumble as Dave placed me down on the ground; the grass shivered at the opening of the underground chamber.

'Right, be ready for anything here, boys.' I said as Dave reached for the latch on the door, pulling them both open.

The darkness ahead was silent. I took a deep breath and headed into the unknown once more. Thankfully this time, I had a little more back up.

30

'Watch your step,' I said to Dave, as we helped each other down the wooden stairs and into the underground chamber.

There was no light switch, so with our torches, we headed further down the corridor. I realised that the direction we were headed, North-East, was the direction of the hockey club and the strange noises. For now, everything seemed silent though.

We got to the end of the corridor and found a large metal door. It had a large circular device in the middle.

'OK then muscles... after three... one, two, three!' Dave said, and we both twisted hard to the left. The device began to spin, the door moved slightly.

We did it again, and the door opened a little more. We slipped inside, into a cold room. Our breath was visible in front of our faces, and there were candelabras attached upon the walls. Dave pulled out a lighter and lit them to give the place an eerie glow.

There was another door with the symbols 'IV' on the top of it. I looked again... Roman numerals... this was number four.

'We must be under the hockey club now, it

must be through this door,' Dave said, hammering at the lock.

'Easy Dave, take it easy... anything could be behind there,' I said, trying to calm him, as he had become rather anxious to get inside.

'OK, OK,' he said, collecting himself, reaching for his walkie talkie. 'Jackson, have we got an armed response yet?'

The buzz of white noise then,' Yes, just arriving. I'll send them down.'

'OK, quietly... tell them to head north and follow the open doors...' Dave said, turning his attention back to the old lock. A few moments passed, as Dave worked his magic. I noticed the cold and shivered. Five coppers in full black protective gear with guns surrounded us.

I intimated for them to back away a bit and they did reticently.

'OK, here goes...' Dave pushed, then pulled it towards him and slowly, the heavy door opened.

The first things I noticed were low whimpers and human crying. As the dim light entered the room, we could not believe what we saw.

I counted seven girls, all teenagers most likely, slowly getting up and making their way towards us. The feeble crying continued, one girl said 'help me...' as she got near me, her face was contorted, she flung herself into my arms.

She was cold to touch, her skin white as snow and as cold as ice.

'Blankets, we need blankets!' I screamed at the Armed Response, who slowly withdrew and went back towards the staircase.

'It's OK; you're safe now.' I said while Dave went into the room to help the rest of the girls get up and out.

'Jackson, we are going to need ambulances right away,' I breathed into the walkie-talkie.

'No problem.' There was the muffled sound of Jackson giving orders to someone, 'what have you got down there, anyway?' he said.

'Seven girls, emaciated, no clothing… no obvious signs of physical harm from what I can see. We need warm clothes, covers…' I said into the walkie-talkie.

We continued to get the girls to their feet. They were like zombies and seemed to be drugged by the way that they were moving slowly and with no real response. In one corner of the room, there was a body, no pulse, no response… somebody's daughter.

In the other corner, what looked and smelt like faeces, urine and vomit.

After I helped the last surviving girl up the stairs and back to humanity, I went back to collect the remaining body. Jackson came with me.

'Oh, Jesus,' Jackson said, as I turned the body over.

The girl was naked, ice-cold and from my guess, barely thirteen years old.

'Animals…'

'What the hell is going on?' Jackson said.

'It's some form of cult. A twisted branch of Christianity gone horribly wrong. Look above the door, 'four.' Copenhagen was 'seven.' You know what that means?'

'There's more. Chrissake…! OK, let's get out of here and get forensics in.'

31

'Bring that hockey club guy in, now!' Jackson said to Dave and I. He was foaming at the mouth over the scene he had just witnessed.

'OK, for what though?' I asked.

'Are you having a laugh, Stone...?'

'No, but technically he's not even connected to this... in any way. We all think he's weird, but...not this... this is bigger, surely?' I said.

'Wait, boss. I got these...' Dave reached around into his backpack and pulled out the files he collected.

Jackson took a brief look, 'for goodness sake, bring that scumbag in!' he boomed. 'Actually, hold that thought for one minute...'

David Miller was walking up the drive towards the police cars and ambulances. I could sense this wasn't going to go well for him.

'What the blooming hell is going on?' he said.

Jackson looked at me, bemused, 'Is he for real?'

'Well, this is my livelihood! You lot come here and...'

'...Shut up, Miller! You are under arrest!'

Jackson grabbed him, threw him on the bonnet of the nearest vehicle and read him his rights. Miller continued to protest his innocence. He flapped like a fish under Jackson's strength. He was swearing quite loudly now in his strong Kentish brogue, as Karl and Jimmy went over to provide assistance that Jackson didn't really need.

Miller was wearing a pair of Slazenger shorts, a plain white cricket top and a baseball cap. Dave and I looked him over.

'Do you think he did it? All of this?' I asked Dave as an aside.

Dave raised his eyebrows. 'Not sure. The evidence doesn't look great for him though.'

Miller was placed in a squad car, somewhat calmer now. However, a young woman was bustling up the street in dressing gown and slippers.

'Let him go; he hasn't done anything wrong! It's not true what they say about him!' she spluttered.

Dave pacified the woman, who upon closer inspection couldn't have been much older than nineteen. She had long brown hair, soft white skin and was probably a substantial size sixteen.

I noticed that the priest had come out from his home next door, thanks to all of the noise and kerfuffle, so I approached him, holding my badge.

The priest nodded at me, nervously.

'Good evening,' I said, realising the time was probably well past midnight, 'apologies for all the hoo-ha.'

'What on earth is going on? Why is the church all lit up?' he said softly.

'Do you recognise that man in the car over there?' I asked.

'Of course, Dave Miller. He runs the bar.'

'Do you see him often?'

'Well, yes. Going in and out of the club. I spoke to him last week about noise from one of the parties, but apart from that, not really.'

'I see. Do you ever see him around the church, in the graveyard…walking or anything?' I wanted to find out if he was the one accessing the chamber.

'Not Dave, no… he keeps himself to himself as much as he can, doesn't bother us. We get all sorts of kids in here. When their parents are drinking, and they get bored, they often come over here and run around.'

'I see. Nothing else suspicious? I mean anything that could help us at this stage?' I said.

'Well… it's probably nothing…'

'Try me, Mr…?'

'Fred. Fred Groves...' the vicar extended his hand, which I took.

'Try me, Mr Groves.' I continued.

'A few weeks ago, I found a whole heap of

rubbish, just dumped out the back of the building. Old cupboards and bits of wood, you know, just thought some lazy so and so had fly-tipped somewhere quiet.'

'Yes…'

'Well, a nice chap who goes in that hockey club came around and said he would move it for me. Which was good of him, I must say. Anyway, he did… I can't remember his name now, what was it… erm… Craig… no… Carl, that's it, Carl… something or other,' he continued.

'OK, so Carl from the hockey club saw the rubbish and offered to clear it?'

'Yes, for free! I was dead chuffed!'

'So, what seemed odd about it?'

'Oh, nothing really, I think maybe, I'm thinking too far into things…'

'No, please. Go on.'

'It's just that… there is no through way behind the church. No path, no woodlands… just the fence. So how did he know about the rubbish out the back?'

'Hm… perhaps playing with his kids? Or he had a dead relative out there?'

'No dead relatives, those gravestones are hundreds of years old. But, yes you may be right, I think he has children,' the priest mused.

'Worth chasing up though, so thanks. You can't remember Carl's surname perchance?' I asked.

'Not off the top of my head, but everyone knows him. He's often in there, next door. People know his partner too, what's her name now? Sam.... Sam, I think…'

'Is she someone who helps in the community…?'

The vicar bellowed with laughter.

'Oh no, quite the opposite. I don't like to speak ill of people, but she is… well… let's just say trouble always finds her, and with two young kids too…' he shook his head.

'Go on vicar; this is all in confidence…'

'You know I shouldn't say… just that she has a bit of a reputation here and in Folkestone for being a bit wayward… if you know what I mean, very wayward in fact.'

OK, I scribbled her name down in my notebook too.

'Well, that has been very helpful vicar. If there's anything else, here's my card, don't hesitate to call me,' I said smiling at the kindly old man.

'Oh, that was it; he left a ladder. A good one too, old and wooden. An antique really…'

'Where?'

'When he cleared all of the rubbish for me, he left a ladder, standing up against the side of the church,' the priest added.

'Show me. Show me where please,' the vicar noticed the urgency in my voice then hurried me around to the side of the building.

'It was here… right here, just under the cross…'

The ladder was no longer there.

The doors to the chamber below were wide open; the vicar peered inside.

'Fifteen years I have been here and I never knew that was there,' he said.

'Want to know something even crazier…? That Gold cross up there opens those doors…'

'Give over!'

'They do. Twist the red flower in the middle, and they unlock. This is not the only church that has this… secret chamber…' not wanting to sound like the next Harry Potter book, I struggled to define what it was. Also, I wasn't sure how much the vicar knew about the medieval crimes that were being committed, literally on his watch. *Here goes…*

'So, you had no idea about this?' I asked.

'Absolutely no idea Detective. Wish I had though, would keep the wine cold and fresh… that's what they say now, red wine to be served cold. Well, I'm not a fan of that, and I'm not sure the parishioners would be either if I'm truthful.'

'No. So you can see that forensics are in and out of here…'

The light in the vicar's eyes dimmed as men and

women in boiler suits left with clear plastic bags. One had human hair. Another had blood and what looked like bone in it.

'Oh, no… what the… what on earth was going on… at *my church!?*'

'We are not sure yet, but we found seven girls down there earlier. One of them was dead.'

'Girls… why?' The vicar put his hand to his mouth and seemed visibly perturbed. 'How did I not know...?'

The vicar fell to his knees and seemed to hyperventilate.

I picked him up and told him to breathe.

'It's OK, Mr Groves. Breathe… relax… It's OK. We don't suspect you of anything. Don't worry.'

He looked at me bemused, pushing himself out of my grasp.

'You cocky bastard, I couldn't care less about *your* judgment…' he said, looking up at the stone building. 'Shame on you…' he said, as tears fell down his cheeks.

I urged him to go back to his house to get some rest. One less suspect to worry about I guess.

32

I got a text on my phone from Jackson, 'In tomorrow at 7 am.'

Dave was waiting in the car and drove me home. It was now 1.12 am. I would try and get my head down for at least a few hours before tomorrow came.

I snuck in hoping not to wake T, but as I crept into bed, she stirred.

'Where have you been?'

'Babe, you don't want to know. Work stuff. Just to let you know, I think our trip to Hamburg may be put back until the afternoon or evening.'

'Hm.' She rolled over and went back to sleep. I moved the red, velvet book that was on the bed onto the floor and closed my eyes.

I had a feeling Jackson wanted to pin this on Miller. That's the problem with being the big boss, pressure from above to get a conviction. I just wanted to get the right man, and I was pretty confident Miller wasn't in on this cult stuff, I just needed to prove it.

+++++++++++++++++++++++++++++++++

Dave picked me up at 6.45 am and we drove to

the station to meet up with the rest of the team.

Jackson was waiting in his office when we arrived; he called Karl and Jimmy in.

'OK, so this is the situation. That was one hell of a racket we made last night. The press has already picked up on it. Luckily, for now, The Rattle murder is locked down, but it wouldn't surprise me if that got out soon too. Our line is that this was a bust on a local paedophile, yes? And we pin Miller for it.'

There was an awkward silence.

'Is he here?' I asked.

'Yes, he is in the holding cells here, Charlie, and you can talk to him in a moment. But, having looked through these folders, there is something quite odd about the bloke.'

'That may well be, Darren, but does that mean he is to blame for the girls under the church?' I asked.

'Well, who knows? But what we have is a gaggle of missing girls under *HIS* cellar. Doesn't look great, does it?' Jackson returned.

'No, it doesn't, but what if he had nothing to do with it? I mean, I don't think the two crimes are connected.'

'It's a mighty fine coincidence, Charlie…'

'I know, but it's not him. He might be an oddball, he might have bad intentions, but this sect? Copenhagen? He hasn't got the minerals for all that, surely?'

'Charlie, when this gets out… everyone will be terrified. Terrified and angry. We need a nick to keep the bloody peace.'

'We also need to find the actual culprits and permit me, but it's bigger than David bloody Miller! I spoke to the vicar… he said he has never seen Miller in his church or on the grounds. There is only one entrance to the chamber. If Miller was squirrelling children away down there, the vicar would have known about it!'

'Is that evidence… is it, Charlie…?'

'No, but… you have no evidence that he has done it either!' I said, getting flustered by Jackson's attitude.

'I don't need evidence! I need probable cause, and I reckon we have it!' he said, waving the folder at me.

'Shall we talk to him?' Dave said, looking up at Jackson, yet directing the question at me.

'You can talk to him, but you lead it,' he said, pointing at Dave. 'Charlie, watch it here pal,' Jackson said, flashing me a warning glance. I turned away and left the room with Dave. Outside the door, I challenged him.

'What's the matter, mate? You lost your voice in there?' I said.

Dave gave me a sideways glance. 'There's no need to be like that, Charlie.'

I took a deep breath. 'Sorry, but I don't want to ping this guy if he's not guilty and I don't think he's guilty!'

'Let's have a chat with him. Stay cool, honey bunny,' Dave said, smiling.

I was raging, but sometimes Dave could see the bigger picture, and that's why he wasn't as annoyed as me. That's also why we were great partners, we learned from each other and rather than lose it with Jackson, talking to Miller was the best plan for now.

33

We went down to the holding cells and I was pleased to see Rod, the holding cell manager who used to work at Folkestone Police Station.
'Hey, mate! No longer at Folkestone nick?' I asked.
'Hey, Charlie. No mate. It's all about Ashford these days. They say "Oh Folkestone this and Folkestone that." All Creative Quarter and Harbour Arm, but it's dead really,' Rod said.
'And Ashford is better?' I asked.
'Oh, hell yeah! Bowling… the outlet… half an hour from the mighty West Ham…'
'Yeah, I guess you're right mate,' he had a point.
'More people… cheaper housing… the new brewery… new cinema… great for kids…'
'Yeah… fair enough, Rod. That said though, no seaside in Ashford…' I said, playing devil's advocate.
'True, but how often do you go to the sea? I mean it's nice to look at, but Folkestone's only great for three months a year when the weather is warm. Ashford… twelve months a year…family fun times…'
'You know what, Rod? You might just be right,' I agreed.
'And the best thing…? Pizza Express… not just

one of them… two!' Rod looked off dreamily into the distance, thinking of pizza.

'You know what, I'm going to get T to look at properties here…'

'Oh, no. Don't do that, not now,' Rod said, his tone changing.

'Oh, OK. Why?'

'Next year, there will be a global pandemic, that's going to close everything down.'

'*Pandemic*…are you sure, pal?' I asked, wondering where Rod was going with this.

'Yes, Charlie. The whole world will be on lockdown. No overseas travel anywhere, people dying, empty supermarkets, the economy completely knackered…'

I listened but was beginning to lose interest. I mean, I think Rod had been watching too many zombie movies.

'So yeah about September, next year… all house prices will be way down, that's your time to move…'

'OK! Well cheers for that mate,' Dave interjected. 'The err… suspect...?'

'Oh, Miller? This way,' Rod said.

'So, Rod, was he a sleeper or a panicker?' I asked. Rod had a belief that if a suspect came in and slept, he was guilty. If he was up and about, pacing the room, innocent. The guilty are going to need the sleep was how Rod dealt out justice in his head. I have heard worse theories to be fair.

'Oh wow, massive panicker… a real fresh fish… I will bet you my house in Ashford he didn't abduct those girls,' Rod said, opening the door to the cell.

'Morning, Miller. Follow us.'

We took the suspect up to an interview room on the first floor of the building. Depending on the nature of the interrogation, we chose where we did it. If we wanted to keep it sinister and claustrophobic, it would be in the holding cells, if we wanted it a bit more professional, the shop floor it was.

Miller seemed a little dazed and glassy-eyed, but despite my belief about him, I had to remain impartial.

We sat him down in the little room and turned on the recording device.

Dave did the necessaries, I kept my eye on Miller, looking for any giveaways in his body language. Currently, he sat with the thousand-yard stare, hands clasped. He looked like he hadn't slept.

'Morning, Mr Miller. Can you tell me about your job at the Hockey Club?' I asked.

'I run the bar. That's it really. I play in the team sometimes when they are short of players, but that's it.'

'I see… do you have employees?'

'Yes… three girls who help me out…'

'How old are they, if I may ask?' Dave interjected.

Miller looked across at him, and Dave met his gaze.

'Not sure, all old enough,' he said.

'Old enough for what?' I asked.

'You know what I mean! All over eighteen,' he continued.

'Is that where you met your girlfriend, Mr Miller?' I asked.

'Yes, she was working behind the bar for me, and we got close…'

'Her age…?'

'Nineteen.'

'Last month, yeah? She turned nineteen in October, right?'

'Yes, I don't see why that's relevant?'

I continued unabated, 'and you are…forty-three… giving an age gap of twenty-four years?' I said.

'That's right. It's not illegal, is it?' Miller asked, sarcastically.

'Well, no. It's not. Some people might find it odd, and it might be frowned upon, but no… not illegal.'

'I get it, you know. People whisper behind their hands. People make jokes about me being 'a paedo.' I laugh along, but I'm not a… one of them…' he said.

'One of what…?' Dave asked.

'A… paedo…'

'For what it's worth, Mr Miller…. I believe you…' I said, laying my cards on the table but keeping my ace firmly up my sleeve.

'Oh… OK…'

'I mean, Dave here isn't sure, and my boss thinks you are a cast-iron wrong un. He's desperate to send you down. You know what will happen to you in Belmarsh, don't you?' His eyes widened, terrified.

'But… but… I've done nothing wrong! I mean, what about Emma? She…I…'

'…Relax for a minute! Hold it together, Mr Miller!' I said, he was close to tears already. 'You need to help me understand these…' I pulled out one of the folders with the pictures of the young girls and boys: nothing lewd, nothing of a sexual nature, just photos.

'I…I…have never seen them?'

I looked at Dave, who currently was doing his best poker face.

'But they were found in *your* back office… and with the seven abducted girls next door… one of them dead, this does not look good,' Dave said in a soft tone.

'Wait… what? Those aren't mine!' he pointed at

the folders.

'But they were in your back office at the hockey club,' I reminded him.

'What back-office…?' He was either very dense or a great actor, I thought to myself.

'Through the beer cellar *in your hockey club*…'

He thought for a moment, 'oh the locked door? Not mine, I have never even set foot in there. Check it, check for prints...!'

'So, who's is it!?' I asked incredulously.

'I was appointed by the committee to run the club. But when I got shown around, I was told it was out of action and not to use it. So, I never bothered with it…'

'You were never curious to look in it?' I asked.

'I never had the time, and after a while I forgot it was there, to be honest.'

I took a deep breath. Dave whispered to come outside with him for a moment.

'Give us one second, Mr Miller.' I said.

'But, I…I'm innocent…' he started again.

Dave shut the door on the interview room and Millers protesting.

'You're right, he didn't do it,' Dave said.

'Thank you.'

'He was up all of last night, bricking it. If he had any inkling about that office and those photos, he would have come up with something. I don't think he has ever been in there. We can get one of the boys to test for fingerprints and DNA in there, but I would bet my mortgage, his won't come up.'

'Jackson will want something though,' I said, concerned for Miller.

Dave opened the door again and went back in. Miller was rubbing his hands nervously.

'Just a quick one, did you hear anything odd in that cellar? Funny noises in the walls? The floor?'

'There was some knocking and scratching, but I thought it must have been rats… there's a sewer underneath the club that runs the length of the pitch.'

I looked at Dave. 'Is there really?'

'Yes, that's what I was told anyway.'

'By?'

'The Committee when I started…'

'Who, Miller? I need a name…'

'Well, the head of the management committee… Pensborough. Steve Pensborough.'

Dave and I looked at him incredulously.

'Right, we need an address for him. You will have that won't you with all your committee papers and so on, yes?'

'Probably…'

'One final thing, Mr Miller,' Dave said, Miller looked deflated entirely now.

'Show me how one of these works.' Dave tossed him a walkie-talkie from a CB radio across the table.

He slowly picked it up and began to look at it obtusely. He turned it upside down before pressing the button on the side. There was a loud hiss of white noise. Miller looked startled. Dave looked at me to wrap it up.

'Do you know any 'Carls' who drink in your club?' I asked.

'Yep, there's one, a bit of a wally, Carl Blewett.' Miller said.

'OK, interview terminated at 10.43 am,' I pressed the button to stop the tape. 'Right… get Jimmy and Karl to take him back, get the address for Pensborough, and he's free to go,' I said to the constable on duty.

He nodded.

'What about Jackson?' Dave asked.

I looked at my old pal. 'What did you always teach me? What's right. To do what's right. This guy is innocent.'

'He won't be happy,' Dave said.

'Well, so be it. Miller, you're going home.

34

'Have you gone insane?!' Jackson said. 'I mean seriously? You have let him go? Without my say so?'

'Darren, please listen to me…' I started.

'Everyone thinks the guy is dodgy…'

'Yes, but…'

'Photos of kids in his office…'

'It's not his office…' I said.

'A girlfriend barely out of nappies…'

'Well, nineteen…'

'What the hell, Charlie!?'

'Well if you will let me finish, Darren!' I shouted. There was quiet, Jackson took a breath. Dave sat quietly, firmly on the fence for now.

'Go on,' he said.

'The back office is not his. We are checking now for any fingerprints and whether or not he could have accessed it. Think about it, if he knew about the office and the weird photos, he would have thought of a reason why he had them. He didn't have a bloody clue.'

'So, what you are saying is it's just coincidence that this known… bloody… paedophile…'

'He's not a paedophile!'

'This known *oddball*… just happened not to

know about the missing girls under his floorboards and just happened not to know about hundreds of pictures of young kids? Targets, Charlie. Potential victims…'

'Darren, he is too bloody stupid to be involved! This is co-ordinated, professional and downright awful. Miller isn't involved. He's a dirty old man who likes a bit of younger flesh; it's as simple as that.'

'To be honest, guv, he's not the only one. For what it's worth, I'm sure Charlie is right,' Dave added.

'Oh really, you're sure? Thanks for that, that's really insightful,' Jackson said sarcastically. Unperturbed, Dave pressed on.

'The person we are looking for is communicating via a CB radio. Miller hasn't got a clue. He drives a top of the range Land Rover, has a nineteen-year-old girlfriend and runs a bar. He is not knowledgeable at communicating across countries with a CB radio. Facebook or TikTok is more his thing.'

'He can give us the address of the management committee's chairman, guess who? Pensborough,' I said.

'Pensborough? Really? The old DCI?'

'Yep… apparently so,' I said, proud of myself, hoping to quell Jackson's raging fires.

'And therein lies the problem…*apparently*…

What if it's a ruse, Charlie? What if it's a lie to buy him some time so him and his bit of flap can leave the country? Did you think about that?' Jackson said, moving firmly into fourth gear, engine revving.

'No… because if you trust me, Dave and our judgment, he's not guilty. He was told that there were rats and a sewer underneath the cellar. That's why no alarm bells rang. As long as he was selling beer and could go home at midnight with his new girlfriend…he was happy…'

Jackson looked directly at the constable in the room. 'Tell Fletcher to have an unmarked car watch Millers house. If he so much as twitches a curtain, I want to know. As for you, Charlie, this is a cock-up. You have dropped the ball here. You both have. Going in without a warrant and now letting go of our chief suspect… our only suspect!'

'Right, I know we are all worried here, but this is getting out of hand,' Dave's voice was stern and cut through the accusations. 'Millers is not involved, end of. I know this is horrible and we're all worried, maybe subconsciously… that we don't have a lot to go on… and about these girls… but we need to pull together. Yeah, we shouldn't have gone in, you're right, Darren. We're sorry, but we saved six lives.'

Silence. Everyone took a breath.

'What have we got then? A pattern of these underground lairs attached to churches?' Jackson asked.

'Yes, Catholic churches so far,' I added in tentatively.

'OK, good…they are targeting the young… we will get ID's on these girls, check them against missing persons…' Jackson continued.

'They could be trafficked; did anyone hear them speak?' Dave asked. There was a collective shaking of heads.

'Nothing meaningful,' I added.

'We now have a link to Pensborough, and we know Green is in Hamburg, yes? My suggestion is that Charlie, you go to Hamburg and bring in Green. No easy task. Dave, you chase this Pensborough lead. Tidy up, get the ID's on the girls, find out what the hell was going on here.'

'We need to compile a list of Roman Catholic churches in the area… maybe across the region if we can and investigate them… the crimson cross, that's the key… if the church has the crimson cross, that is the trigger. Copenhagen was seven, and this is four. There has to be more.'

Dave and I got up to leave.

'Hey, Charlie. Good luck in Hamburg, OK? Don't do anything too risky,' Jackson added softly.

I guess in his way that was him making peace. I was worried. I didn't want to go to Hamburg without Dave. Last time I would have wound up dead if he hadn't have been there. This time, who knows? We are getting closer to the source, and Green will know.

Before I left, I ran a quick background check on Carl Blewett, the guy who cleared the rubbish for the Priest. Dave stayed with me. 'Oh, wow…'

'What's that?' Dave said, turning towards the screen.

'I know this guy… had a couple of arrests for possession of class 'A' substances. He's the one who cleared the rubbish and left the ladder.'

'That rubbish had to be planted for the ladder to be left and not raise eyebrows,' Dave said.

'Absolutely. And guess what? He is also on the hockey club's management committee. What do you know?'

'Print that out for me, Charlie. I'll get him too. And yeah, stay safe out there. Doesn't look like I'll be there to bail you out this time, eh?' he said, punching my shoulder.

'Yeah, I know. Don't worry, I learnt from the best,' I said, trying to stay as brave as possible.

'Seriously though, don't be stupid. That bitch is dangerous. If you're in trouble, walkaway, there

will be another opportunity.'
I nodded.
'See you in a few days, buddy.'

35

We touched down in Hamburg in the late evening. With the time difference, it was getting on for 10 pm, so it was straight back to the hotel for a bit of food and bed, or so I thought.

Tara had packed all of our stuff and I took my police bag. Even though it was a relatively short flight, she had managed to get some sleep during it.

'Come on, let's drop the bags and head out,' she said, grinning from ear to ear.

Having thought about it, she would have been keen on a night out; police protection, then two weekends with Maddie. It had been a while.

'This isn't a jolly, you know?' I smiled at her.

'Yeah, I know. But why not get a feel for the place?'

We headed to the front of the hotel and hailed a cab.

'Where to?' the cab driver said abruptly.

'Erm… take us to the main nightlife, please,' I said.

It was a liberating feeling, like a tourist, not worrying about anything except a few drinks and some fun. The work could wait until tomorrow.

Where we got out of the cab was pretty far from scenic, or pleasant. It was quite the opposite of what we would look for in a city break destination. We were on the Reeperbahn, Hamburg's main drag, which reminded me more of Blackpool on steroids than Germany. Bright neon lights flashed up lurid images of naked women, men in groups swayed and staggered across the pavement, women called out flaunting their wares. If there were ever to be an apocalypse, it would look something like this.

I looked at Tara, who was enthralled.

'Come on, Charlie!' she said, grabbing my hand and walking swiftly up the street.

We walked past at least three or four 'sex shows' and just when I felt I was safe, a lady who shouted at me in English came away from her leaning post and pinched my bottom.

I refrained from producing my badge and explaining that what she did was a criminal action; instead, I smiled at her as she chewed her gum ferociously and stepped back into the shadows.

'Right, that's enough of that,' Tara said, leading us down the nearest side road.

As soon as we were away from the Reeperbahn, Hamburg became far more civilised.

I looked on Google maps and we were in an

area called St. Pauli. The names and styles of the bars changed significantly, from Chug and Heaven on the Reeperbahn, to Café Havjana and Johanna, off the beaten track.

We found a bar that was quiet and lit by candle glow. We went in and sat at a round wooden table, with two leather stools. I went to the bar and ordered two Steins of lager, noticing that the bar had only a handful of people in it.

'So, did you tell Jackson that I was coming?' Tara asked.

I shook my head.

'Probably for the best. Especially after the Hawkinge bust. He may be feeling a little vulnerable,' I squinted at her, confused.

'What do you mean?'

'Well, I guess despite the outcome, you and Dave kind of did your own thing. He specifically asked you not to… I mean, I know you did 'the right thing…' but…'

I always shared with Tara. I implicitly trusted her. I kept the sordid details of the cases from her, the things that would keep her up at night. I needed to let her in a bit though; for her and my sanity.

She also provided insight. I never thought that Jackson would be feeling a bit hurt by us going maverick, but it made perfect sense.

'Oh, wow, here comes trouble,' Tara said,

thrusting her thumb at the door. 'Quick, I'll get another in before they get to the bar.'

That was my girl, noticing the band of burly football fans plundering through the entrance like a group of thirsty pirates.

Tara came back with the drinks, just in the nick of time. The fans seemed in good spirits though; I'm guessing their team won.

'If you want me to help at all while we're out here, Charlie, I will. Or I can just do my own thing. It's entirely up to you.'

Again, this was a difficult one. Tara had a lot of skills, some that truly complimented mine. Whereas I was a maverick and quick thinker, trusting my intuition… she was more methodical, working things through…providing balance.

'Yeah, I reckon you could help tomorrow, sweet,' I said and noticed the light in her eyes brighten a little more. She would have made a good copper… a good partner, even.

'Well, I don't want to get in the way,' she said out of politeness.

'Look, you want to help, and I want you to. Just keep it quiet, OK?'

'OK!'

'There are two leads tomorrow, the Catholic Church in…' I checked my phone, '… Pinneberg, outskirts of Hamburg. The second one is Green's address; she's been spotted in both places recently.'

'Sure. You know, Charlie, Troy's book talks a lot about this city.'

'Oh, really?'

'Yes, he came here when he was a teenager. He talks about the church again, like in Copenhagen, but also mentions…'

'…Hey guys… you from England?' a rotund German man approached our table. He had his hair in a bright purple mohawk and had small, round-rimmed glasses on and introduced himself as Rolf Finke.

'Oh, erm… yeah?' I said.

'Oh, I love it! Your football, you have the best in the world! I like West Ham United in England…'

'Oh cool, me too!' I said.

'Oh great, how do you feel about the move to London Stadium… I hear it's not going too well?'

Before I could give my opinion another St. Pauli supporter interjected, visibly drunk but in high spirits, talking about Tottenham Hotspur. Immediately I lost interest and went back to supping on my large stein of beer.

'I leave you… but nice to meet you!' the German man said, dragging his drunk friend away from Tara and me.

'Well, they were friendlier than I thought they'd be! Anyway, it's operation find Jennifer Green tomorrow?' Tara asked. She had downed her first two pints and was giving me a look that I hadn't seen in a while.

'Yes, I guess so. And find out more about this weird, religious thing that's going on,' I returned.

'Well, let's not worry about that now. Save it all until the morning. Take me back to the hotel, Detective Stone,' she purred.

I hailed the first cab I saw which took us the short distance back to our room. I suggested a nightcap, but Tara wasn't interested. As soon as I shut the door, she was kissing me and heading for the bed.

The calm before the storm, the ecstasy before the laundry.

I would enjoy tonight. Tomorrow we had work to do.

36

I woke up early, the alarm said 6.23 am to be precise.

Tara was asleep on her side of the bed, snoring lightly. I got up, put on a pair of shorts and a t-shirt then went for a morning jog.

The city was quiet on this sunny, Tuesday morning. Rush hour had yet to kick in, and it was amazing how much a city changed overnight. The Reeperbahn seemed timid and calm in the early morning sunshine; likeable even! There was history, culture and character in Hamburg.

I ran past the St. Pauli football club, which brought a smile to my face. The symbolic skull and crossbones were worn proudly on a black flag across their main stand juxtaposing the jovial bonhomie we witnessed from the St. Pauli fans last night.

I got back, sweaty, but feeling great and dived straight in the shower. Tara was stirring, so I left her. The shower was disappointingly tepid but did the job. As I was finishing off, Tara came in naked and pulled across the shower curtain.

'So, where have you been?'

'Running!'

'What a good boy! Room for a little one?' she asked, getting into the shower, with me.

Showers for two were never as glamorous as they looked on TV, I found. Bums hitting each other and water flying in your eye and other crevices. I decided to get out and leave Tara to it.

Once she was finished, we went over the road to a coffee shop.

'I am going to the church shortly, you should come. With that book of Troy's in mind, it may ring some bells.'

Tara nodded eagerly.

'When I go down to the Green home later though, I think you should stay behind,' I said, genuinely worried for her safety. Green's cronies would know that we busted the chamber in Hawkinge. They would be looking for revenge. I knew it was a little dangerous to have Tara out here, but these people have targeted my family, whether I was with them or not. Part of me thought it safer to have her near.

'There is a car waiting at the Police station in Hamburg, so let's get a taxi up there,' I said.

Tara finished her coffee, caught between two worlds now. Excitement and trepidation; an alluring elixir.

Another city, another VW. This time an SUV

called a Tiguan. It was a reliable vehicle, and I always enjoyed driving in Germany. In fact, in many ways Germany was so similar to Great Britain, I felt it was a home away from home: the road system, weather, football and cuisine had several similarities for me.

We were headed north-west out of town, and the sat-nav indicated a twenty-four-minute drive. Here I was, once more into the unknown, I felt at peace though having Tara next to me, a help rather than a burden.

'Hey, Charlie, your phone's ringing. It's Jackson,' Tara said.

'Answer it, but keep quiet please, darling,' I said to her. As I was driving, she answered and put it on speakerphone.

'Good morning, Charlie. How's it going?' Jackson said.

'Good, boss. Got out for a run this morning, cleared the head so good to go.'

'Where are you now?' he asked.

'Just picked up the car and en-route to the church, my first stop…'

'OK, good. I have a contact who is going to meet you there. In fact, this lady contacted me, said they might have some information for you about this case.'

'Contacted you? How did they know I was here?' I wondered.

'I don't think they did know, but they have some information on Green that they want to share. It could be good for the case. Sounds to me like a little old lady, so I'm sure you will be fine.'

'Oh, great. What's the name?' I asked.

'Francesca Gruttel,' he spelt it out, and Tara wrote it down in her little notepad.

I nodded at her.

'OK, buddy, work hard and stay safe. Give me an update later on.' Jackson said.

'Always…'

'Oh, and before you go, those girls in that chamber in Hawkinge were all trafficked. None of them were English. Some Romanian, some Slovenian, one Montenegrin…' Jackson trailed off.

'OK, so what happens now?' I asked.

'Well, nothing changes except they become someone else's problem. We need to know why our friend in Hamburg is involved in this though. The girls in the chamber could now be completely unrelated to Brian and Laura's deaths,' Jackson said.

'Yes, it certainly seems that way. Completely different plan of attack, ethnicity, everything. OK, let's see what I can dig up. I will call you later.'

'Ciao, amigo!' Jackson said, doing his best

Italian accent. People are strange, I thought, but at least every day was different with these guys.
'Is he normally so chipper?' Tara asked.
'Chipper? And a bit weird? Yeah! I guess we all are. Comes with the territory. So, let's find this Francesca and see what she has to tell us.'

++++++++++++++++++++++++++++++++

I parked up outside the church in Pinneburg. It was large, brick-built with stained-glass windows, the complete antithesis to the ones in Hawkinge and Copenhagen.
The building was open, and people were milling about. An old lady with a large shopping bag went inside, as a truck roared by the entrance. I went up to the front doors, which were made with high-quality, dense wood. I stroked the smooth wood and noticed that the Priest was inside and chatting to people. The organ played softly, and the ethereal glow briefly beckoned me within.
I remember being forced to go to church when I was younger: the welcoming feel, the warm hum of the choir, the aromatic scents and life-size statues.
I wanted to go in and light a candle for my father and my nan. The warmth of the church pulled me in, but… I couldn't; I would feel like

a fraud having spent years having some belief, but rejecting the institution that came with it. The overall package just didn't ring true to me. It was like anything: the force, education, church, add people and the message becomes tainted; diluted.

'You must be Charlie?' a voice said from behind me.

I turned to see a well-groomed woman in a business suit, smiling.

'Yes, hi. Francesca?'

She smiled and held out her hand towards me, which I shook.

'This is my partner, Tara,' I stated.

Tara smiled and shook the lady's hand. 'Pleased to meet you,' she said.

'Can I ask you to walk with me?' Francesca asked as we followed her lead around the building.

'I understand you are investigating a murder case?' she asked, furrowing her brow, looking concerned.

'Some murder cases… yes. There's been more than one,' I returned.

The woman tutted, 'terrible business this; it must be stopped.'

'Yes, that's why we're here. To find out more information about the suspects and to try and find the killers,' I stated, hoping Francesca would open up and reveal what she knew.

'You think that the killers are in Hamburg?' she asked.

'Well, we are looking for…' Tara interjected. I held my hand up, and she stopped mid-sentence.

'At this point, we have some suspects, but any information would be of use. Is that why you wanted to meet us?' I continued. I felt rude silencing Tara. She looked a bit sheepish, but for all we knew, despite this woman coming forward, she could be anybody.

'Yes, that is why I wanted to see you. I believe you have a suspect in mind that you need to find the whereabouts for?'

'Erm, not so much whereabouts, but any information that could help with the case?' I was beginning to get a little frustrated at how evasive Francesca was being. It was like she was trying to get information from us.

'I'm sorry, Detective. I don't want to be difficult. It's just… these people are dangerous…' she whispered.

'Oh, I know, but I'm sure any information you give us, we can ensure your safety. I can speak to the Polizei…'

'These people, this lady…she isn't worried about the police…'

'Which lady?'

'Green. Jennifer Green.' she said looking off into the distance. 'You know, she comes to a place, and she takes over. Everywhere she goes. Relentless and will stop at nothing to get what she wants… you know that is what this is all about Detective?' she said, now on a roll.

'No, tell me? What do you mean? Power?'

'More than power…control…everything the men have always had, she wants, it's her thing, that's why the sacrifices…'

I made a mental note. *Sacrifices?* Is that what Bryan Rattle and Laura Unsworth were? We had walked around the building, and I could sense Francesca's nervousness as we were back at the entrance.

'Do you have anything more to tell me?' I asked.

'Yes, but not here, it's not safe. Come and meet me later, at 8 pm at La Locanda Restaurant. It's on Wex Strasse.'

'OK…'

'I'll see you there. Come alone, Detective.'

With that, Francesca left us and scurried up the street and to her parked car. We watched her drive hastily away as if she had done something wrong.

I felt confused and felt Tara's eyes boring into me.

'Going on a date then, "detective?"' Tara said

suggestively.

'Give over,' I said.

'Make sure you, *"come alone,"* she continued. 'She was spooked. She clearly knows how dangerous these people are.'

'Hm, well it sounds like a date to me. I think that Francesca wants to see a little bit more of Charlie Stone than I'm comfortable with!'

'She's scared. And she doesn't even know we are together,' I added.

'Good point, "partner!"' she said, looking pleased with herself.

'Oh, you liked that, did you? You'd make a good policewoman…'

Tara thought about it, 'maybe one day, after I've raised our kids,' she said.

I looked at her, and we both burst out laughing.

'Come on. I think I need a drink after that comment!' I said.

37

We stopped for coffee and felt re-energised. We had a lot of the day left and knew we would probably be seeing more of the city this evening, despite my 'date' with Francesca Gruttel, so we needed to get to work.

We stopped at the hotel and grabbed Troy's book from the room before heading to Hamburg library.

'If I can read more of this book, it may give us some insight into what the hell is going on here,' Tara said.

'Exactly. Did you notice how she called the deaths, "sacrifices?"' I asked.

'Yes. That's where I think you should start. Think about it. You have got: the crimson cross, torture, sacrifice, Latin… erm, you know. They're your key elements. Get searching on the computer and go from there.'

I looked at her and smiled, 'You know no-one likes a bossy detective, Tara,' I said, tongue in cheek.

'It's not a popularity contest. Get cracking, Stone!'

We laughed, and she opened the book and got to work. I started on the computer and found my search to be limited. Nothing had the same level of organisation of what was happening here. I decided to go old school and look for actual books.

The library was extensive and old. The fittings were made with dark oak and to walk around felt like being in Hogwarts or Eton! Despite feeling out of place, I continued with my search up the winding stone staircase and into the furthest corner of the library, where I found a small section on 'The Occult.'

I fingered the old, leather-bound books, but there was nothing that seemed to be of much use. I went back to Tara, who was far more upbeat.

'Charlie, check this out…. Troy has gone to meet a guy here, a mentor, that's to do with the church. When he goes to meet him, he says he feels all of the same things as before… *'I felt light-headed like I was in a hazy dreamworld. I didn't know why… but I remember seeing lots of shiny gold and open fires. The number one was written as a Roman numeral on the wall…'*

'So maybe number one is the first chamber created? The original?'

'Yeah. I mean we must be talking thirty years ago as Troy is still a youngster, like fifteen here…' Tara mused.

'Quite possible that this is the original place then. Any suggestion of where he is?'

'Ah… it's so frustrating! He doesn't say. Just that he is in Europe somewhere… It's cold and icy…the buildings look old-fashioned…'

'That could be half of Europe… potentially northern Europe, but doesn't narrow it down.'

'Listen… '*when I met him, despite the lucid haze I was in, I felt immediate fear. His voice was a deep, slow monotone. His hair was long and dark, mixed with grey… his beard was long, but mostly, his eyes were piercing, like black pebbles, that seemed to look straight into my soul…*'

I did a quick check on my phone for cults (my thinking being that cults have leaders), matched with the crimson cross.

'Jesus! I saw something about this!' I ran back up the winding stairs to the small section of books at the back, found the one I was looking for and brought it back to Tara.

'See when I added the words 'cult' and leader to 'ludibrium', 'crimson cross' and the rest of the search, it came up with this…'

I put the old, leather-bound book in front of Tara. It read 'Rosicrucianism: The Mysteries' by Mitt Goddel.

'This is a mystical, religious order that was around in medieval times…perhaps this is what all of these killings are about?' I suggested.

Tara took the book. 'The guy who wrote it is from Copenhagen…'

'Excellent, we can look him up.'

'Hm, probably not, he died fourteen years ago.'

'Ah damn!'

'But he does talk about the leader of the Rosecrucian Order. A Christian Rosenkreutz… a German nobleman from the fourteenth century… and you are not going to believe this…' Tara went on.

'Try me,' I said.

'Rosenkreutz is German for crimson cross, Charlie. It all makes sense now. They're bringing back the Rosecrucian Order, that's what this is all about!'

'But if Troy's book was talking about a leader of an Order thirty years ago, perhaps it never went away?'

'Perhaps not, so there must be a reason that this is suddenly coming to light and so…'

'Violently?' I finished her sentence for her. 'My guess is someone wants a change of leadership, and that person is you know who.'

'Jennifer Green,' Tara stated.

'Bingo. We need to find out who this 'mentor' guy is in Troy's book, and also I need to meet Francesca,' I checked my watch, 5.54 pm. 'OK, it's getting late. Shall we grab some dinner and have a walk around the city? You can drop me off…'

'…For your hot date…'

'And you can…'

'I'll head back to the hotel and see if I can work out who this guy is and where we can find him. That's if he is even still alive,' Tara said.

'If he's not, someone who is running the show will be. We need to get to them.'

'I'm on it. Gosh, this is exciting! I can see why you put up with all the other stuff…' Tara said, visibly buzzing from the investigative work.

'We are nearly there. Let's eat and then see what tonight brings,' I said, giving Tara a big kiss.

She had truly become my partner in all senses.

38

We took a long walk back from the library and found a local Italian for dinner. Despite Francesca Gruttel wanting to meet at a restaurant, I wasn't going to leave Tara hungry. I phoned Dave and put him on speakerphone when I got back to the hotel.

'Hey Dave, I've got some good news,' I said into the phone.

'Oh, excellent, we need some. Go on,' Dave said, sounding somewhat deflated.

'Well, it appears that this is all to do with an old religious order, a mystical version of Christianity called Rosicrucianism.'

'Right.'

'So, a lot of it fits. Places, people and also Troy's book which seems to be weirdly giving us clues along the way…'

'OK.'

'So, we are looking for a descendant of a guy called Christian Rosenkreutz – that's German for crimson cross, incidentally, somewhere in Europe…'

'I see.'

'And tonight, well, in fifteen minutes, I'm meeting this woman to see what she has to say about Green and her operations…'

'Wait, what woman?'

'This…. Francesca Gruttel, or whatever her name is…'

'Oh right, never heard of her. Well, be careful. I wouldn't trust any one of them, Charlie,' Dave said cautiously.

'Noted. But to put your mind at ease, she is terrified of *them*.'

'Well, she's right to be.'

'How are things your end?' I asked.

'Went to find out more about the Laura Unsworth girl. Honestly, this poor girl. Poor, poor girl…' Dave trailed off.

'Go on, mate.'

'Same type of stuff, body in one piece this time though. Still an unfortunate and untimely death. Drugged in the same way, barbs found in her system, but this girl was subject to what they call….' Dave took a deep breath, 'the pear of anguish.'

'Oh, *Jesus*…' Tara said; I remember she studied A-level history, so would know about some of these devices.

'What's that? Do I even want to know?'

'You probably should. It is inserted into someone's body and is opened, causing extreme pain. No prizes for guessing where this was…inserted.'

There was silence.

'The Cross was also left there, this time in the marshland nearby.'

'Any leads?' I asked.

'It all points back to chamber four and Steven Pensborough. He doesn't think he is on the radar because he is communicating in such an old-fashioned way. But I am certain it's him and this branch of the Order. I am also convinced that this Carl Blewett chap is his right-hand man, but I'm going to need more time. Anyway, you'd best go, or you're going to be late for your date!'

I looked at Tara, who was not amused and hung up the phone.

+++++++++++++++++++++++++++++++

La Locanda was a small restaurant on a busy street in Hamburg, although tonight the street was quiet. It was located on the corner of Wex Strasse and Virgil Strasse and was fairly nondescript.

There was an eerie stillness to the night. An odd mist hung over the city and the streets. This part of town seemed empty tonight.

I was ten minutes late by the time I had left Tara and jumped in a cab to get here. As I got closer to the restaurant, I was surprised to notice it was pretty much empty too. Was there something on in Hamburg tonight I wasn't aware of?

I saw Francesca facing the door, looking nervous. There was another table with one diner, a male.

I approached the door and went to push it, but thought I heard someone speak to me from further up the road.

I looked down the dark street, 'Charlie, Charlie! Come here! Herr Charlie!'

I noticed a black hummer a little further down the road with the passenger door left wide open.

'Charlie, quick!' the voice came again.

I walked towards the door of the hummer, worried I was going to be kidnapped or something worse, but also intrigued by who was calling me.

I kept my distance from the vehicle but as I got adjacent with the front seats, saw the overweight body of Rolf Finke, the football fan from last night.

I relaxed and started laughing.

'Hey buddy, how's it going?' I asked.

'Charlie, you're being set up. Get in the car.'

'What?' I looked back at the restaurant.

'You have a couple of seconds until they realise… GET IN!'

Rolf looked severe, so I jumped in the car. As

soon as I did, there were deafening gunshots, and the glass of La Locanda shattered as a man came running towards me with a firearm.

'Quick!' Rolf pulled closed the door of the hummer which had its engine running and was now speeding through the backseats of Hamburg.

'How did you know?' I asked.

'I am interested in your case. I've been tracking you. That lady, she works for Jennifer Green.'

'Jeez... I should have guessed.' I felt like I had let myself down here.

'No, these peoples are brilliant criminals, Charlie. They have fooled lots of people, very professional, very dangerous. Oh, scheisse...'

I looked back and noticed two black Mercedes were tailing us and appeared to be catching up. More gunfire followed, one bullet hitting the side of the car.

There was a loud explosion in the background; La Locanda was engulfed in flames.

'Hold on, Charlie,' Rolf said.

I put on my seatbelt as Rolf handbraked down a narrow side street, losing the black Mercedes briefly. Rolf knew what he was doing. He was focused and driving with skill.

'Were you in the forces?' I asked.

'No...'

'Oh, you're Polizei?'

'Erm, no…'

'So…' I looked around at the dashboard of the hummer. There was a radio, walkie talkie, advanced GPS… Rolf wasn't a civilian.

'So, I run…hang on…'

The second black Mercedes appeared in front of us and handbraked hard. Rolf braked heavily and swerved past it, narrowly missing a parked Skoda. He wasn't fazed. He felt my hard Paddington stare as he looked at me and remembered our conversation.

'Oh…yeah, I run security for St. Pauli…'

'What? A football club?'

He looked at me like I was mad.

'No, not a football club…. *St. Pauli* football club…' he said. I had touched a nerve. 'This is as I thought, Charlie. That lady, Francesca Gruttel, she works directly for Anna Gibson, Green's deputy.'

'Yeah, I know all about Gibson,' I said.

'They want you dead, Charlie. Getting you out of here is not going to be easy…'

I immediately picked up my phone and called Tara. What if they had got to her? It rang and rang, but there was no answer. I left a message to call me straight away.

'Is that your girlfriend?' Rolf asked.

'Yeah, I just want to warn her.'

Rolf nodded. 'She is staying in a hotel?'

'Yep, the KiezPiraten.'

'Ah, the St. Pauli Hotel!' Rolf beamed a big grin at me. 'Wait one minute.'

Rolf made a call which was picked up after one ring. He spoke in German, and it sounded like he gave unambiguous instructions to whoever he was talking with.

'Ja, relax. She is safe.' Rolf said.

'Who was that?' I asked.

'The owner of the KiezPiraten. Being part of St. Pauli has its benefits.'

39

'Let's go somewhere busy, where you are safe, and we can talk,' Rolf said.

We were back on the main road, Budapest Strasse. It was a wide road with lots of traffic and people; I immediately felt more relaxed. Parking was at a premium, so Rolf pulled the car to one side, blocking a lane on the two-way highway. He got out and spoke German to a man who was outside, smoking a cigarette.

The guy nodded and jumped into the driver seat of the car.

'Charlie, come with me,' Rolf said.

We went towards a small bar called 'The Jolly Roger.' There were colourful stickers splattered on the outer shell and some punters outside drinking, smoking and talking loudly. Rolf nodded at the security guard, who stepped aside.

As soon as the door opened the sound of seventies punk music blasted out; the lighting was dark, with various coloured spotlights around the room, but the main thing, it was packed out. Rolf indicated me towards the back of the room, and I followed, easing past the evening drinkers as I went.

It was an exciting crowd. Mainly miscreants,

punks, anarchists and skater types. There were St. Pauli skull and crossbones t-shirts worn like a uniform, but the vibe of the place was friendly. Rolf stopped at the back of the room where there was a little space.

It seemed like this was a part of the bar customers weren't allowed to stand, but as I was beginning to notice, Rolf seemed to transcend these petty rules.

He ordered two steins of local lager and passed me one.

'So, you are probably wondering what is going on here, Charlie?' Rolf laughed a big, hearty laugh and gulped a few inches of his drink down.

'Yeah, uh… I got the Green bit. Just where do you come in?' I asked, trying not to sound rude to a man who may have saved my life.

'Good question. As I told you, I run security for St. Pauli's home matches. It is a small community really, but the club is heavily linked to the local area, so as such I have to be like… how you say in English… eyes and ears of the place.'

I nodded, impressed by Rolf's ability to understand and articulate English idioms.

'That must be quite a job… it's a big city…'

'Oh, no, St. Pauli is a small section of the city, but what we lack in size, we make up for in character!' he said, looking around the busy pub. 'Yesterday, remember when I saw you in the Chug bar with your girlfriend? Well, when you left, the barman was talking into a headset, and he said you were leaving for the hotel. I went out to see what was going on, but luckily, you got straight into a cab, but the barman was watching you.'

Rolf finished his beer, and before he had time to ask for a new one, a fresh one had arrived.

'There was a cab, literally outside!' I mused.

'Yeah, I think you were lucky! From what I understand, as soon as you touched down, she's been gunning for you.'

'Green?'

'Of course! Who else?' he laughed.

'Right. So?' I asked. I liked Rolf, but he did seem pretty forgetful, especially when it came to important things such as helping me stay alive!

'Yeah, sorry. So I did some ringing around, and I heard about the English policeman who was staying in the Kiez. I asked them to track your movements and tell me when you left. I saw you meet Gruttel at the Pinneburg Church. If you're from St. Pauli or involved in the football here, you would recognise her. She is the new 'media operator' at the club.'

'Jeez, I should have done my research!' I said.

'No, Charlie. How could you know? They only told you about the meeting, what, ten minutes before? You were driving to the meet point. How could you research?'

'Fair enough.'

'But it's a panicky move from Green, you must have really upset her or her plans for this!' Rolf laughed again. I was glad that he could see the funny side. I was panicking about Tara still. I picked up the phone to call her.

'Charlie, she will be OK. If she is at the hotel, my people will keep her safe. And if she has gone out, she will be somewhere busy. Nothing will happen to her. Relax.'

But I couldn't. Why wasn't she picking up?

'Can you keep her safe though? Green is powerful. You know that. If she can pretty much shut down a Hamburg street to have me killed, she can get to Tara. No offence to your guys.'

One of the barmen came towards Rolf and spoke in his ear. He nodded and downed his drink.

'OK, Charlie. We need to go,' he said, getting up to leave.

We went out through the back, via the toilets. Rolf's trusty hummer was sitting there, as if by magic. We jumped in and were back on the move.

'Take me back to the hotel, Rolf,' I said, increasingly worried.

Rolf looked at me and put his hand on my arm.

'Charlie, come on. You know you must drag them away from her, not lead them to her. They don't want Tara; they want you. Murder is their game, but not random or unnecessary killing. Every single body is accounted for, every death part of their puzzle, your girlfriend would be collateral. Sorry to be so mercenary, but it's true.'

He was right. I needed to think like a copper, rather than a lover. I needed to keep a civilian safe and no matter my feelings, had to leave her.

'Where to then?' I asked.

'My friend just told me they are looking in the town to find you. There is some good news and bad news.'

'OK, the bad news?'

'There are six guys now, all armed, with the mission to *kill Charlie Stone*,' Rolf said bluntly.

'But the good news...' he continued, trying to sound more upbeat, 'they are easy to spot... these are professional hitmen, hired killers: dark clothes, slick vibe, an eighties look.'

'Sorry, what was the good news?'

'This is Hamburg, Charlie! Home of the hobos!

They stand out a mile, that's why we are two steps ahead of them. They are heading to the Jolly Roger now. My guys will try and put them off the scent, send them out of town, but for us…'

'Let me guess, into town?'

'You guessed it. The best place for you is into the eye of the storm.'

'Not being funny, Rolf, do you think it might be an idea to ditch the car? It's not like, your average, blend into the crowd-type vehicle,' I suggested.

'Sure. Good point. But it is bulletproof!' he said.

'Really? Why?'

'You won't believe me if I told you,' Rolf laughed.

'Well, I need a good story, Rolf, something to cheer me up.'

Rolf smiled, 'it was sent to me by the president of Gabon. He came to one of our matches as a business guest. I ran security for him.'

'So, he bought you a bulletproof hummer?'

'I think he had it going spare, but yeah. I mean, the match was just the start. I then took him out in Hamburg. It is safe to say he had a good time,' Rolf said.

'I see, enough said about that…'

'I mean he *really* got his rocks off…'

'OK, gotcha…'

'Like, naked on the dancefloor, a bottle of Cristal in his hand. Two girls…'

'OK, OK! I get it!' I said, and we both laughed. We pulled over and got out of the car. Rolf parked a few streets away from our destination, and we walked the rest of the way. We both kept our eyes open for the hitmen, but if there was something sinister in the air, the Reeperbahn hadn't got the memo.

'You ready for this, Charlie?' Rolf asked, grinning from ear to ear.

I am glad he could remain so upbeat given the current circumstances.

'Yeah sure. Let's see what Hamburg has got to offer,' I returned, Rolf laughing.

'Welcome to the Sinful mile!' Rolf shouted into the neon night.

40

I began to wonder about Rolf. Perhaps he was working for Green, and I was being drawn into another trap? But why would he go to the trouble of this elaborate story?

It was times like this, I had to trust my instinct, and it told me he was genuine. If I was being led to my demise, this would be an interesting place and quite the opposite of Green's first attempt, the deserted La Locanda. We were in the biggest club on the Reeperbahn, and it was chock full.

Rolf was at the bar ordering drinks.

He came back with two cokes, which pleased me given our current situation. I gulped at mine, not realising how thirsty I was.

'So, what's the plan?' I asked Rolf as we took a seat in the VIP section. I looked around at the packed dance floor down below. It looked hellish; groups of lairy lads leering at half-naked dancers hanging from cages above them, like fallen seraphim.

We were a floor up, and it was far less busy. I had excellent visibility all around me. There were two entrances to the VIP section on either side, with a bouncer on each access point. The bar was behind me, but after scoping it out, there was no real threat that I could see. There were also three strippers working the room, selling their wares.

Rolf must have already had a word, as the girls stayed well clear of our table.

'I think we need to wait for the situation to calm down. Then you need to get Tara,' Rolf said.

'I need to know where she is,' I said.

'Relax, Charlie. She is at the Piraten with the owner, Max. He is a friend of mine. She is at the bar, drinking, relaxing.' Rolf leaned over and showed me his phone. There was CCTV coverage, and I could see Tara exactly how he had described, sitting at the bar with a long drink in front of her. She was chatting and smiling.

'Why hasn't she called me? She must have left her phone upstairs.'

Rolf sighed, 'Max has told her you're with me having a drink. She's happy, Charlie. Don't worry.'

I calmed slightly, the beat of the nightclub was like a mantra, and I felt content for a moment. It had been a long time since I had been in a place such as this. People often talk about missing the bright lights and the glitz, but I really didn't. This drummed it home. In a way, I enjoyed the journey of the music, particularly house music. The rises and falls, the crescendos and bass drops, in its own way it was theatre… drama.

But with it came the inevitable pitfalls. I only had to look down from this VIP room to see where the fights would occur later into the night.

Drunk lads, possibly British, on the dancefloor. Ravers high on MDMA or pills in one part. Burly bouncers looking surly, eyeing the slightest bit of trouble… it wasn't for me anymore. The hangover for me was never worth it. What I mean is, big nights out were never as satisfying as they should have been. I just didn't enjoy them or see the point. Unless you were single or wanting to take drugs or drink and I was past all of that now.

'Wish you were down there, huh?' Rolf asked, watching me while I was miles away.

'Uh, no. Quite the opposite. Give me a quiet hotel bar any day… hey, Rolf, thanks for doing all of this for me. You have kind of saved my life.'

He gave me a wry smile. He probably thought that he saved my life, but I backed myself to get out of that set up at the restaurant. That said, he was a good guy for getting me out of a situation I didn't need to be in.

'Hey, are you definitely not police?' I asked him

again.

'No, Charlie! Can't a guy just be a concerned citizen these days?' he returned.

'Well, yeah., It's just rare is all. But thanks, Rolf. It's proving harder and harder to catch the real criminals these days. Jennifer Green is a case in point. She moves around so much we can barely get near her.'

'OK, I have to level with you, there is how you say… an ulterior motive?' Rolf said.

'I see, there usually is,' I said, somewhat deflated. I genuinely thought Rolf might be doing it all just because it was the right thing to do.

'I want to bring down those bastards too. I hate that Green bitch and her Doberman henchwitch Gibson too,' Rolf hissed.

'Why? What's your interest if it's not work-related?'

'It's a long story…'

'Well, until we hear gunshots, we have time?' I suggested.

I could see Rolf was uneasy, and he shifted in his chair.

'So I don't know what you know about Hamburg, but in particular the district of St. Pauli?' he asked, testing my local knowledge.

'Well, I know that St. Pauli has a big football following all over the world, which is weird for such a small club… aren't you in like the second division?'

'Yes we are, and it's not weird, Charlie. Do you know why we have such a…' he took a deep breath, 'a global brand?'

'No…not really?' I didn't want to guess and upset Rolf, the look on his face told me he took this very seriously.

'I'll give you the short version as I could talk all night about this…but St. Pauli is the poor, working man's football club of Hamburg. It is built on the Hamburgerberg, which historically housed all of the unpopular and poorer trades of this rich city.'

'OK…'

'But with that came history and culture. Lots of free thinkers, anarchists and rebels settled in the area. During the Second World War, we saw more devastation than possibly anywhere else in Germany…'

'No way! What about Dresden, what ab…'

'Trust me, Charlie. What the British did here was borderline war crime territory,' I didn't question Rolf, he sounded like he knew his stuff.

'When the country was moving towards more right-wing and Nazi movements, we championed anti-fascism as wc know how war can truly destroy a community. But out of that, we grew resilient: anti-racist, homophobic, fascist. They are the principles of the club.'

'Sounds awesome, Rolf! No wonder the club is so loved. Still, how does this tie in with Green?'

'Our CEO for the past six years has been Gotte Ubblich, a beloved man. Gotte runs music bars in Hamburg with his boyfriend and has helped secure the club's security. He helped many of our poorer fans who were squatting on the east side of town keep their homes. He is a good man.'

I nodded.

'Last year he disappeared in peculiar circumstances. There was a change of personnel on the board of directors, including an Anna Gibson who became a trustee of the St. Pauli Charity Fund. She started making a lot of trouble and divided what was otherwise a united board. I did some digging and knew that Green holdings PLC totally funded her. They wanted the club to themselves and the revenue it brings.'

'So, Mr Ubblich. They uh…?' I indicated with my fingers a gunshot. Rolf breathed heavily.

'No one knows. Green effectively runs the club now through Gibson though. That's why Green is so often here in the city. She owns buildings on the south side of Budapest Strasse and wants to expand. I believe knocking down the stadium, and building properties here is her long-term plan.'

'I know that feeling…'

'Yes, I know the same thing happened to your club in England, Charlie.'

'It is disgusting what happened to West Ham, but at least we still have a club; it's just not recognisable to most of the fans.'

'It is a tragedy, Charlie. In our case, she plans to get rid of the club completely! St. Pauli is more important than life or death to some of our fans!'

I nodded, I understood. There were fans at West Ham who bought season tickets because they always have but watch the match in deepest, darkest East London as they can't face the new stadium.

'So, you want to find Gotte?' I asked, getting back to the point.

'I don't know about him. Some say he was murdered so they could take the club. Others say it all got too much and he left Hamburg with his boyfriend. I don't know. What I do know is that I want Green gone. Locked up. And her mate Gibson.'

So that's why Rolf was so keen to help me. He leaned over and put his hand on my arm.

'It's not the only reason, Charlie,' as if he had

read my mind. 'You are doing the right things. Doing the best you can. I read up about you.' Rolf smiled at me.

'That's all we can do, Charlie. Our best.'

The touching moment Rolf and I were having was interrupted curtly by the deafening sound of automatic gunfire that rang through the club. The music stopped, and the lights were killed, the safety of the nightclub was now in total darkness.

41

The rat-a-tat was blistering through the gloom. There were shouts and screams as through the darkness civilians climbed over one another, desperate for the exits.

'Fire exit, Charlie. Get out of here, I will find you!' Rolf said. In the darkness, I saw his large frame head in the opposite direction.

'Rolf, no! Come back!' I said, genuinely worried for his safety.

'GO! It's you they want, not me. I'll stall everything, but go!'

I ran past the bar, which was on a different relay or powered by a back-up generator as the multi-coloured neon lights gave me a path to the emergency exit. I followed the green lights, down a few stairs and burst through the black double doors. I was on a metal emergency staircase, two floors from the ground.

I toyed with the idea of heading upwards, but it led to the roof, which would give me no options for escape.

So down it was and into the alley that ran alongside the nightclub. People were now running along the Reeperbahn and to safety. The assault rifle sounded again. This time outside, but definitely further away than it had been.

As I got to the bottom of the stairwell, I looked towards the Reeperbahn. There was a man with dark hair and a roll neck, appearing to keep guard. I crept down to street level, and because the alley I was in was a dead end, no-one was coming down it. I had to find a way past the man and back into the melee of people.

I moved up as quietly as I could. Just before I returned to the street, I slipped on a green glass bottle that had been left on the ground. The bottle skidded and smashed into the wall to my left. The guard turned around and saw me, we made eye contact, and he shouted something loudly in German.

I ran down towards the dead-end, not knowing what my next move might be.

I kept going, but there was no exit. All I could see was the back entrance to what appeared to be a Chinese restaurant. The white light beamed out of the doorway, and there were loud Chinese voices. I could hear steps behind me, so I took a deep breath and headed through the kitchen.

The chefs were shouting at me but could see I wasn't stopping. One bigger, older man tried to manoeuvre himself in front of me, holding out his hands, but I pushed him to one side.

I didn't know much German apart from

'danke,' so I ran through repeating it loudly, smiling at the apoplectic kitchen staff. Next, I was in a restaurant. There were two toilets to my left and right, but I continued into the main room, now jogging while trying not to look too out of place.

Despite some peculiar looks from the waiting staff, I made it out of the front door of the building without any issues. I turned and looked through the large bay window of the restaurant and saw the man who had been standing guard. Another man who was armed was standing by the diners.

They saw me, and before I turned to run, I heard gunshots again. This time a handgun, definitely aimed at me.

There was the sound of shattering glass and more screaming as I turned and sprinted as fast as I could back along the Reeperbahn, which was now empty, apart from the odd drunken straggler and homeless man.

I took a left and a right from the main road and found myself by a side street that was covered by large metal sheets, hiding what lurked inside.

I had fallen upon the infamous 'Herbert Strasse.'

I slid between the metal panelling and onto the main drag. It was quiet, and the mood was certainly calmer and more relaxed than I expected.

There were women dressed in underwear looking out of the windows of the buildings. Some seemed nonchalant towards the public, others spoke in thick Eastern European accents, promising the world for the right price.

'You come in, mister? Good looking man, you come in with me…' the lady in a leather policeman's hat purred at me. I tried to look for an exit route, but the road was wide and clear. It was only a matter of time before my pursuers arrived on Herbert Strasse.

'Oh sure, yeah! I'll come in…' I said nervously, despite having no intention of any form of activity with the young lady in question.

'Yes, good…' she opened the glass door slowly and out of the corner of my eye, I could see commotion at the entrance to the street.

I got in as quickly as I could and closed the door behind me.

'Oh, mister! Very keen! Quick, quick, come and lie down!'

I went behind the curtain and watched the lady as she shut the door behind me. I had no idea what lay beyond this room but was pleased to feel a door handle in the small of my back. The lady turned and smiled at me. She had black stockings to match her leather police hat and bra. 'What are you doing, you nervous? What's your name? Come and lie down, take off your top…'

'I…uhm….Dave?'

'Dave… Dave! Good name, masculine! Come and lie down with me…' she said, kneeling on the makeshift bed that was in the small room. I smiled and stood stock still, except for my hand in the small of my back, slowly managing to open the door.

Suddenly there was a knock at the curtained window, 'Polizei! Open up!'

The lady turned, suddenly panicking, rushing to put on clothes, as I slipped from her metaphorical clutches and through the back door of the tiny room. I was swiftly transported from the lurid, red cupboard of seduction, to the realities of backstreet Hamburg.

There was a foul smell of damp in a corridor that had peeling paint and many broken floorboards, which must have once resembled a corridor. At the end of it was a door with two shattered windows on either side.

I made it to the door carefully, choosing the strongest floorboards to stand on, mercifully I did not fall into some rat-infested underbelly. I made my exit and was in a dank alleyway that led back to the bright lights of the Reeperbahn.

At the end of the alley, I checked both ways and couldn't see anything dangerous or suspicious. I put my collar up and walked swiftly along the Reeperbahn, which had filled up once again with revellers. It didn't take long for the party people to forget about the gunfire and threat of imminent death, did it?

As I walked, I kept my eyes and ears peeled for anything suspicious. I was desperate for a cab to get out of there, but there were none to be seen.

Nervous, I went to cross the street as there was a McDonalds and groups of people milling outside.

As I did, I heard a car's brakes screech behind me. It sounded like a handbrake turn, and the vehicle was heading this way. I refrained from looking which was hard and nestled into the group of people, who were outside McDonald's, praying that this wouldn't be my final visit to the Golden Arches.

The car braked again just behind me. I was anxious; this could be it.

'Hello, stranger! Get in!' a voice I recognised; Tara.

I turned, and she was hanging out of the passenger side of Rolf's hummer. Boy was I pleased to see these guys.

42

Tara manoeuvred herself into the backseat, and I sat up front with Rolf. I took a deep breath and had time to recollect my thoughts. I was caked in sweat; my t-shirt and jacket were soaked through, but I was alive, and Tara was safe.

I felt a hand on my back, stroking my neck. I turned and smiled at her.

'Hey you two, no time for that,' Rolf said.

'Play him the tape, Rolf.' Tara said.

'What tape?' I asked.

'Listen to this, my friend,' Rolf said, rewinding an old-fashioned tape recorder and hitting play. It was muffled, but after a few seconds a female voice came in... 'that's right. The businesses will be closed along Wex... yes... that's right. He will meet you at eight along the Wex...' it was a telephone conversation, but who was talking? '... yes, we will have men there, one in the restaurant and others waiting... of course not, you will be completely protected... no, it's an order from above... listen, if you're not up to it... that's fine, but remember that video Jennifer has... and you can kiss goodbye to any shareholding... OK... good, then meet me there at seven-thirty, no later...'

'Anna Gibson?' I suggested.

'Yes, giving orders to Francesca about tonight at La Locanda. My friend also has CCTV footage of Gibson and Gruttel entering the restaurant this evening.' Rolf continued, his voice filled with excitement.

I tried to think logically. Was it enough to convict Gibson? These people were as slippery as eels, but thanks to Rolf what was supposed to be a simple murder on a deserted street became very public. The Polizei, along with everyone in town, would know that there were gunshots and a car chase in the district. If we could place her there, giving orders about it, she is bang to rights as far as I could see.

'That's good. How reliable are these sources, Rolf?' I asked.

'The tape comes from my friend at the phone exchange. CCTV is from the town security force, directly. It is watertight,' he added.

'Man, you do have some good connections here, huh?' I added, shocked at how many favours Rolf was able to pull in when required.

'It's not me, its St. Pauli. We are a family. A strange, disjointed super tight family,' he added.

'My sort of people,' I added.

'Me too,' Tara said emphatically from the backseat.

'Yes, I saw you had fun this evening. Slightly

less insane than my evening,' I said, goading her a little.

'It would have been rude to turn my nose up at the fantastic hospitality, plus I knew you had Rolf on your team so you would be OK,' she said, smiling.

I thought it best to leave out the Herbert Strasse part of the evening from my war stories.

'So what's next then, Charlie?' Tara said.

'Gibson? It's not who we wanted, but it's an excellent start. What do you say, Rolf? Want to help me arrest her?' I asked.

'How you say in English? Do bears shit in the woods?'

'Yeah. Something like that, mate! Come on then, let's find her!' I said.

++++++++++++++++++++++++++++++++

The time was past midnight now, and Rolf planned to head to the football stadium at St. Pauli to decipher her location.

Rolf parked the car outside of the main gates of the stadium and turned the engine off.

'You see, Gibson currently has the role of acting-CEO in Gotte Ubblich's absence. Green and her are trying very hard to change the people in charge. But they can't do it as quickly as they want. A number of the board still want Gotte back, and a lot of people have held onto their old roles.'

'Like you, I guess?'

'Exactly. I have access to the whole building. I know they are planning to install a new security system and I am sure my days are numbered under Gibson and Green, but for now, I have the keys to the kingdom.'

'Can we just walk in off the street?' Tara asked.

'You can if you hold the keys. I'm sure there will be some extra layers of security she has installed, but…'

'If this provides information leading to the arrest of Anna Gibson, it won't be an issue mate. I promise you,' I said. He looked at me and nodded.

He was a really good guy. He knew the risks of getting himself involved, but he was so keen to get rid of this scourge that he was prepared to help, no matter the personal cost.

We left the car and walked up to the cast iron double gates at the front of the building. The large circular logo "St. Pauli – 1910" stood proudly in front of us.

'Interesting,' Rolf mused. 'The gates are unlocked.'

I looked up at the enormous new stand, a typically modern football creation: shiny, new and corporate. Tonight though it was shrouded in darkness.

'Someone must be here,' Rolf continued.

'Are you sure the head of security didn't just forget to lock up?' I said, joking, of course. Rolf laughed.

'Wait here,' he said, skipping back to the car. He came back a few moments later, with two 9mm guns.

'Oh,' Tara said, looking decidedly more nervous.

He handed one to me.

'Just in case… you know,' he said.

Tara looked at me, scared.

'You wanted to be a cop,' I said.

'Yeah, after our kids, Charlie! At this rate I won't make it that far!' she said sniggering. I think the mix of adrenaline and excitement was powering her through.

I went to push the main gate, and Rolf's tattooed arm came out slowly and halted me.

'Come to think of it; there's a better way.'

We left the car, and he led us around to the back of the main stand. The perimeter of the ground was surrounded by metal rails and climbing spikes, but towards the furthest corner of the field was a small workman's entrance. Rolf, like the jailer, jangled his extensive set of keys and found the right one for the large padlock.

'We come in this way; it's a back way. If Gibson and her goons are here, we will bypass most of the security cameras and locks,' Rolf said, pushing the door open.

'Most?' I asked.

'Well, you can't have everything, Charlie! I have to keep it interesting!'

I wondered once more about Tara, and whether a mission such as this was somewhere she should be. The thought of asking her to go back to the car did not appeal either. I was sure I would receive very short thrift.

Anyway, I had to remember I couldn't control everything as much as I liked to. I wanted to keep everybody safe, but as I had gotten older, I realised it was impossible.

'OK, we go up the stairs here, I will unlock the top door. There will be an alarm code for the utility room, and once I've done that we are through the stock room and into the bar; the corporate area. They could be in there. If they are not, they will be in one of the offices off it,' Rolf garbled, he was breathing heavily.

'Relax, you haven't legally done anything wrong, OK? I mean, you could have left your wallet here, and that's *why* you're here, right?' I said, trying to quell his fears.

He gave me a sideways glance. We both knew

that if Green, Gibson and their hitmen were here, we were walking into grave danger. We steeled ourselves; then Rolf made his way up the metal staircase.

43

I followed Rolf, and Tara followed behind. We tried to keep our footsteps light on the metal, but however hard we tried, they echoed slightly in the still night air.

Rolf got out the keys again, this time holding the large bundle in his hand and ensuring he didn't jangle as he did. He pulled the door open and slid in. We heard him push five buttons on a keypad by the door, and then he motioned us to enter.

As we walked through an automatic motion sensor light turned, and I froze, but Rolf nodded, and I knew it wasn't a problem. We were in a storage room filled with stock. There were industrial-sized cans of sunflower oil, pots of powdered gravy and cartons of premium apple juice.

Through the stock room we came to a large black door. Rolf signalled for quiet and leaned his head against the door, listening for any sounds. I couldn't hear anything, nor could he, so he slowly pushed the handle.

Behind the door was a large wooden bar, presumably the corporate bar for the football club. On either side, there were large bay windows. One looked out onto the pitch and stadium; the other out towards the lights of the city. The room was illuminated by the pale glow of the full moon; the calm was disconcerting. Gold fittings and champagne glasses were hanging from holders. It certainly did not fit with the anti-establishment image of St. Pauli that Rolf epitomised. I could see why he was so disdainful for Green and Gibson.

Through two double doors at the end of this room lights beamed beyond, suggesting that was where our targets were. We snuck forward and kneeled behind the bar.

'Those lights shouldn't be on, so whoever is here is behind those doors,' Rolf whispered. We nodded collectively.

'You are not going alone, I'll come with you,' I said.

'You are not leaving me!' Tara chimed in.

'OK, looks like we are all going,' Rolf said.

'Let me lead,' I said, but I was already off before he had a chance to reply. The way I thought about it, I was the policeman, I should take the lead.

There were two exits to the bar on the left and right; I went left. I snuck around the side and crept towards the light through the door, leaning up against the wall. Rolf had moved to the right-hand side of the bar.

I could hear the low murmur of voices beyond

the door; there was also a soft pounding on the floor. I turned to see Rolf moving up as quietly as he physically could; the voices stopped. What Rolf wouldn't have realised was that his large frame caused minor rumbles through this new build addition to the old St. Pauli construct. Also, the angle from which he came from caused the moon that hung gracefully over the ground to cast a faint but visible shadow over the glass panels of the double doors.

'Rolf! Cover!' I shouted as the sound of silence was replaced by gunfire through the double doors.

'Tara, stay down!' I yelled.

The sound of a bullet hitting Rolf's fleshy frame and him hitting the ground made two thuds, but the shots continued unabated. I pushed away from the plasterboard wall and began to fire back.

It was Russian Roulette. I knew this could well be it for me; for all of us.

I ran to Rolf firing my gun with my left hand. I slid his firearm towards Tara through the left side hatch of the bar. I saw her scrabble on her knees to pick it up.

'Tara, cover me!' She grabbed the gun, and there was a moment's pause from both sides, each waiting for the next move.

'Leave me, Charlie. Get her out, now!' Rolf

said, blood appearing around the sides of his mouth.

I dragged his heavy frame towards the bar as gunshots filled the room again. I managed to pull Rolf behind the bar and sat him up. The wound was in his chest and was bleeding heavily.

'Tara, hold this on him,' I had taken a bar towel and was pointing towards his chest. She nodded and passed me the gun.

I looked around and noticed that a large hole had been blown through the door behind me. I saw some dark hair with wisps of grey. I craned my neck to look further, and his eyes met mine. Then there was the smile.

'All right, Charlie! Saved your arse again, old boy!' It was Dave. How did he keep managing to do it?

A woman's voice boomed, 'Jennifer Green! If you are in there, come out now, hands up!' There was a foreign twang to her accent. Rita emerged from the storeroom brandishing her gun.

Silence. I checked that both my guns were cocked and loaded.

'You need to come out now with your hands up, and this will all be over!'

Silence again. I looked at Dave and then at Tara.

'Stay here, sweet. Don't move.'

Dave and I moved up together, quietly. I made it to the side of the door frame again and could see an angle into the room where we believed Green was. I noticed Dave was in the full body kit, a bulletproof vest which read 'Politi.'

I saw Rita Germann behind him, with her gun pointed directly at the door frame.

There was a muffled movement from inside the room. Dave and I agreed to go in on the count of three.

One…Dave used his fingers to intimate silently to Rita and the rest of the police force behind her.

Two… we waited… poised.

On the count of three, there was an ear-splitting bang, and the corridor filled with smoke. I couldn't see anything, so retreated towards the bar to protect Tara and Rolf. Rolf was semi-conscious, Tara was whispering to him to try and keep him awake.

The smoke cleared a little and Dave appeared in the doorway.

'Well, that's one down,' he said. 'Not the one we wanted.'

I entered the room that was now decorated in shattered glass from the bay windows of this once-majestic office.

Behind a large oak desk, slumped in the seat,

was Anna Gibson. Her blonde curls a new addition, but the face was recognisable. I quickly went to her and checked for a pulse. I opened her eyes… and waited for the pulse. It was faint, but definitely there.

'Quick, we need paramedics! She's alive!'

44

Rolf was taken away on a stretcher and then blue-lighted to Hamburg – Eppendorf, the University Medical Centre.

The paramedics on-site managed to resuscitate Gibson; much to Jennifer Green's chagrin, I'm sure. When they set off the flashbang and escaped, my guess was they presumed Gibson to be dead. Either way, we had a starting point. I looked around the office and tried to find anything that would be of help to the case.

I managed to get a different Hamburg address for Green from the one we were given. Despite sending the Polizei to both places to find her, I didn't hold out much hope; she would go way underground now.

The local police chief put out a call to all local officers regarding Green and the henchmen, as they must be somewhere on the streets of Hamburg. Again, I didn't hold my breath.

Tara and I went to the hotel and packed our bags. Dave went with Rita to the police station to start the paperwork for the case. It was interesting to note that Rita had joined up with the German force despite being part of the Danish one. She (with the help of Dave) was able to give them the heads up about Gibson,

Green and their plans to have me killed.

'I think I'm about ready for home now,' Tara mused, while placing her toiletries bag in her suitcase.

'I bet. Listen I'm sorry you saw what you did and were involved to such an extent, babe.'

'Oh no, Charlie! I loved it; it was exhilarating! It's just I'm tired now and want to sleep in our bed.'

'So, knowing what you know now would you still have come to Hamburg?' I asked, smiling at Tara.

She didn't take long to answer, 'hell yeah! That feeling when you know you have stopped a bad person from doing these things. I mean that woman tried to kill you, Charlie!'

'You're not wrong. Let's get a couple of hours sleep, darling. In the morning I'll have to question dearest Anna.'

'Oh, really? She's going to be up to it?' Tara asked. A good question. A couple of hours ago, I thought she had shuffled off her mortal coil.

'Apparently so. Text came through from Dave.'

'Well, no worries. I'll hold up in a coffee shop or something…'

'No way. You are coming to the hospital with me. Gibson's still there, and I'm not letting you out of my sight.'

'Fair enough, Detective,' Tara said sleepily, as she lay on the bed and closed her eyes.

We woke up four hours later, and it had just gone seven in the morning. After showering, brushing my teeth and zipping up my bag, we were ready to leave.

I liked Hamburg; it was a city with a lot of character. The people were kind and friendly; there was no pretence. I hoped I would come back but thought honestly it would be unlikely. There was just too much world to see. Also, holidays now had to factor in kid's entertainment. As much as Hamburg could cater for all, the X-rated stuff was too much for Maddie to be around.

Tara finished her packing and said her goodbyes to the manager of the hotel. I grabbed a coffee from the shop next door, and we headed up to the hospital where Rolf and Gibson were. Rolf's condition had stabilised from critical when I went to sleep last night. I had no update since, so was guessing no news was good news.

Gibson was conscious and wanting to leave; however, she was under arrest. Once the doctors said she was fit enough to leave, she would go straight into custody. Dave and I wanted five minutes with her before we flew back to Blighty later on today.

I left Tara in the hospital café while Dave and I went to the second floor for Gibson. She was in a secure unit and had a policeman on the door. We showed him our credentials, and he nodded us entry to Gibson's room.

It was bright with a view of the trees and park to the south of the building. Gibson was sitting up in bed, her blonde curls now slightly more tamed and she was looking healthier. She was going to survive the clutches of Jennifer Green and face justice rightfully. Sometimes, despite all of the darkness, everything worked out as it should.

'Good morning, Anna,' Dave said.

She looked at me, 'You going to let your sidekick lead this, are you?'

'Sidekick? Well, that's a bit rude. Happy to be Robin though, he is a bit younger, eh Charlie?' Dave replied, not giving Gibson take the upper hand.

'It is the only way you would be younger than me unless you had a time machine. A time machine would be nice, wouldn't it, eh? Go back and put right all of those mistakes? Save all the lives that you ended? The kids you've murdered… that sort of thing?'

Gibson smiled and looked out of the window. 'You will have to do better than that Charlie Stone,' she replied.

I looked at Dave, who took up a seat by Gibson's bed, directly in her eyeline.

'Oh, please…' she said. She would be a tough one to interrogate.

'Ms. Gibson, you are now in police custody, and we have evidence that suggests you helped organise the failed murder of Detective Stone, who it seems you are already aware of.' Gibson was unmoved, Dave continued. 'Added to the connection you have to Paul Wadham's prostitution ring in England earlier this year, you will probably spend the rest of your life in prison…'

'Is that a fact, *Dave?*' she said, raising a small smile.

'No, no. It's not a fact. You will, I'm sure, have a super lawyer who will try and negotiate a better outcome, but it is incredibly likely given the evidence against you. Anyway, we don't want to argue over your impending incarceration. We just wondered whether you had anything you wanted to tell us, given you're going down.' Dave added.

'Not to mention, you were kind of thrown under the bus, by your good pal, Jennifer,' I added.

'Really?'

'Well, she left you there last night, while she and her security guys escaped. Hardly what you would expect? You have been a loyal servant to Green for years… doing her bidding, whatever she asks. Yet it's you now who will take the fall. Seems a bit unfair to me, don't you think?' I surmised, hoping she would bite.

'I guess, but that's the Order of things. It's the way it's been for centuries, Charlie old boy. You know that. There is nothing *I* can do about it.'

'But you can. You don't have to take all of the heat. You can tell us, tell us what she told you to do. Share the burden. You don't have to be her lapdog now. It's over. A judge would look more leniently on you if you could help us bring her in.'

Gibson turned her head to look at me.

'It's already in motion, Charlie. She is going to destroy your life, in ways you can't imagine, and you can't stop it. You have no bloody clue.' She smiled at me.

I tried not to show my emotion, but my heart was pounding. 'Come on, Anna. The noose is tightening. We nearly got her, and we've got you. We are finding out about the chambers underground. Is that what you want to be *your* legacy? Your abiding memory as you rot in prison? The faces of the innocent kids, innocent prey that you gave to those old men, the murders haunting you?'

'That's better, Charlie! Pull on those

heartstrings! Much better!' Gibson laughed. 'You are so far off the scent, it's worrying. So, I'm going to give you a bit of help, but you are going to have to work faster, Charlie, much faster.'

'Go on,' Dave said.

'Acht Straat Mampero...' she said, as she pulled out what appeared to be a shard of glass from the side of her bed and began cutting and jabbing furiously at her neck. Dave and I flung ourselves at the desperate lady, but it was to no avail.

'Help! Quick, get a nurse, now!' I called.

PART 3

45

'Maddie, careful on that!' I shouted after her, beginning to develop a sweat. She was up and down the assault course as if in a trance, my words passed by her like a ghost.

'Maddie! Can you hear me?'

'Yes, Dad, but I can do it, I know I can,' she returned, red-faced and frustrated.

'I know you can do it too. But you are more likely to do it if you listen to what I have to tell you,' I said, wanting her to be able to grab the swing in front of her but knowing that in her current frame of mind, it would be unlikely.

'I can do it!'

She was stubborn, bless her. Just like her Mother and her Father, in a number of ways. Luckily, she got her desire for physical activity from my side of the family; her mother's side was mostly sedentary.

The assault course in FlipOut! Ashford was a lurid affair. I loved it though, it had green graffiti all over the wall, and they had taken some of the key elements of the area and put them into the murals. For instance, there was the McArthur Glenn Designer Outlet depicted, with the HS1 train speeding past in front of it. The more I thought about it, the more Rod was right. There was a real buzz about Ashford. Also, no-one knew me here, and I liked that.

'Dad, Dad! Look, I did it!'

There she was grinning ear to ear, my stubborn, beautiful seven-year-old, hanging from the metal beam she had been trying to grab for the best part of an hour.

'Yes, darling, well done!'

'Err, Dad, how do I…'

'…Get down? Here I'll get you,' I offered.

'No, it's fine, I'll jump,' she returned. I waited as Maddie looked down to the ground.

'Actually Dad, do you mind helping me?'

+++++++++++++++++++++++++++++++

Later on that day we were back in the flat and Dave had come to the house for a catch-up. We had been home a day and a half since the Hamburg trip and to be honest, I think we all needed a break.

I had seen people die in the line of duty. The nature of Gibson's death was a little traumatising, to say the least. They gave me a freephone number to call in case I was struggling; I hadn't used it.

We had a tiny courtyard garden in the

Folkestone flat, so Dave and I took a couple of beers and sat out in the late afternoon sun.

'How are you feeling?' Dave asked.

'I have felt better,' I replied.

'Gibson's death?'

'I have seen enough in the line of duty to prepare me for that, although it wasn't pleasant. I mean, I wanted her to face justice. Death is an easy way out for her.'

'Yep, she knew what she was doing. What else is it, Charlie? Because, if it's the threats and so on, we can get Jackson to…'

'I know mate, I know. It just feels like we are always behind. She has given us that information. We are struggling to find what we need ourselves, you know?'

'Look at it this way; we've done well. We have got Gibson, and the rope is tightening on Pensborough and this Carl guy, who is part of this thing too.'

'It's too much guesswork though, we are always nearly there, but not quite.'

'Charlie, get a grip, mate! We are in the middle of the case, and we are making progress!'

'Yeah, but I need to know we can get these guys before there are any more deaths, Dave! You heard what she said; it is getting closer to home… something big is going to happen, and I'm worried about it.' I took a breath and composed myself again. 'Anyway, what do you make of this address Gibson gave us?'

'It's an address in Amsterdam, the nice part, owned by Green Holdings. Looks residential,' Dave added.

'Well, looks like that's our next stop,' I said.

Dave nodded, 'I'll speak to Jackson.'

46

The rest of the weekend passed peacefully in our trusty threesome: Tara, Maddie and me. We chilled and watched a film after Dave left on Saturday and went for a roast dinner at the Earl's Hotel on Sunday. We dropped Maddie back, and she was tired but had a good weekend. One of my primary responsibilities as her father is to keep her safe, and for her to feel safe; that was also important to me. As far as Maddie was concerned, she had no idea of the danger that lurked around the corner.

Kids are so resilient; she didn't really remember the time in the safehouse in Dover. As much as I missed her, these days I breathed a sigh of relief when she went back to Jo as I knew she was away from the danger I brought to her world.

Still, Green was on the run. We had a further clue too. At least I hoped it was a clue and not a trap. As a force, we were taking it as Gibson's guilty conscience rather than her final trick to finish me off.

Like roulette, the odds were fifty-fifty, but I had to hope and pray that deep down all humans are good, despite their evil deeds.

Tara had packed my bag for me; she wasn't

going to make this trip.

'I need you back in one piece, Charlie. Tomorrow, I mean it,' she said half-joking.

'I have no desire to be out there any longer. My Amsterdam days are well and truly over, sweetheart. I can guarantee you,' I meant it too. A night of Netflix and chill with Tara was far more appealing currently than an overnight coach trip with Dave.

Thar's right, Jackson's thoughts were that it would be safer to travel via coach, rather than plane. We were more likely 'to slip under the radar,' apparently. Great. I just prayed that it wasn't a coach filled with revellers and that we could get our heads down.

Fortunately, the travel wasn't hellish. I placed my trusty Beats headphones on my head and listened to three podcasts, which ate up a majority of the journey. Dave napped, and we only came together really to eat the sandwiches that Tara had prepared for us, before going back to our respective pastimes.

Around 4 am, I woke to Dave nudging me and we had arrived at Centraal. The area was quiet at this time, although the late-night shenanigans are hidden further into town, south of Centraal Station.

'Wakey, wakey young man, the hotel is this way,' Dave said, leading the way.

We were staying in Amsterdam – Oost, in a plush new hotel called Yays Oostenbergengracht. The idea was to stay for a maximum of one night as this was intended to be a brief mission.

I wanted to get a cab back to the hotel, but Dave insisted on walking to wake us up. I had to admit by the time we had walked the fifteen minutes with our bags, in the cold November air, I certainly felt more refreshed.

There was an espresso machine in the kitchen. This was all the rage on the continent and most welcome on our arrival. Dave and I sat down by the window that overlooked the canal.

'I remember the last time I came to the 'Dam,' I mused.

'The Dam, eh?'

'Yes, it was a rugby tour, 2006. Very different type of trip,' I chuckled.

'I bet. We can take a walk in a bit and get our bearings if you like. Might bring back a few memories, Charlie?' Dave smiled.

'To be honest, I want to forget most of the memories from that tour. I was deep in my drinking days, and our hotel was slap-bang in the middle of the red-light district. There was a weird guy selling magic mushrooms over the road from the hotel and dealers coming to our rooms to sell their stuff during the day.'

'Mad times. Did you see those bicycles out the front? Shall we take them into town and grab some breakfast?' Dave asked.

'I don't see why not pal. I mean the land is pretty flat over here, right?'

'Yeah, that's what they say. Leave it with me.' Dave left the room presumably to speak to reception about the bikes. We had two beds in the room, one makeshift mattress upstairs, which I took. At Dave's age, I worried about him and his knees. The stairs were rickety and a bit old; it was potential for disaster, in my opinion.

I flopped on the bed and closed my eyes, drifting off far, far away...

'Wake up sleeping beauty!' Dave's voice came from downstairs.

I must have been in a pretty deep slumber as for a moment I had no clue where I was. These days that caused a bit of a panic, but I talked myself down and calmed; eventually, my brain slowly caught up with my body.

I groaned and slowly moved from the bed and down the stairs. Dave was beaming, standing at the front door, ready to attack the day.

I think that's the thing as you get older, the morning becomes far more valuable. Get out and active while the day is young. Dave must have been pushing sixty years old, although it was a bit of a mystery to me what his exact age was. I never asked, and he never wanted to talk about it, so it would probably remain a mystery to his dying day.

That said, he was agile on the rental bike we picked up from Yays and watching my old mukka cycle along the canal routes in the morning sun, that big grin across his face, was quite something.

One of the joys of Amsterdam is it's well geared for cyclists. So even though we were on the wrong side of the road for Brits and were hardly avid cyclists, it didn't prove too treacherous. One thing we both agreed on is that Amsterdam, if not hilly, is most certainly 'slopey' and when we stopped for coffee near the Hortus Botanicus Amsterdam, we certainly knew about it!

'This is the life, eh Charlie? Out on the bike every morning, decent coffee… ever thought about living somewhere apart from England?' Dave asked, sipping on his double espresso.

'Oh yeah, all the time. It's Maddie, though. I couldn't leave her.'

'Couldn't she come and visit? It would give her insight into a new culture and take her, you, Tara away from all of that… grime in East Kent?'

'Yeah, but how would that work? I have her

two weekends a month and half the holidays. If I lived here say, she has to get planes, with a minder and so on, it's just not logistically possible I don't think mate.'

'I see what you mean. Shame though? Better quality of life on the continent,' Dave mused, sipping his water now.

'Agreed, but it is what it is. I suppose it makes you appreciate it more in a way. So, what's the plan for the address? What do we know?'

'Not a lot. It seems to be a residential address, probably one of Green's, rarely frequented. We've had the police monitor the place and in the last few days, only some very minor activity.'

'OK, like what?'

'Well, they said they possibly had some movement in and out a couple of days ago. But we need to remember this is Amsterdam. They have other priorities here.'

'Yeah, and I guess relations between them and us aren't as positive, given the whole Brits abroad thing, maybe?'

'I guess so.'

'Speaking of that, how are things with your new pal, Rita?' I asked, watching a smile spread across Dave's face.

'Good. She's… you know… it's good. When this is all over, we might go away somewhere together. Perhaps you and Tara can come with?'

'Oh, *that* good! Well, it would be nice to pack for a trip where my life is not in danger, so yeah when it's over, count us in!' I said, genuinely excited for it.

'Right, let's go find out what's going on at Mampero Straat, eh?' Dave said, dropping a ten euro note on the table and heading for his bike. He was quite the man of the world.

47

When we got back to Yays, we changed and got some small work-related items together. As this was a day job, we had to dress sensibly, not inconspicuously.

We both wore dark clothes, but simple shirts and trousers. Dave had glasses, and I wore a grey beanie hat. He had a small utility belt that housed the intricacies of his cat-burgling life: lockpicks, UV lights, tiny torches etc.

I just took my good humour and what was left of my detective's brain.

The road was a typical residential road in Northern Europe. It was somewhat upmarket, you could tell by the quality of bicycle and vehicle parked by the side of the road.

Also, there was a large, metal gate to the residential block and almost certainly a second layer of security.

Typically, the second level was a standard Yale or bolt-lock; it was getting in through the first door that would be difficult.

'Here, Charlie. Head into that coffee shop and grab a couple of cans,' Dave said.

I meandered off and did as he asked. Then we sat at a bus stop which was a few metres away from the gate of the block.

'Let's just scope what's happening here, mate. It is what? Nearly three in the afternoon and this is a big, residential block. Something will happen soon. Just look like your waiting for a bus and drink your drink!' Dave said chuckling.
'I can't remember the last time I waited for a bus mate,' I said.
'You snob!'
'I didn't mean it like that! I just… haven't!'
'Well, sit quietly and talk to me like were off to town. Hasn't the weather been a little mild for this time of year, don't you think, Charles?' Dave said, putting on a posh English accent.
'Oh indeed, Stephen. It is playing havoc with my wardrobe choices I must say,' I returned, Dave laughed. I was never very good at putting on accents.
By the time I had drunk a third of my apple Fanta, a large truck had pulled up near the bus stop. A short, stocky man bustled out of the cab with a piece of paper in his hand, looking around at the buildings in front of him.
'Where are you looking for, pal?' Dave said.
'Number forty-two, you know where it is?'
'Oh this one, here.' Dave pointed to the locked, metal gate.
'Ah thank you. Only have a short amount of time, see?' he said, we nodded and smiled, getting up from our seats.

243

The man went over to the giant buzzer panel and couldn't find the number he needed.

'It's not here?' he said a little cross.

'No, it is, just ring number seven and tell them you have a delivery. The larger numbers are through the building, but they don't have a buzzer yet.'

The man did as he was told and the door unlocked. We went through with the guy who halfway up the path turned and looked at us.

'Why did you not let yourselves in then?'

'Oh, I lost my keys, and he's my friend who just… you know…stays sometimes,' I said simply.

The man looked disgusted and stormed off into the building. We quickly ran up to the second floor to apartment number eight.

'OK, only polite to knock I guess, just in case.' Dave said.

'What if someone's in there and they answer?'

'They won't. But if they do, we need to check the water meter. You do the talking, and I'll check out the locks for later.'

'Right, water meter, eh?' I said.

Luckily, I didn't need to recall my GCSE Drama qualification and Dave went about picking the locks of the apartment door.

I stood, keeping watch. There were no cameras in this lobby area, and I just hoped and prayed that the delivery driver, who we sent on a wild, goose chase, didn't come up to find us in a rage.

Luckily, Dave had opened the door reasonably swiftly, and I headed in.

'Patience, dear boy. Wait a minute while I sort out the alarm,' Dave said quietly.

He was right, there was a high-tech alarm in the room, but with Dave's skills and black magic, he was able to decipher the code and disable it. He motioned me inside.

'Just go steady, buddy. We don't know what other trickery dearest Jennifer has left for potential intruders,' I said to Dave, pretending he didn't know this already.

We were standing now in the hallway of an upmarket apartment. Directly ahead was a bathroom that was made of grey slate and glass. I had a brief look in there, but there was nothing of value to us.

To our right was a kitchen/dining room area which I went to explore, while Dave took a left into what can only be a bedroom. Everything in the kitchen was exactly how I would expect it. Kitchen utensils were hanging from a central breakfast bar area. There were all the mod cons and not a dirty plate or cup in sight.

It was clear that this place was rarely used. I checked the cupboards for any letters, bills, papers but there was nothing.

Again, the front room was clean and functional. TV in the corner, vase of plastic flowers, a painting of a seaside scene on the wall. It was more like a hotel room than an apartment.

'Charlie, I think we have lift off. Come through here,' Dave said.

I went through the hallway and into the only bedroom at the other end of the apartment. A double bed was placed in the middle of the room, immaculately made and certainly not slept in. A black lamp stood on a bedside table. Black shutter blinds hid us from the outside world.

'Talk to me mate, this place is like a sterile hotel room,' I said.

'Dave was halfway inside the glass-fronted wardrobe. I couldn't see his head as he burrowed further inside. I went around to see what he was working on, and it was a small black, computerised safe. It was like a hotel room, I thought, no personalisation whatsoever.

'Anything in the rest of the flat?' Dave asked. Despite thinking of himself as a man of the world, he still used English lingo like flat, which made me smile.

'No nothing, mate. It's like a showroom. You wouldn't know anyone even lived here. Maybe they don't. Anything in here?'

'Not a sausage, except this safe,' Dave said.

'Any chance of you getting it open sometime today please?' I said, winding him up.

'Very funny. Unless you want to try, mate?' he said, laughing. 'Do us a favour, go and double lock that front door and pop the kettle on. This could take a while.'

48

Breaking into a safe is not easy.

Given that we went armed with virtually nothing, just Dave's Batman utility belt, the job of cracking a modern safe was virtually impossible.

We toyed with the idea of buying a blowtorch and heading back to do the job. This was flawed though, as how would we secure re-entry? What if someone came back?

I offered to go for Dave, but then we would be compromised and given how dangerous things had been, I didn't want to risk it.

Besides, a regular blow torch from a hardware store may not get the job done; these modern safes by nature weren't designed to be opened forcibly.

'What are you thinking, matey?' I said to Dave, who was looking at the safe and starting his third cup of coffee.

'We can't get into it here, so we are going to have to take it with us,' he said.

'This is more my kind of job mate! Like, break it off from the wall?'

'Yes. But, we need to be careful about noise and too much damage. Remember, we aren't supposed to be here. The police aren't even a hundred percent with us,' Dave said.

We decided to call Jackson, and I put him on speakerphone.

'Hi, lads. Please give me some good news,' Jackson said.

'Well, there is nothing at the place, except a brand new safe, locked. I can't crack it. I can't blowtorch it. It's a tricky one,' Dave said.

'So it's someone's apartment?'

'Yeah but honestly, boss, you wouldn't know. There is nothing here to say who owns it: no clothes, letters, devices. Just the poxy safe,' I added.

'I see.'

'So, we don't know how much time we have. We've been here…' Dave checked his watch, 'two hours and a bit. I don't think someone lives here, but still, anyone could come knocking or looking…'

'Well, you don't have many options in my opinion, lads,' Jackson stated.

'What leave it?' Dave asked.

'No! Don't leave it! Break the damn thing off! What is it, bolt connected to the wall?'

'Yeah, I think so. Two bolts that probably came with it. It will be possible. May make a little bit of noise though.' Dave added, angling for some support if this went south with the Amsterdam Politie.

'Just do it. Figure something out! You're workmen; this is essential building work or something, you had to come in or the… I don't know…building would explode. Come on, box clever lads, you'll figure it out.' Jackson joked. With that, the phone went dead.

'Well then, let's find something strong and big,' Dave said.

I went on the hunt, and in one of the kitchen cupboards, where all the cleaning products were kept, I found a small hammer.

Ten minutes or so of banging and coercing, and we were able to prize the safe from the wall. We caused a considerable racket, but we could finally get out of this place.

It was evident to anyone that it had been taken. A foot-wide chunk had been removed from the wall. Paint peelings decorated the floor.

Best to get out as soon as we could. Dave and I got up and headed for the door, but just as Dave went to unlock it, I stopped him.

'Listen,' I whispered.

There were murmurings from the other side. I could hear echoey footsteps coming up the communal stairs.

'Bugger!' Dave said.

'It might not be anything, relax,' I said, looking through the spyhole.

Unfortunately for us, it was two politie, one

male one female coming towards the door.
'They must be here for the noise. Charlie,
quick,' Dave ran with the safe to the bedroom.
He looked out of the window, tutted and then
ran to the front window in the living room.
'There we are, Charlie. Get yourself down that
drainpipe now, and I'll throw the safe to you,'
Dave said, somewhat excitable.

There was a loud knock at the door.

'Have you gone potty, mate?' I asked.

'Charlie, it is the only way we will get this safe
out of here. Listen…' he shook it, and I could
hear a sound, like papers shuffling. 'We need to
get the thing out of here.'

I looked down. Another knock on the door;
louder this time.

'What are you going to do?' I asked.

'It will be fine. Wait for me on the corner of
this street, by the tram stop. Now get gone!' he
said, opening the window.

Against my better judgment, I moved out of the
window and looking completely, one hundred
percent like a burglar, walked along the window
frame and onto the metal drainpipe by the side
of the apartment block.

I grabbed on to it sweating and started to slide
down. I let go accidentally and fell to the
concrete with a huge thud. My knee hurt, but I
was OK.

'Right on three, catch,' Dave said.

On three, he threw the safe, which after travelling two floors was a massive beast, but I caught it. I wondered if I had have let it drop, would it have opened on the concrete? Probably not, that would be too simple, I thought.

I walked as calmly as I could, trying to put to the back of my mind that I was a man in dark clothes and beanie hat, carrying a battered safe, that had obviously been robbed. I walked past the parked police car and waited at the corner of the road at the tram stop, ignoring the sideways looks I got from pedestrians and cyclists.

I took a deep breath and wondered, what was hidden in this safe? I prepared myself for it to be nothing of note, that way I couldn't be disappointed. Maybe though, Gibson was right, and it held the key to bringing down the Rosicrucian Order.

'Charlie! Run!' I turned and saw Dave running towards me, being chased by the two policemen. For an old boy, he was sharp across the concrete. I turned and saw a tram on the other side of the tracks about to pull off.

'Quick, quick get on it!' he said bolting past me.

I caught up with him and managed to jump on

the moving train, much to the irritation of the two out of breath coppers we had left behind.

49

We got off near Centraal and stopped for a scooner of beer in an Irish pub called 'The Rover.'

The beauty of the Centraal district is that *nobody* looks out of place… anything goes. So two grown men in dark clothes carrying a battered safe is OK, plus we could mix into the crowd. It was getting to around six in the evening, and the pubs were getting busy.

'Right, so for our next trick… opening the magic box!' Dave said.

'Hang on a minute, before we get onto that, how did you evade those coppers, back there?' I asked, genuinely intrigued.

'Well, if I told you that would be revealing my tricks of the trade. High level, top-secret, MI6 types of tricks,' Dave said, maintaining a straight face through the whole sentence.

'Oh, really?'

'Well, no. Between you and me, Charlie, I used the old 'there he is over there trick' and ran the other way! But we won't tell the boys back home that, eh?'

'No, course not. So, you blamed it on me?'

'Yeah, sort of. Good old Charlie Stone taking the rap!' Dave added, ordering a couple more beers to the table.

'So, I've been thinking… using the police is a no-go, but also we don't particularly want to take it back to England.'

'No, we have to open it here,' Dave said.

'So, what about an industrial factory? Flash the badges and get them to open it for us? Then we can drop it in a skip or whatever over here and get back home with whatever is inside?' I said.

'That, my man, is a good plan. Cheers to that.' Dave picked up his beer and saluted us.

'Another cross-channel trip that I'm chalking up us a success.'

'Well, let's not get ahead of ourselves, brother, we aren't back home yet.'

While we finished our drinks, I found a place near Schiphol, that looked like it could help us. Schiphol is also where the airport was, and I found two flights back to London Stansted for us. Stansted wasn't ideal as it's the least accessible London airport for Kent, but hell, I was so keen to get back before we became wanted criminals in Holland, that I would worry about that later.

We grabbed our bags from Yays and asked reception to call us a cab out to Schiphol. Twenty minutes later, we were outside a large, faceless industrial building in the backstreets of nowhere.

Dave handled the discussions with the burly factory worker, which made me happy. He certainly didn't seem so glad to see us, churning out what seemed like swearwords in Dutch as he took us through to his machinery. I think he was about to knock off for the day, working overtime, so his rage was somewhat understandable.

He put on a pair of plastic goggles and fired up the giant torch. Within a few moments, he had split the metal, and the contents of the safe was accessible.

Inside, we found five letters, all sent from the same address in Luxembourg.

'Well at least we will have some reading material for the flight,' Dave said, as I grabbed them and stuffed them in my gilet pocket.

50

The flight was not full and thus Dave and I could sit together for its duration.

'Well go on then,' he said eagerly, as the plane started to taxi.

I pulled out the letters. The address was written with an old-fashioned ink pen, probably a fountain pen, and the writing was reminiscent of my year four teacher, Miss. Williams, who wrote in calligraphy.

'Ooh, fancy!' Dave said as I pulled out the letter inside the envelope.

'OK, here goes:

11 Rue Munster
Grund
68140 Gunsbach
Luxembourg

Tuesday 10th September 2019

Dearest Jennifer,

Just a quick note to say, it was essential to see you last week; the plan must forge ahead as we agreed. There will be without doubt challenge from the board, there is always opposition, but if we are to drive our Order into the future, we must not err from our plan.

I was impressed by your understanding of the fundamentals of the order, the history of the elders and your vision for the future.

What we must do is be clear about how to maintain our power and you are the person to do this — regardless of your sex.

Regards,

Pieter

So, the apartment was Jenny's, but who is Pieter? This is someone entirely off our radar, who we had never even heard about. I continued onto the second letter, passing the first over to Dave.

11 Rue Munster
Grund
68140 Gunsbach
Luxembourg

Thursday 3rd October 2020

Jennifer,

I am pleased to hear about the accession in charters 1 to 4 of the Order. You don't need me to remind you that you are the head of the most critical and profligate chapter of our Order. In short, without your sterling work, what we have provided to our associates would not have been. This is why, I am determined to ensure that you will succeed me as the head of what we do.

As you know, the issue of you being a female has not gone away. I have had kickback from a number of our clients, many of whom I have straightened out and some I have given short thrift. Jenny, you must not take this personally, it will happen, regardless of what some of the older people think.

I have reminded them of the sacrifices you made, your own daughter given up, to preserve our sanctity.

Wadham and Beddle sacrificing themselves for the cause was down to their loyalty to you.

This will be honoured, but first, there will be trouble ahead. I need to see you before the initiation. Come in the usual way.

I look forward to meeting this Carl Blewett, I have sent him the times.

I trust you will straighten everything else out.

Best

Pieter R.

The final piece of the puzzle, as Anna Gibson alluded to…. Pieter seems to be the one pulling the strings. We always believed it to be Green, but no. It looked like we would be going overseas again, this time to Luxembourg.
I passed the second letter over and opened the final one. There were two other documents, but these were unfinished drafts, written back, that had no importance. This letter was the most recent:

11 Rue Munster
Grund
68140 Gunsbach
Luxembourg

Tuesday 5th November 2019

Dear Jennifer,

The plan is in place. We will initiate your new man this time next month. He has the details, as you do. Please ensure he is ready and he understands the sacred nature of the Order and the work we will ask him to carry out.
I take you at face value that he had nothing to do with

the issues at chapter four. Why that policeman is not dead by now I have no idea and to be honest, that is something you do need to address. I hope you can ensure something most foul happens to that man. Something that hurts him more profoundly than the end of his own life…

Your decision to move all of our work between one and three now is a good one., especially since the authorities seem to be closing in. Luckily, they seem to be one step behind; nothing can stop the plan from going ahead. Two more sacrifices and the succession will be complete; the order passed on.

See you on the 3rd.

Pieter.

I took a deep breath and felt my walls closing in on me again. I prayed for the journey to go quickly; I needed to be home to protect my family.

51

From Stansted, I shared a taxi home with Dave.

It was expensive and extravagant, but the letters had affected me. Dave too. He wouldn't say it, he would always try and put a brave face on for me, but he was worried. The letters were pointed, and although I wasn't named, I was an explicit target.

I rang Tara to check in with her. At first, she didn't answer, and my heart raced for a few minutes. However, she missed the call as she was in the bathroom, and she called me straight back.

'The reason I didn't answer was that I bought that car I showed you,' she said, sounding pleased.

'The massive one you texted me last night?' I asked.

'Yep, the seven-seater. It looks like a tank!'

'Tara, why do you need such a massive car?'

'I like being up high. Plus I will need it to carry the army of kids that we have,' she said.

I blushed a little, 'well good to be prepared. Tara's tank for her army, eh?'

'Tara's tank, I love it!' she said.

'Love you, see you soon,' I said, and we hung

up.

A few hours at home, that was my lot and then tomorrow at 7 am we would meet with the others, show Jackson the letters and decide on a plan moving forward.

This time something felt different. Dave had a glassy, distant look in his eye since reading the letters. I knew something dark was coming. Nothing normally frightened me, and despite the fact the end was coming for Green and the Order, I knew it wouldn't be without recompense.

I got indoors and cuddled Tara. I just wanted to be close to her, hiding under the sheets, before tomorrow.

+++++++++++++++++++++++++++++++++

The alarm went off at 6 am. I turned it off and rolled back into bed next to T. She was warm, and I cuddled her for a moment while steeling myself for what lay ahead. I was ready, though, excited even, to try and complete this case for good.

As I went to wriggle out of bed, Tara held me there close to her. I told her I would be back from work as soon as I could, but we both knew that it could be a long while. I stayed with her and held her for a moment before the familiar pull of my work tugged at me and told me it was time to go.

When I arrived at the Ashford Police Station, Jackson was already set up in the conference room with Karl and Jimmy. Dave was en-route from Folkestone, so I fixed myself a cup of black coffee and waited.

I put my hands around the warm cup and watched the steam rise from the black liquid. I breathed the smell in and thought that really, this isn't a very appealing thing, but I drank it religiously, every morning.

How many other things that we do are by-products or a force of habit? The number of women I have dealt with in this line of work that refuse to prosecute their violent husbands due to loyalty and habit. They are scared and call the police when he gets violent and then when it's all calmed, and he's calmed, they go back and continue in the same way. Habit. That's why despite my underlying feelings about Jo, one thing I liked about her, was the fact that we called it a day when we did. The rows were getting worse and worse. When you know each other that well, you know how to raise the demons and Jo did that with me.

Now, I had Tara, and Maddie had Tara, which showed her how a positive, healthy relationship could be. It also taught me how important it is to not go back to the toxic relationship when it gets tricky. If Jo and I had, then I wouldn't have met Tara, and we would be stuck in the same cycle of rows and bitterness. Habit. Habit's a real killer.

'Greetings, apologies for my tardiness,' Dave said, 'But I have some information that I think you all will be interested in.'

'Well, I guess that's the meeting started, eh?' Jackson said, slightly bemused and a little miffed that his role as big boss and chair of our gatherings had been taken.

'Oh sorry, boss, but you're going to like this,' Dave continued, pulling out a tape recorder.

'The Order is going through some interesting changes at the moment. As you know, the first part of the acceptance is commitment… through the initiation…'

'Who is this talking?' Jackson asked.

'That is our old friend Pensborough, Green's underling.' Dave confirmed. 'The voice you're about to hear is Carl Blewett. The lad from Hawkinge who is on the committee at the sport's club.'

'Yes, I understand… I need to go out to Luxembourg, yeah?'

'Well, yes. But before the initiation ceremony, you are going to meet him… first…'

'What before the initiation?'

'Correct. That's what he wants, it's never been done

before this way, but these are unprecedented times. The Order is facing…significant challenges, and he wants to meet you beforehand.'

'OK…'

The voices went fuzzy, and Dave clicked the tape-recorded to a halt. I looked at him; he was grinning ear to ear.

'You've got a plan, haven't you?' I asked him. He nodded slowly, the smile not leaving his face. I knew that this would mean some form of danger for me, that's for sure.

'Hold on a minute… so on that tape, you've got Pensborough and Blewett preparing him for his initiation?' Jackson asked.

'Yes, but normally these things are in their weird chambers, and we would have no access to it, but this one is different.' Dave stated. 'They are meeting beforehand.'

'Let me guess, I go to the initiation as Carl Blewett and meet this leader guy… Pieter or whatever and infiltrate the gang?' I asked.

'Yes! Exactly! They don't know what Carl looks like, all they know is that he's English and he is coming over to meet them and is one of Green's lackies,' Dave replied.

'One small issue, if I may…' it was Jimmy, I think it was the first time in one of our meetings that Jimmy had ever become involved.

'Go on,' Dave said.

'Well, if Charlie goes, won't Green and her people recognise him? It was only six months ago you were at her house with her. It won't work,' he continued.

'That is a very annoying, very intelligent point, Jim,' Jackson added.

'I could do it,' Jim continued.

'I don't think so, this is serious business,' Jackson said a little off-handed. Dave shot him a glance.

'What are you saying, boss? Can't I handle it? Or I'm not up to it?' Jimmy returned angrily. He wasn't ordinarily confrontational, but Jackson had hit a nerve.

'Calm down, Jim. I meant that Stone is a DS and you're a DC, this is...' Jackson stuttered.

'No...go on? What's your point? What have I done wrong? I'm only a DC because my poxy DCI won't promote me!' Jimmy's voice raised.

'You haven't done anything wrong. This is just a massive case,' Jackson continued.

'Yeah, and if we go in, whoever goes in, if they mess it up, won't come out.' There was a sombre silence at Jimmy's words. He was right.

'So, let's bring this Carl in and make our decision from there. We need him anyway to find out the details of this initiation and so on,' I said.

'Is it worth getting a search warrant for his place?' Dave asked, but he knew the answer. 'Yeah, the emails and comms we will need for sure,' I said.

'Karl, go to Blewett's address and bring him in. Jimmy can you speak to Folkestone Magistrate's Court and get that warrant ASAP,' Karl nodded, but Jimmy left the room without acknowledging Jackson at all. Dave, Jackson and I were left in the conference room.

'He's a good copper to be fair, Darren,' I said, watching Jackson who looked a little perplexed at the situation.

'Have I been harsh on him?' Jackson asked.

'Not that I have seen. But you don't know what's going on at home. His wife might be pregnant, or he's saving for a deposit or anything. It's not always personal,' I continued.

'It seemed a *bit* personal,' Jackson said, looking at Dave for an answer that wasn't forthcoming. 'You've sat here, Dave, what do you think?' he asked.

Dave paused. 'See how he is tomorrow. Give him time. He may just want to prove himself.'

'Would you use him here though?' Jackson asked.

'I don't know. I would always want to do it myself if I could. This is a tricky one that requires experience. It could go either way.'

Jackson looked at me.

'I want to do it. It's always been my case really, and I want to get these guys. That said, as I get older, I need to stop shooting from the hip, and maybe I'm too close to it.' I said, unsure of what to think really.

'Let's find out from the suspect what he knows about this whole process and go from there,' Jackson said exasperated.

We both nodded, and Jackson left the room for the safety of his office.

+++++++++++++++++++++++++++++++++

Dave and I went to get some food at The Phoenix pub in Ashford. It served simple pub grub, but the owners were a down to earth married couple and the place was friendly.

The more time I spent in Ashford, the more I grew to like it.

We took a slow walk back hoping that Blewett would have been brought in by now and the search warrant had been secured; we were right on both counts.

We headed straight down to the cells and saw Rod.

'Greetings from the underworld!' he exclaimed as we went in.

Dave smiled, and I couldn't help but laugh.

'How is life up there in the light?' he continued.

'Good, mate. Well, it will be better if we have a new arrival. Do we?'

'This is Ashford, Charlie! Always new arrivals! But the one you are looking for is in cell seven, I believe.'

'You still loving Ashford, Rod?' I asked, his comment made me wonder.

'It's like anywhere, Charlie. People. It's all about people. If you have good ones around you, you will be OK. Some good folk here, especially out where I am…' he said, drifting off into the distance.

'Well, that's good mate, glad you still like it!'

'Don't get me started on the Pizza Expresses too… and a Haribo Store, next to the Lindt store. It's dreamworld pal.'

'Certainly sounds it,' I agreed.

'Come on, Rod, take us to Mr Blewett please!' Dave said, hurrying up the process. I liked Rod and enjoyed his child-like humour and banter. Dave was a bit longer in the tooth, and his patience a bit thinner.

'Of course, Detective Woodward. Right this way, sir!' Rod said doing a mock salute as if he were in the army.

'Careful now! I may not be your gaffer anymore, but I can still give you a run for your money in the boxing ring,' Dave smiled and pretended to spar with him.

Rod laughed and opened the door to cell number seven.

52

Carl Blewett sat opposite the door on a wooden bench. He was a short man, relatively well built. He was wearing a long overcoat with an all in one tracksuit underneath it. He had a baseball cap on that read 'Stussy', a brand that he presumably liked.

He wore white trainers. If I were honest, he didn't look anything like I expected him too, but I knew also, you must never judge a book by a cover; he may dress like a twelve-year-old but wolves often reside in sheep's clothing. Dave looked at me, and I nodded at him, we knew the drill. Dave started, and I got heavy if needed later on.

'Good afternoon, Mr Blewett,' Dave began. His eyes didn't move from the closing door. He was in a daze.

'How are you?' Dave often asked a direct question early on to see whether the suspect was playing ball.

Carl sniggered, but then refrained from speaking. He was going to try and play hardball with us.

'You know, it is in your interests to talk to us. We don't have the time and energy to mess about with people like you. As we speak, they are tearing your house up and finding out what they can about you. We know what we need to know, and you are in a lot of trouble,' Dave continued.

'Yeah, you won't be going to Luxembourg or anywhere soon, put it that way,' I interjected. Carl shot a glance at me before going back to stare at the back of the door; his fragile walls were beginning to break.

'Come on, Carl. Don't be silly here. You have got your little life in Hawkinge. You don't want to throw it all away for these guys,' I added. He was breathing deeper and deeper.

'We can help you, Carl. We can protect you from Green and her people,' Dave added.

'It's not Green you need to worry about,' Carl said, his eyes not moving from the back of the cell door. He was terrified at the gravity of the situation. I thought back at his convictions, all relatively minor: drug offences, drink driving, GBH.

This was a different ball game altogether.

'Is that so? What about your pal, Pensborough?' Dave said.

'He is even lower down the order,' Carl blurted out.

'So why the girls in the Hawkinge chamber? Pensborough was involved in that, seems like a big thing to trust him with?' Dave said.

'And he messed it up…' I added, just to turn the knife a little.

'So, he's in trouble with us and with the Order,' Dave continued.

'Carl, you're in a better position. Give him up and tell us what you know, and the judge will take pity on you. You have got your girlfriend and your daughter, do the right thing,' I whispered to him.

He pondered the situation, but he wasn't fit for this level of criminality. He was panicking, and he knew this was a serious moment; a crossroads.

'Pensborough is gone. The girls he trafficked, he shouldn't have done. He didn't have the permission…'

'What happened?' Dave asked.

'He went over with Green to Luxembourg and met a few connections. He wanted to create his own 'club' in Folkestone, like a dance/brothel type place. He always had ideas…trying to make money and all that. But he was twisted. There was something entirely wrong about him, you know?' he continued.

'Was? What do you mean… was?' I asked.

Carl smiled at us, 'Oh wow, you guys are so behind! He's gone, they finished him. Chamber One: too much bad publicity, the girls were the last straw, it was totally off-grid and Green couldn't have it, you know? Jeez, I can't believe you are so far…'

I had enough of this and grabbed Carl by the arm, pinning him against the wall.

'Get off, what are you doing?' he protested.

'Stop playing with us, Carl. And stop telling us we don't know anything. That's why you are here because we caught you, right? We know you left the ladder, we know you knew about the girls in the chamber, and that makes you an accessory.' I pushed his arm further up his back. 'I also know it's your initiation you little twerp. When, where, how? Tell us!'

'Charlie, leave him now,' Dave said, putting his hand on my arm. I had Carl's arm bent behind his back, and I was twisting it. He was almost in tears at the pain.

'Tell me now!' I repeated.

'Ahhhh, let me go!' he said.

I pushed myself away from him and sat back down. He reorganised himself and sat back down. I was irritated now; it wasn't the first time in this case we had been told we were far off the scent. All I cared about was saving lives; the game meant nothing to me.

'It's all happening in Luxembourg, the capital. The initiation is in Chamber Seven, but he wants me to meet them in the club out there.'

'This… *Pieter?*'

'Yes, him and others. Green will be there too.'

'Where is the club?'

'He has a place there, Rue de Treves. That's where I am meeting him, Saturday night. The initiation is on Sunday morning, midnight.'

'What is the initiation?' Dave asked. 'Like, what are you doing there?'

Carl again looked bemused because we didn't know. This time he kept his thoughts to himself.

'It's…. erm… well, it's a sacrifice. You have to sacrifice…someone…' he said sheepishly.

'To show what? Your commitment to their 'order?'

Carl nodded.

'Jesus… right. Let's go. I've heard enough,' I said.

'What about me?' Carl said.

'What about *you?* You're staying here for now, mate. Have a nice little think about all the things we have on you, and you just admitted too. We are going to see if we. can save your sacrifice from an unpleasant death.' I added.

'One final thing, Carl…. have you met any of these people? Pieter for instance or Green?'

'Not Pieter. Green once, although I doubt she would remember,' he added.

Dave went over to Carl and whipped off his baseball cap. He was shaved bald.

'Do you always wear your hair like that?' Dave asked.

'Since I was a kid,' Dave looked at me and nodded.

'Thanks, Carl.'

We were back up in Jackson's office with Karl, Jimmy and Jackson.

The mood had relaxed a little. The warrant obtained quickly, and as we knew, Blewett brought in with little issue.

'He told us everything: the where, when and who. We have our way in,' I said.

'He also told us that Pensborough was dead! Our old DCI!' Dave added.

'He's dead?' Jackson asked.

'Apparently so. By order of The Order,' Dave finished off.

'Blimey,' Jackson muttered. 'They mean business.'

'Yes. But Blewett is bricking it. He knows he's in too deep. He can barely hold it together in there. He was going for this initiation which in effect is murdering some bright young thing to show your commitment.'

'But why? What's the point in all of this?' Jackson exclaimed.

'Well that's the question we need to answer,' I said.

'Blewett is as bald as a coot. Has been since he was young. So, whoever is going in is going for a trim first. He also said that Green would be there, but he didn't know any of the others. He barely knows Green at all,' Dave said.

'Jimmy, step outside with me for a second,' I asked, moving towards the door. Jimmy got up and followed.

'Listen, I know you're chomping at the bit to get involved on a deeper level here. This one isn't for you though, pal. I need to do this. This is some very, very dark stuff and I think for your first big undercover... on your own... I wouldn't risk you. So, I want you to know this isn't Jackson's decision; he hasn't got a problem with you. This is my decision. And I promise that I will put a word in on the next one for you, OK?' I put my arm on his shoulder.

'OK, Charlie. I just want you lot to trust me.'

'We do, mate. I promise. Help me finish this and then we will go from there, all right?'

'All right,' he said.

I opened the door and went back in.

'Right, we've had a chat. I'm going in as Carl Blewett. I suggest Dave comes to Luxembourg. Karl and Jimmy, you need to find out everything we can about who we're meeting, the buildings, entrances and exits… full reports on all of it… Jackson… I guess you just sit there and look pretty as usual, eh?' I said, knowing I was riding my luck.

He gave me a sideways glance, 'very funny, Charlie. You do know who relays all of this to the Super, explains all the mess and collateral damage, organises your overseas permits, firearms…?'

'OK, OK. It was just a joke, mate. Keep your wig on!' I said.

'You two go and get packed, I will book you on the next flight I can,' Jackson stated.

'Yep, because tomorrow we have a meeting in Luxembourg,' I confirmed.

53

The plane touched down at Luxembourg Airport, and immediately everything about the place gave you a feel of luxury and expense. It was an interesting place. I mean, having done some very brief research on the plane, Luxembourg City is the central hub and the only city within the country. In short, it is a small country, although well connected and bordering five other European countries. Teachers get paid on average around 60, 000 euros a year. Once Tara had finished that book, I would drop Troy Wood a line and tell him!

'We have got a driver for this one,' Dave said, pointing to a car that was sitting silently up from the taxi rank.

'Sweet,' I replied.

As I approached, a man in a suit got out and took our bags for us, placing them carefully in his boot. Whether he was doing this because of excellent customer service, or the fact that he didn't trust us with his shiny new car, I wasn't too sure.

I got in the passenger seat and noticed the car was electric and very modern. The control panels stretched the length of the dash; everything was electronic.

'What car is this mate?' Dave asked, his passion not stretching to new, modern beasts of the road.

'Tesla, here….' he said, slipping the car into a new gear and putting his foot down.

'Hm,' Dave grunted at the driver. 'What sort of engine has it got?'

As Dave and the driver engaged in car talk, I took a moment to steel myself for the mission that was ahead. What was the goal and the outcome? I mean, we knew we were going to infiltrate and find out more about the Order, but how did Jackson want them taken down? The way I saw it, there were two more pieces to the puzzle; Green and Pieter. This Pieter guy seemed like the head of the Order, judging by the letters. If we got him, would the rest of the cards fall? Tonight, we would rest; tomorrow was the meeting.

We made it to the Sofitel Hotel, and despite Dave's initial disdain for all things modern, he ended up liking the driver and taking his number.

'Developing a habit, eh mate? Picking up numbers when we're abroad?' I said.

'Well, you know,' he tried to think of something funny, a witty quip, but it didn't come. I smiled at him and rubbed his shoulder. I loved him and all his quirks and foibles.

'Right then, let's get up to the room. I'm in the bathroom first,' Dave said.

I checked my watch. It was 9.15 pm. *Yes, good idea. Time for a couple of beers, maybe.*

'Why can't I go in the bathroom first?' I replied.

'Mate, the state you leave a bathroom, no chance!' he laughed.

'What do you mean?'

'I think you get most of the water on the floor, rather than on your body. I'm going in first,' he said forthrightly.

'Charming!' I thought to myself, but I knew deep down he was right. I wasn't the neatest or tidiest. Hey ho.

We got very loosely spruced up, before heading to the rooftop bar on the Sofitel. It was quite a sight. Upon exiting the lift, there was a man in a suit to greet us and take our jackets. The panoramic view across the city of Luxembourg was extraordinary.

We sat at a window seat, and an attractive young lady in a minuscule mini dress furnished us with two cocktail menus.

As she left the table, Dave and I glanced at one another and couldn't help but giggle.

'I tell you what, I could get used to this!' I said.

'Here, I'll be telling Tara if you start chatting to any young ladies out here,' he said, waggling his finger at me.

'Seriously though, how have we afforded this on our budget?'

'Don't know really. We are in the same room, I guess. And it's Luxembourg, Hardly a popular tourist destination. Perhaps that drives the prices down,' Dave mused.

'Well, either way, happy days for us!'

We ordered drinks and looked out across the skyline. When the cocktail waitress brought the drinks to us, Dave went to work.

'Sorry love, could you tell me what that old part is called?' he said, pointing over to the medieval buildings that seemed etched into the gorge below.

'Ah, yes sir,' she purred in a deep, French accent. 'That is the quarter called Grund, built into the valley by the Alzette River. It is a medieval city, very beautiful. You must visit.'

I think Dave was a bit in awe of the lady and his conversation stopped. So, I paid the lady and thanked her. Dave watched her as she wiggled away.

'Listen, haven't you got a girlfriend these days?' I said to him, I refrained from waggling the fatherly finger though.

'Well, I guess… in a long-distance kind of way,' he said.

'How is Rita?' I asked.

'Oh, very lovely. We have some enjoyable WhatsApp video calls. She is planning to come over soon too.'

'Well, well. Trips to Hamburg trips over here. Must be getting serious, old boy?' I ribbed him, but he was having none of it.

'Changing the subject slightly, are you on board with the plan of attack for tomorrow, Charlie?'

'Not really…'

'Well, while you were packing your bags and doing your hair before we caught the plane, I sat down with Jackson…'

'Lovely…'

'The good news is we can extend the time we keep Blewett in custody for an extra forty-eight hours. He has agreed to help us pretty much; folded like a deck of cards and wants to do as little time as possible,' Dave said.

'Understandable…'

'Yes. And also of course, he knows the whole plan. So we, I mean I, will have him in my ear as we go to the meet.'

'OK, so what do I need to know beforehand?'

'Well the meet is at 10 pm in the Gentleman's Club on the Rue de Treves, just down the road from here apparently,' Dave said.

'You could ask your new lady friend?' I intimated at the waitress.

'That wouldn't make the best impression now,

would it? It's a glorified strip club and brothel…'

'Good point… so meet at 10 pm? Bit late buddy. I like to be in bed with a nice chocolate biscuit by then,' I said.

'Sadly the international criminals of Luxembourg are not going to pander to the nightly regimen of Folkestone's finest, Charlie Stone,' Dave smiled.

'Well, I suppose it could be worse.' I said tongue in cheek. 'So what is the purpose of the meetup?'

'Remember, you are Carl Blewctt, desperate to be inducted into the Order under Green. You are after the financial security it provides and the camaraderie, the weird sex ring stuff, but ultimately, you agree with their guiding principles…'

'Right, brutal murder and savagery? Good thing I can act…' I replied.

'No, that's not it. This is all about spiritual redemption and sacrifice. In this case, a sacrifice, to bring the world back into line…'

'Oh, OK do carry on…'

'So, the sacrifices they use are kids as we know. They all go down 'the wrong path' and then apparently, have the opportunity to atone…'

'Like, what do you mean "the wrong path?" like sex and drugs and stuff?'

'Not even that bad. I mean it could be screens. Being on your phone too much or creating profiles and posting sexy photos when you're too young. Even to have social media, that sort of stuff. Although, that's like an example. It's not all to do with social media. It could be other stuff too, according to Carl.'

'We got all of this from him?'

'Yes, he became surprisingly lucid when we discussed the search warrant and the sort of time he might do if there were any lewd pictures of minors on his computer. He suddenly became very keen to strike a deal. This guy has got a lot of previous remember. Anyway, the team back at home are compiling a document for some fun time reading tomorrow.'

I pondered what I'd been told.

'Go back to the atonement bit... how does that work?'

'Well, again this is all second hand, but apparently, once the person has been captured they are given the opportunity to change their ways... but how this works who knows.'

'So this initiation... this is a girl or boy for all we know. They will have had the chance to atone but haven't?'

'It would seem that way, but whether the atonement bit is just rubbish to make them seem less…evil, I don't know,' Dave concluded.

'The whole thing is very sinister, and it gives me the massive creeps. So much so, I'm having another cocktail,' I said, signalling for the bar lady to come back over.

'Careful mate, don't overdo it,' Dave said watchfully. He refrained from a second drink, but after I had finished mine, we headed back to the room.

54

I had a clearer picture of what tomorrow would look like. By the time I had got back to the room and into bed, Jackson's file had arrived, and Dave and I both perused it individually, before hitting the hay.

In the morning, I woke before him at around 6ish, but I was too nervous to go back to sleep and didn't want to turn the lights on and wake my old pal. So I leafed through the electronic document once more.

One thing that struck me about this, was it is an old established order that had been around for years; hidden in plain sight.

Those murders we see so regularly all over the world; some of them were down to the Order. The reason it had become public this time, Bryan Rattle, the poor kid from Hawkinge, remains a mystery. Had that not have occurred, we may not have joined up any of these dots. It was like a freemason's party or the darker elements of the Illuminati, but in plain sight, we had the opportunity to starve and kill it.

The leader Pieter Rosenkreutz came from a long line of family members who it appeared were part of the wealthy aristocracy. Born into money and financial security and also a history in the Rosicrucian Order, Pieter was a fearsome character in his day.

Although his twenties were not documented in the file, he seemed an angry and intelligent youth. He was arrested twice for extreme brutality and faced prison at one point, before his father and the connections he had got him out of trouble.

He has invested in some businesses that lay in the dark arts: the deep web, extreme pornography websites and underground sex clubs. This was Pieter's schtick. Match that with a physical presence and intelligence, and we were facing a formidable opponent.

From what we could see, Green had done some terrible things that she needed to face justice for, but Pieter was the driving force behind it all.

'Stop thinking so loudly,' Dave's voice was around an octave deeper in the morning.

'Sorry mate, a lot going on. With my little brain, I'm finding it tough!'

'Hm, well we got a day ahead of us, supposed we can do the tourist thing for a bit, take our minds off it?'

'I suppose we could. I'll jump in the shower, you get the coffee on,' I said, jumping out of bed.

'Wait, hang on… you will flood the place!'

By the time he had finished protesting about my shower habits, I was in the bathroom and had the door locked.

Fool me once, Dave Woodward!

++++++++++++++++++++++++++++++++

We tried to get our minds off tonight by walking around Luxembourg City and stopping at a few places for drinks and food. We went to the Rue de Treves and saw the club, which by day you could mistake for any abandoned business; grey shutters and no-one in sight, tonight I daresay would be quite different. We went to the central part of town and stopped in a Dortmund FC bar, which was good fun. We had coffee and watched some Bundesliga on the TV, before finding another pub to have some lunch.

Afterwards, we strolled to the Old Quarter, where the municipal buildings were and admired the old, gothic architecture. There was a constant fire burning outside the civic hall, to symbolise hope. I shivered when I saw it as it brought back memories of the chamber in Copenhagen. *Be strong Stone…more is coming tonight.* Murder, always more murder.

'Charlie, look over there. I know you have been putting it off,' Dave said.

'What do you mean?' he was pointing at a barbershop, it looked empty.

'See, no-one is waiting. You might as well go now.'

We had decided that to imitate Carl best I would have to get my head shaved bald, as he wore it. I wasn't looking forward to it. *What would my girls think?*

'It will grow back. Plus, you have a fine collection of hats, you'll be OK,' Dave said grinning.

'Thanks, mate,' I said, walking tentatively towards it.

After my cut, I was pretty sad about my curly locks being savaged, so we found one more bar and had a smoothie each.

It didn't take our minds from what was to come. Dave started getting itchy feet at around 6 pm and wanted to head back to check all of the electronics and connections back to Blewett and the team. He went ahead, and I decided to take a slow walk back and ring Tara on the way.

'Hey, you! How's Luxembourg treating you?'

Tara was in good spirits which was pleasing to hear, but she didn't know of the full extent of our enquiry and that we were going to infiltrate the Order directly; it would only worry her.

'Yeah good, working tonight. It's going to be

cold. It's like nearly freezing already over here!' I replied, trying to remain jovial.

'You're in luck because I packed you a pair of my leggings at the bottom of your case to keep you warm!' Tara said. I had got into the habit of wearing her leggings on super-cold West Ham nights, and she clearly didn't seem to mind.

'Thanks, hun. What have you been up to?'

'Oh, not a lot. Seen my Mum today. Apart from that just reading…'

'Anything interesting from Troy's book?' I asked.

'Well, there are lots of riddles. It's all a bit… how can I describe it… everything means something, is a message. At the moment there is some discontent, and he's sending a coded message using letters and words to his headmaster at the school.'

'Oh, I see. So, gone a bit off tangent? No mention of Luxembourg?' I asked.

'Not yet, but I'll keep you posted.' Tara confirmed.

I said my goodbyes and that I aimed to be home in a day or two. Tara was fine, and I think getting used to my time away. She knew it was for the job, and in a way, it was healthy for us to co-exist without each other there all of the time. It gave us something to talk about at least!

It reminded me of lockdown when we were in Dover. People think they would love some paid time from work with their family, but it quickly becomes a difficult time, especially when it's forced, you know?

I got back to the hotel and went straight to the room. I placed my key, wallet and phone on the side and had a final shower.

When I got out, Dave still hadn't looked up and was twiddling with some electronics on some form of a panel.

'Here, Dave. Do you remember when I told you about that Troy Wood book? Did you… did you ever look into getting it?' I asked.

'It doesn't exist, mate,' he said, beavering away with some wires and cords.

'What do you mean?'

'Well, you can't buy it anywhere. It's not out. No word of it on Amazon or Waterstones,' Dave said.

'Really?'

'Check it out. Google it.'

I could see he was busy, so I did as he said and he was right. No trail whatsoever on the internet, Troy's Facebook page, nothing.

'But I've got a copy… signed to… me…' I said to myself. What was the message on it again? I texted Tara and asked her to check and then got changed.

We checked in with Carl to see what the dress code was. He suggested smart-casual, so I wore an open neck shirt and a black suit.

It was too dangerous to wear a wire or an earpiece in this situation, so we agreed to stay in communication via text. I began to get that cold, nervous feeling running through my veins. So, I suggested a quick drink on the top floor. Dave could see my disposition, so agreed. Just one.

When we arrived at the bar, I checked my watch... 9pm. One drink, then I would take a walk through the town and to the Gentleman's Club.

I took a deep breath and said a little prayer to myself.

55

'You have ID?' the burly bouncer on the door said in a gruff voice.

I did and passed it to him. Jackson had gotten Blewett's ID from him before we travelled.

'Hm, wait here.'

The bouncer disappeared beyond the velvet curtain and inside the club. The loud bass of the dance music from inside hit my chest. It was a welcome sensation that distracted from the endless, bitter cold of this country.

The bouncer returned. 'Mr. Rosy is waiting for you in the back,' he said, moving to one side.

Mr. Rosy, eh? It must be a shortening of Rosenkreutz; *a nice pseudonym to make this man seem like a friendlier person, maybe.*

I walked forward and lifted the velvet curtain; it was heavy yet smooth to the touch. As soon as I entered, the bass hit me again; harder, intoxicating. It was dark inside, the wild spray of coloured disco lights filled the room, mirror balls glistened, but the pervading hue was a crimson red, deep red, blood red.

There were a few groups of men dotted about, sitting in red cushioned chairs, watching. There were dancers in cages at either end of the room and a stage with a large silver pole. I went to the bar which ran along the left-hand side of the room, and a dancer immediately approached me. She was tall and her scent intoxicating, making me feel a little intimidated by her. She smiled at me.

'Have a seat, sir. We will bring drinks for you,' she said in a thick accent, in the noise I couldn't make out where it was from.

'It's OK,' I said like a true Brit, cash in hand, waiting at the bar. I loved Europe and being abroad, but that's one thing we will never agree on. Brits like to get their drinks, whereas table service was customary in Europe.

I smiled at her, and she departed, unimpressed. Hey ho.

I bought myself a soda water and pulled up a stool, scoping the room.

It was clear to me who the group of men I needed to approach were. They were towards the back, four of them and they exuded the confidence that not many civilians do in places like this. I knew that they knew I was here too, as the bouncer will have checked with them, so I needed to approach soon. I took a deep breath, the bass hard once again in my chest.

I strolled towards the group. One of the men noticed me coming and raised himself from his seat.

'Carl?'

I nodded.

'Good to meet you.' He took my hand, shook it and told me to sit down.

I met the rest of the group but was a little in awe of Pieter Rosenkreutz. It was clear who he was. He nodded at me and did not offer his hand.

Long black hair with grey streaks, partly tied back, framed his long, thin face. He had grey stubble and a leathery, brown face, with piercing brown eyes; eyes that had seen too much. Where the others were wearing shirts and blazers, Pieter had a t-shirt and light chinos on. But it was his aura, you could feel it: overpowering, immense and terrifying.

'Tell us, Carl, how are you finding Luxembourg? Where are you staying?' One of the men asked.

'Good. It's cold, colder than England! But yes, nice. In the Sofitel,' I said, somewhat nervous like I was at an interview. The men nodded their approval.

'And your flight, everything OK?' another of the men said.

I nodded nervously and made small talk again, wondering where all of this chat was leading. Pieter remained silent for now, looking down at his glass, untouched.

'We wanted to say we were very pleased with

your work, with David Pensborough. He spoke very highly of you, as did Jennifer,' a voice said. I nodded and smiled.

'Is Jennifer coming here?' I asked.

Pieter, who was fingering the crystal etching on his glass, spoke, 'She has some loose ends to tie up in England.'

His eyes met mine, and I shuddered. The piercing gaze ripped right through me, and I felt immediately he knew I was a fraud.

'Pensborough is no longer with us now, of course,' another of the men continued, 'and we need someone to run Chapters One to Four.'

Again, I nodded, waiting like Carl Blewett would, listening.

'Jennifer likes you, Carl. She wants you to take it over, but it requires…'

'Commitment. Real commitment.' Pieter interjected.

'Of course,' I said, clutching my drink anxiously.

'We have had too many charlatans, Mr Blewett. Too many without the skills to maintain the Order. Seven hundred and forty-six years, we have been here. We are merely custodians of a greater power and the people we work with now, have access to the elite, something that no one else has access to, a power unparalleled. It comes, though, with sacrifice.' Pieter continued.

'Yes, Jennifer has explained. I understand.' I replied.

Pieter looked at the man to his left and nodded. He opened a small satchel by his feet and pulled out some pictures, passing them across the table to me.

'This girl, Iona Usero. Take a look,' he said. I leafed through the pictures, mostly taken from Instagram. Photos of her in bikinis and cavorting with other girls by a pool, one close up of her sucking her finger... I understood what they wanted and as I passed the photos back, I shook my head in mock disgust.

'This girl, sixteen years old, she sells her body on the internet for likes. Rather than use her brain, she uses her God-given vessel to tempt and seduce, she is but a child...' the man continued. I nodded again in agreement.

'She has been offered a chance to atone, but she will not accept the path, she chooses the wrong one. Tonight for the sanctity of the Order, we will offer her to the Gods...' the man said.

'You will offer her to the Gods.' Pieter clarified. I looked over and again his eyes bored into me, asking my soul: can I hurt, can I torture, can I murder?

I looked at him and smiled, 'Thank you. This

would be an honour to me. She will suffer and then she will die,' I said.

The men looked at each other and smiled.

'The ceremony starts at midnight; we will take you there. Have a drink on us. Have a dance if you like. Relax.'

I smiled at the men and nodded, my gratitude. I ordered a double whiskey from one of the dancers and let the bass wash right through me, take me somewhere else, but it was no use, I wasn't going anywhere.

56

I drank my double whiskey slowly; I didn't want them to think that anything was up. I knew I would need to get to the bathroom and contact Dave. I relaxed and made small talk, trying to pretend that the slaughter of an innocent child was not the only thing on my mind.

I made my excuses and went to the toilet, getting out my phone to contact Dave.

I noticed that I already had two messages on my phone when I opened it.

The first text was from Tara wishing me luck and hoping that everything went well. She also sent me the message from Troy's book: *Dear Charlie,*

As you know, I left teaching to become a writer. Well here it is, my first book. Hopefully, it will help you. Best, Troy.

Help me? What the hell did he mean? Why send *me* the only copy of his opus?

The second was from Dave saying that Jennifer Green would not be there at the club tonight. I went into the cubicle and rang him straight away.

'Mate, they want me to kill a girl tonight. I can't do it.' I said.

'Well, to be fair, you knew that you would be

part of the initiation process. We didn't know that you would actually have to do it. We will work something out Charlie,' he said.

I wasn't sure, but I did know that I would not be able to go through with what they wanted me to do no matter how much Jackson wanted to crack this case.

'I need to go, mate, I don't want to create any suspicion, but we need to think of a way to get me out of this sooner rather than later. The plan is to stay here for about another hour, and at midnight we're going to go to the chamber. That's when the murder will happen.'

'OK, Charlie. Leave it with me, we're going to work something out don't panic buddy. Hang in there, we will think of something.'

I put the phone down but didn't feel any better about the situation. If Pieter was not on to me now, he would be soon. I was not convincing, as I did not want this.

I washed my hands and made myself presentable in the mirror, before returning to the table of men.

'These girls, Carl, do you like them?' Pieter asked, waving his spindly fingers toward the waitresses and dancers that were floating around. He was smiling at me.

'Well, yes. They are beautiful,' I said, not knowing what to say.

He called one to the table, and she smiled at him, despite looking wary. He called for her to come closer and he put his hands between her legs, groping her. She smiled, although incredibly uncomfortable as he ran his old, grey hands around her abdomen.

He smiled and whispered something in her ear. 'Come with me,' she said, looking at me. There was a look of desperation in her eyes. She held out her hand and pulled me from the chair.

'No, please it's OK,' I protested.

'Go with her,' Pieter said, an order not a request.

She took me by the hand and led me through the club and behind another red curtain. There were private booths, mostly empty. There were gold chains across the booths, and the young lady undid one and ushered me in.

'Is he your friend?' the lady said, beginning to dance and undress.

'No, I… uh…'

'He's a real asshole… all the girls can't stand him,' she continued.

'Oh yeah?'

'He is a bully. You shouldn't be with these men; these men hate women,' she continued.

'You know, I think you're right. But I have to see these men…'

'Let me guess, *business?*' she said sarcastically.

'Yeah, something like that, you know I don't want to be here… and I…have a girlfriend, so I… you can leave this. I won't take offence,' I said, trying to get her to stop dancing without being rude.

She laughed. 'Everyone here has a girlfriend or wife, baby! You're sweet. You don't belong here, pretty boy,' she said, her breast dangling precariously in front of my face.

'Seriously, you can stop this,' I said, raising my voice slightly.

The girl, who couldn't be much older than nineteen, was genuinely shocked.

'I'm sorry, I just…don't really want to be here,' I said.

'You and me both…'

'Then leave! I can get you out of here, I need to go with these men, but I will come back and get you later,' I said.

She put her skimpy clothes back on and looked at me sideways.

'Ah, you sweet innocent man. You have no idea!' She laughed loudly. 'I started this when I was fourteen. This man took me from my family. He killed my brother. I will never leave this life…' she said, putting her undergarments back on.

'I will take you, let me do this thing, and I will come back and get you, what's your name?' I asked.

'Hm, you're funny! Layla. Nice to meet you. Are you going with these guys? Where do they go?' she asked.

'Somewhere worse than here,' I looked into the distance, hoping for an answer. I remembered my phone and checked it while I was away from Pieter; nothing yet.

Layla put her hand on my shoulder. I must have looked worried.

'Here, take this. I keep it for pricks like him out there. If you're taking him away, I guess I'll be OK,' Layla said, passing me a small, sharp implement.

It was a makeshift blade she had carved together, and she kept in her stocking; it looked like part of her intricate garter belt.

I took it without question and put it down the front of my trousers.

'Thanks.' I said. She was a sweet kid, destined for a life of jerking off old, rich men.

It was disgusting, but for now, there was little I could do.

The velvet curtain twitched and the booth darkened, Layla got to her feet and scurried away.

'Carl, its time.'

57

The Black Mercedes purred along the Luxembourg freeway, eating up the sub-freezing darkness. I felt like a criminal going to the gallows, but it was worse than that. I wanted to check my phone but couldn't as Pieter was sitting next to me.

We got out of town, and the darkness thickened around the car. I felt progressively worse in myself. I put it down to the impending situation, but it was deteriorating rapidly. I felt dizzy and fuzzy. Troy's book, I thought to myself… he could never remember where he went as he was… had I been drugged?

I looked at Pieter who had put his spindly, talon-like fingers on my knee, I guess in an effort to calm me. It didn't work. I faded to black.

++++++++++++++++++++++++++++++++++

The phone rang. I didn't know who it was. My tubby, eight-year-old body ran to it. I picked it up, and it clicked off. I heard the click as soon as I answered. Annoying. I went back to watch the end of Home and Away. Home and Away at ten past five, followed by Neighbours at five thirty-five. Dad watched the news at six.

The phone rang again. I ran back and answered it.
'Hello.' Click.
I put it down again. Why was no-one else answering it?
'Mum? Dad?'
I went back to the TV, the phone rings. I answer it,
Click.
Mum!? DAD!?' I scream, there is no answer. I check
the driveway. There are no cars on it.
I panic, I blub like a girl. My sister must be here. I
went up to her room. She wasn't.
The phone rings. I leave it. It rings and rings and rings.
I cry. I have to answer it. It asks me too.
I answer it reticently. I scream into the phone telling the
person on the other end to leave me alone. Click.
I cry. I pace the front room.
The phone rings relentlessly, like an orchestra of neglect
in my mind. Neglect. Violence. Silence. In that order.
Ring! Ring! Ring!
At some point in the next ten minutes, an adult returns.
I think my Mum. She consoles me. I'm inconsolable.
The voice in my head, with its welcoming warmth, tells
me I am not good enough; no one cared enough. Dad
takes the phone out of the wall.
Mum hugs me. I cry. Never, ever good enough.

++++++++++++++++++++++++++++++++

'Carl? I think I may call him Carlos? A bit more

exciting… Carlos, we're here,' Pieter's voice breathed. I slowly came back to reality; I wished I hadn't.

The aura had changed; the feel had changed. The spiky, frantic nature of the strip club replaced with spiritual calm.

Chamber five; Pieter's chamber, I was finally here.

The gold glow of the candlelight, the cold, damp of the earth and brick walls, the lack of light, the feeling was back as I opened my eyes; Copenhagen all over again. Except this time, it wasn't me who was the prey.

That blurry, fuzzy feeling was replaced by cold nausea. I tried to regain my sight, but it came in fits and starts, blurring every thirty seconds or so and I would drift back into unconsciousness.

Get a grip, Charlie….

There were a lot of people here, more than I expected. I counted eight, but it could have been more, their robes all looked the same. I looked down; my gown was white, theirs black; initiation time.

'Carlos, come to me,' Pieter purred, like a real-life Saruman, his long hair down now and his dark eyes glistening lustily in the candlelight. I walked towards him, taking deep breaths, remembering what I had learnt, trying to regain my senses as quickly as possible from unconsciousness. My phone was in my pocket. I could feel it. I could feel something else a little sharp, pressing into my groin. What was that? Pieter said some words that echoed around the room. I think they were Latin. They reminded me of the iconic emptiness of church.

There were three white stone steps and then an altar. A girl was sitting in a dark, wooden chair on the platform. Straps forced her soft skin against the wood. Her dark hair hung in a pair of plaits.

Her tears were soft. She looked at me nervously, her eyes pierced and pointed like Pieter's; mercifully drugged.

The men in robes gathered around the bottom of the altar, waiting.

What was the girl's name? Layla something?

'Carlos, to enter the Rosicrucian Order…'

I'm sure it was Layla…?

'…A sacrifice, an offering to be made…'

No wait, Layla was someone else…

'This night and for all…'

Iona Usero… that was it. Somebody's daughter… sixteen years old… this poor child.

'Carlos, here…'

Pieter pointed to an old lever. He showed me how to turn it. The girl shuddered and let out a little yelp. The tears fell from her face onto her white gown. White for sacrifice.

I looked around for help; there was no-one. I looked at the faces of the men, their heads bowed. Except one, one was looking directly at me; I recognised the face.

'Carl!' Pieter boomed, placing my hand on the lever and thrusting it in a circular motion.

The girl shrieked and shuddered. The piercing scream echoed violently through the chamber. The Pear of Anguish… designed in medieval times to make women talk…

'Again, Carl, again!' Pieter continued, foaming at the mouth like a dog salivating.

I had no choice; I had to turn the lever. The girl jolted and screeched again, the pear of anguish, forcing the flesh wider.

'Yes, again!' Pieter bellowed, a broad smile across his face, Iona was writhing in the chair, her legs kicking in agony.

I looked down again at the crowd of men now intently watching the torture. Suffering they could never understand... and there it was, that face, the face I knew; Rita Germann.

She nodded to me; *she must be armed,* I thought.

'OK, Pieter…' I drew the small knife Layla had furnished me with from my trousers and thrust the blade into Pieter's neck. He turned and fell, blood spurting violently from an artery.

I rapidly turned the lever back, closing the Pear

of Anguish and easing the pain of this defenceless girl.

As the men began to ascend the altar towards me, everything felt like it was in slow motion. I went to undo Iona's straps, and a gunshot boomed around the chamber. It was Rita; the shock dispersed the men in robes who ran for the exit.

There was only one way in or out, and as the gaggle of goons ran towards the door, it opened revealing white light, police sirens, Dave and at least a dozen, armed response police officers.

58

There are no excuses for the man or woman
you become.

You could have had the worst upbringing in the
world, but you have two options, bemoan and
pity yourself or get on with it. Improve your lot,
talk to people and get over it.

I was lucky. My parents did their best. It was
hard, but at least they tried. Some people's
parents didn't do their best, didn't care. Mine
tried. So I guess I'm one of the lucky ones.

Iona was the same. Her parents were sat in the
lobby in the hospital of Luxembourg, crying;
caring. They were eternally grateful to me,
although I felt sick inside. What I had to do,
what I had put her through.

'Are you OK, mate?' Dave's dulcet tone
reassured me.

'No. I should have just stuck Pieter earlier. If
my mind had worked quicker and recognised
Rita then…'

'Don't be ridiculous. You were drugged, it was
amazing you could function as you did. This
whole weird thing… fuelled by drugs…. You
overcame that, and you saved her. Saved the
sacrifice, Charlie…'

'But at what cost, that poor girl, she could be

deformed and damaged for life, she hasn't lived, she hasn't loved…'

'Charlie! Get a grip of yourself… what else could you do? You saved her life! She will be OK, and we don't even know whether there is any physical damage to her body. If there is, she will get the best treatment; this is Luxembourg for heaven's sake! Her parents owe her life to you,' Dave said, his words washed over me.

'Where's Pieter?' I asked.

'ICU. He's going to live and face justice, Charlie,' Dave said, clearly pleased. I wasn't so sure if I was. The rest of his life in a cushy jail cell, reading material, workout equipment, three square meals… no, I wasn't sure at all if that was the right thing for him.

'I see. I guess you tracked the phone again to find me?'

'Not this time. Rita had travelled down to see me, and when you rang, we knew we had an hour to get there. We came to the club and followed the black Mercedes to the chamber. We waited outside, picked off a latecomer and Rita got in. We then called for backup, telling them that a kidnapped girl was held at gunpoint; the rest you know.'

'Cool. Well, a job well done, I guess.' I said, although it didn't feel like it to me. I felt different, numb.

'A job well done, Charlie. You saved the girl's life, and we have caught the head of the Order. We have brought it down, this whole evil cult. You did it!' Dave said, patting my shoulder.

'Thanks. Celebrate with a coffee, shall we? Fancy one?'

'Yeah sure, white two sugars,' Dave replied, beginning to get up.

'I know how you take it, pal! No, you stay there, I'll bring it,' I replied.

'OK.'

I went straight to the coffee shop, which looked like it served an excellent coffee, but we weren't going to find out. I checked the hospital map and went directly to ICU.

When I got to the door, it was locked via an electronic buzzer system. There was also a Grand-Ducal Policeman outside the room. Pieter Rosenkreutz was a powerful and important man in Luxembourg. There was no way the nurses would let me in to see him, let alone the copper, so I had to think.

I looked up and down the corridor and noticed that there was a fire alarm on the wall. There was also a security camera hanging from the ceiling, but I figured by the time they had checked the footage, I would be halfway to Blighty.

I checked that no-one was around and I

smashed the glass on the fire alarm. As soon as I heard the ringing, I ran to ICU and pounded on the door. The nurses looked bemused, shrugging shoulders; they were not informed that there would be a fire alarm today.

'Excusez-moi! C'est un emergencie!' I said, the policeman came to the door.

'Qu'est que-ce?' he said.

I pulled out my best A-Level French or what I remembered and once again that GCSE in Drama was required.

'Un petit-fille et un grand homme! Bats toi! Bats toi!'

The policeman looked confused, but I must have been convincing because he ran down the corridor where I was pointing.

'Le café, monsieur!' I continued.

He continued running around the corner.

The nurses had come to the door, looking confused. I showed them my police badge. 'Rapidement!' I said as dictatorially as I could and pointed towards the exit.

They looked a little worried but went out to wherever their designated fire safety point was, talking quickly in French.

The alarm continued to blare. I went into the unit, locking and bolting the door behind me. There were two people in the ICU, a woman and Pieter Rosenkreutz. Either the nurses didn't believe there was a fire or these two bodies were expendable to them; I wasn't sure. What I was sure of was I was looking forward to five minutes alone with Pieter.

I walked into his room. It was dark; the curtain drawn.

I went to it quietly and opened it. His eyes although shut, squinted immediately and attempted to open.

I shut and locked the door to his room; double security for when the fire alarm stopped ringing.

I sat down next to Pieter and put my hand on his to wake him.

He tried to open his eyes again and failed.

I noticed the cut on his neck bandaged heavily, dried blood on the white dressing. His long mane now streaked with red. He had an oxygen mask on, and the tube from it stretched down towards a gas canister.

I followed the tube halfway and pressed the tube shut with my fingers.

Pieter began to gasp, and his eyes opened wide.

'Hello,' I said.

He looked at me, bemused.

'Carl, how did you…?'

'Don't worry about that. Tell me; I need to know, are there any more bodies? Anyone else I need to know about?' I asked.

'What? What's it to you?' he asked, somewhat riled by my query.

I pulled out my badge and showed him. That steely glint in his eye had gone, and he just looked tired and disappointed.

'Predictable. You know ten years ago, this would never have happened,' he said, adjusting himself in bed. 'Mobiles and social media, it's the scourge of our time. How did you…?'

'It doesn't matter how… we did. We got you, and we got Gibson, and we're going to get Jennifer Green,' I said with finality, after all of this time at his mercy.

Pieter laughed. 'Maybe, maybe. But you can't stop what is coming for you.'

'What do you mean, Pieter?' I asked, hoping that on his death bed, he would want to tell me the information that could finish these evildoers for good.

Pieter paused; the fire alarm finally stopped sounding.

'You know… you will never truly get to the top, never find the bottom of the rabbit hole, Mister…?'

'It's Detective to you.'

'Well, Detective, since the beginning of civilisation the people in control have known more, have run things for the proletariat. Kept people in check,' he continued.

'Well if you call brutal murder, keeping people in check, then yeah… you did a great job, Pieter,' I said dryly.

'And this is the problem with the general public. You lack the understanding to see the bigger picture. Everything you see on the TV, everything you hear, it's controlled. You get drip-fed what people like me want you to hear…'

'Go on, Pieter! This is fascinating…'

'We bring violence to your doorstep, focus your eyes on postcode crimes. Break up your communities with Facebook and internet shopping, and still, you don't fight back…'

'Uh-huh…'

'What the aristocracy do with a few lost children concerns you, but you fail like all of these idiots to see the bigger picture. Addicted to computer screens, obsessed by celebrity, cavorting with the same sex… all we do is what has been done throughout the ages… Detective… what did you say your name was?' Pieter asked.

'Detective Stone. Charlie Stone.'

Pieter turned to me, and his eyes lit up. Voices were at the door of the unit, banging loudly; panicking.

He laughed heartily.

'Charlie Stone? *The* Charlie Stone? Oh, this is

marvellous! I can die a happy man…'

'Oh and die you will…' I confirmed.

Batons had broken through the ICU door now, and the voices were getting louder. I'm not sure they even knew I was here, but when they found me, I would not be welcome. Like a number of evil men; Pieter Rosenkreutz was a powerful and respected man.

'Very, very soon, Charlie Stone, you will see. There is a puzzle, and there is one piece left. Nothing will stop that from happening. When the puzzle is complete, the light will shine through the darkness and light up the water. Then you will see.'

'What do you mean? What the hell are you on about?'

'Oh, a village idiot like you, you would never understand. But you will feel it, oh boy, will you feel it!' Pieter laughed once more.

'Where is Jennifer Green?' I grabbed him by his bruised and battered neck. The blood seeped through the dressing; I felt its warmth on my hand as I pushed Pieter's jugular further forward.

He choked and spluttered on his blood.

'Where the hell is she!?' I tried again, pushing harder. He laughed again.

There was the sound of footsteps and loud banging on the door to Pieter's room. French accents, the sounds of gun's reloading; shouting.

I wanted to watch him die… but I couldn't. The door was about to give way, and if it did, my life would be over too. I let go of Pieter and dashed to the second storey window.

PART 4

59

December 15th, 2019. It was the first gathering of Christmas; seven days after returning from Luxembourg.

I was on annual leave, and I had mostly slept and tried to relax. We had cut off the head of the Order and hoped, prayed that this would be the end of the torrid affair.

Whatever happened, I was determined to enjoy my leave and have some semblance of a relaxing family Christmas with Tara and Maddie.

We went out in Tara's tank early in the morning to get the ingredients for the platters and the vast quantities of drinks that would inevitably be consumed.

We were home now, and people were starting to arrive.

Frequently, our eagerness took over, and we started drinking too early; eating our pigs in blankets and brussel sprouts with pancetta and gallons of prosecco.

The low sun through the window, although not warm, was likc an oppressive hand on our pale English skin as Maddie, Tara, and I prepared the snack plates for our guests.

It was only a small affair. We invited Tara's parents and a few close friends, and after the English awkwardness that always seemed to temper these events, the drinks were flowing freer and people seemed to be beginning to enjoy themselves.

Maddie sat on a rattan throne that we had brought in from the garden. She was talking politely with her new, adopted grandparents. They were discussing the benefits of music – in particular jazz and rock. Maddie claimed how she liked the latter more, much to the chagrin of Tara's mother. Maddie looked at me and smiled. I winked and gave her a little nod of approval.

My phone buzzed in my pocket. I was determined to stay out of the firing line for a while, but what if it was Dave? I owed this man my life; he had saved me on more than one occasion, so I quickly read it. *'It's happened again, mate. Dolly Innes, 17, washed up on Sunny Sands beach.'*

It was from Dave. I looked at the tray of hors' d'oeuvres in my hand and my stupid plastic, oven glove. Life felt so futile and worthless sometimes.

The Order? I texted back.

I waited, putting the vol au vents on a serving

plate and the little sausages on cocktail sticks. If I tried to be normal, tried to be like everyone else, maybe the horror and darkness would go away.

My phone buzzed again; who was I kidding, I was Charlie Stone.

Same MO, girl had broken arms and black eyes, they are still finding out information. Looks like we are back to work tomorrow. Enjoy yourself tonight.

I sent back a thumbs-up, took a deep breath and back to the party; trying to forget.

I intimated to Tara to serve more champagne, well Cava, so the guests had drinks. Tara nodded and diligently took the bottle around while I prepared the food.

'Hey!' Maddie said jovially, 'I want one!'

'Dream on, kiddo…' Tara said, smiling at her eight-year-old stepdaughter.

'Well, I have had champagne before in Paris, actually…'

'You what?' I said.

'Yeah, Mum gave it to me on the Eiffel Tower.'

'Hmmm. Expensive tastes. Sorry no champagne for you here, have your apple juice please.'

Maddie harrumphed and complied.

 I brought a further plate of pigs in blankets to the table where everyone was sitting.

I felt content as the patriarch, while the others ate. Maddie was the queen of the party, everyone wanting to spend time with her. The family was here, Tara was happy. I felt my old wounds were healing. A day didn't pass where I didn't think of Iona and the suffering she must have felt.

She is back in her home town of Arlon in the south of Belgium now, recovering well. She is undergoing psychotherapy, and everything had returned to normal. Amazing, what us humans can endure, still it made me feel no better.

I shook myself back to reality. I placed some dipping Camembert in the oven. Behind me, there were laughs and loud chatter, a welcome soundtrack to a successful day so far.

'Maddie? Mad… where are you going?' Tara's voice raised an octave above the melee.

My daughter was now standing by me. She reached for my hand, and I gave it to her. Her eyes glued to the floor, and her face pale. She squeezed me.

'I feel sick, Daddy.' She made her way up the hallway to her room.

'Maddie, wait!' I hollered after her.

'I'm going to be sick, Dad!' Maddie broke into a jog and went into the bathroom.

Before I had time to drop my tongs, Tara had eased past me and after her. I nodded to Tara's father to take up cooking duties which he duly accepted, and I followed the girls into the house.

By the time I had gotten to the bathroom door, there were the sounds of retching.

I poked my head tentatively around and witnessed a vibrant, yellow pool of vomit sitting on the bathroom floor.

Tara was rubbing Maddie's back as she sobbed into the porcelain toilet bowl.

'It must have been something you ate,' I said unhelpfully.

'It must be your cooking,' Maddie said, turning to me dishevelled. Her grin told me she was joking, and we all laughed.

'Probably, sorry,' I added.

'Come on you two, let me get this cleaned up,' Tara said. 'Charlie, you'd best head back to the party.'

'I'm going to lie down in bed if that's OK?' Maddie said.

I looked at her and nodded as Tara wiped her face.

'Come on, sweet. Let me take you,' I took Maddie to bed. She was in a cold sweat which certainly, with my minimal knowledge, seemed like food poisoning.

'I love you, Dad,' she said.

'I love you too,' I gave her Scruffy, her teddy

she had since she was a baby. She smiled and hugged him. 'Have a little rest, close your eyes.' Maddie nodded and faced the wall, her eyes closing.

I closed her window and pulled her curtain before pulling her door to.

'Don't shut it, Dad,' she mumbled at me half-asleep.

I didn't. I headed back to the party to make small talk and grabbed a glass of wine, as all the champagne had gone. It was lovely, after all we had been through, the capture of Rosenkreutz, that we could now have a relaxed Christmas together.

Tara returned from the bathroom, a little annoyed, but she had cleaned the mess and had a quick shower to get rid of the muck. I looked at her adoringly; her gaze not so loving in return. *She did offer to clean up the mess though*, I thought to myself…

We continued to chat, and guests started to leave a few hours later. Firstly, it was my Mum and her partner who always needed to get back for their small rescue dog. He struggled to cope without my Mum after about an hour, so we were lucky really that she stayed so long!

Then it was Tara's grandmother; we ordered her a taxi as she was a little tiddly from the numerous glasses of plonk.

Finally, we were left with Tara's parents, who got a cab into town. Despite her Mum nearing the ripe old age of sixty, she still liked to be seen on the Folkestone scene now and again. We were left with Taylor, Tara's brother, and a few of his friends. We had all had a few drinks by this time and decided to get a board game out; Cards Against Humanity.

'Just let me take a wee and check on the little one,' Tara said. She looked a little tipsy, her eyes bright and glassy.

I had checked on Maddie about half an hour ago, and she was asleep still, facing the wall.

'Hey Charlie, have you heard of that new musician, Michele Kawinisa?' Taylor asked.

I pondered for a minute, pretending to recollect, but I had no idea.

'He's like a fusion of dance, rap and jazz... let me connect to the speaker, and I'll play you some....'

'Sure!' I said, although it sounded dreadful to me.

Suddenly, a piercing shriek rang around the house. It was Tara. I ran to her.

'Charlie! Maddie is gone!'

60

There was no excuse for the man you had become.

I did everything I could to keep my family safe, and I had failed. Now was not the time for beating myself up, I would have a lifetime of that to come, regardless of the outcome.

I went to the front door to see if Maddie was outside, or had gone with one of the other members of the family. I looked out of the door, but there was no-one there, they had all gone.

'Phone your folks, phone Grandma,' Tara nodded and checked in with the in-laws.

I phoned Dave and got out my journal. After Luxembourg, I decided to keep a journal about all the clues I had received. What with Gibson's word, Troy's book and Pieter's ramblings, there might be something to gain from drawing the dots.

'Neither of them has her, and she's not in the garden…' Tara said.

'I'm trying not to panic here, but it's unlike her to go off, especially when she is not feeling well, so we need to be sensible and work this out. If we work quickly she can't have gone far,' I said, opening the journal.

I added in the name from earlier that Dave told me; Dolly Innes, Sunny Sands, 17.

I re-read Pieter's words: *There is a puzzle, and there is one piece left. Nothing will stop that from happening Charlie. When the puzzle is complete, the light will shine through the darkness and light up the water. Then you will see....*

Tara was looking over my shoulder, 'Come on we need to crack this!'

Tara was thinking out loud, 'Troy's book said, "everything is a message. The way they leave crime scenes, the ages of the dead, the names of the dead... *everything has meaning...*"'

Gibson: *I'm going to give you one piece of information., but you are going to have to work faster, Charlie, much faster.'*

I wrote down the names of the murdered in order of how we found them...

Bryan Rattle, Laura Unsworth, Iona Usero, Dolly Innes...

'Charlie, write down the initials,' Tara ordered.

B R L

U I U D I

'What was that word that kept coming up? The one written on the wall in the first chamber you went too?' she asked.

Dave came bustling through the front door that was left open, in the vain hope my daughter may come back through it.

We nodded to one another, and Dave didn't try any further greeting, understanding the gravity of my situation. I was amazed I was keeping it together. Maddie was missing. I was a target. Inhale deeply, stay calm.

'Ludibriums…' I wrote it on the page.

L U D I B R I U M S

'Most of the letters are there, Charlie… there are just…two letters missing…' Tara said.

I checked it M and S were missing; Maddie Stone.

I flung the journal and the table across the room, narrowly missing Tara's leg. Rage consumed my being. I needed to get her back.

'There is a chamber in Folkestone. This new girl, Dolly Innes, washed up on the beach, just like Amy Green did at the start of all of this. Also, we know of the other chambers and that there are four in this sector: Two in Ashford, Hawkinge and now in Folkestone. She will be there.' Dave said, matter of factly.

'Where is it?' I asked.

'That's the problem; I don't know.' Dave returned.

'Who would know… maybe Carl Blewett?' Tara said.

'We don't have time… wait…' I picked up my journal from the floor. '*There is a puzzle, and there is one piece left.* Maddie. *Nothing will stop that from happening Charlie. When the puzzle is complete, the light will shine through the darkness and light up the water. Then you will see…'*

'The light will shine…?' Dave said,

'Water…?' Tara nodded.

'The lighthouse?' I said.

Tara and Dave nodded. 'It has to be…'

'The clues all fit. Everything is a message and anyway, have we got anything better?' Tara said.

'Let's get down there,' Dave said, pulling out two small 9mm guns from his puffer jacket pocket.

'Personal collection?' I asked.

'We haven't got time to go through Jackson,' he said correctly.

Tara was getting a jacket and boots on. I looked up at Dave, who shook his head.

'Tara, this… you can't come with us this time,' I started.

'To hell I'm not! She's my daughter too!'

'I know, sweet, but I can't lose you as well. Stay here… please…'

She sighed, surprised by my honesty and threw herself onto the sofa. Dave passed her a walkie-talkie from his C.B. radio. It buzzed and crackled in her hand.

'Keep that on, hun,' he said, as we ran downstairs and jumped into his Dodge.

61

Dave immediately got on the phone as he drove.

'They've taken Maddie. Meet us at the Harbour Arm; I'll send you the postcode, the entrance to it now, please… yep… got to go… ciao…'

Dave put the phone down and started fiddling with the C.B. radio.

'Who was that?' I asked.

'Oh… Rita, she came over… we had some time off, you know,' he said, still trying to get a signal on the radio.

'Good,' I said. Rita was an excellent policewoman.

'Tara? Tara?' Dave spoke into the radio; it cracked and hissed its reply. 'Bugger!'

I checked the gun was loaded and placed it in my pocket, then took the walkie-talkie from Dave and tried to fine-tune it, I thought I could hear a voice on the other end, talking back to me but I couldn't be sure.

The Harbour Arm was a short drive.

We arrived at the large silver gates and parked up. It was locked up as it always was for the winter, but with the new renovations that had been completed, there was another way through.

We sprinted around through the cream malaise of the Harbour Station, past the signal box and onto the hard, grey concrete of the Arm.

The air was cold, but the sea was calm. There were no vessels on the water.

We ran past the shacks that heaved with hipsters, DFL'ers and wannabe trendy kids in the summer; the crowd that did such a great job selling Folkestone as the 'coolest' place to live in the U.K… It may have been cool, whatever cool meant, for about three months of the year. The rest of the time, it was just cold; our little Summer Town.

At the end of the Arm, the blue and white lighthouse stood majestically.

I went up and tried the door. It was double-locked and was dark inside. I checked the perimeter, but there was no clear and distinct way in. I looked into the water that surrounded the structure, and I could see a light shining bright from under the water level, *the light will shine through the darkness…*

'There. Is that light normally on?' I asked Dave.

'Who knows? I wouldn't have thought so. Why would it be?' Dave said.

We were feeling in the dark, quite literally, but it wasn't for the first time. The buzz of fiery adrenaline kept me pushing forward. If I had to tear the top of the lighthouse with my bare hands, I felt I could. Part of me felt helpless against centuries of the Order, but I would die protecting my family and preventing this evil from continuing.

I looked up at the lighthouse again. The main light wasn't on, but the beam from under the water shone like a beacon. Why? If not for boats, it was a sign, a call to arms.

I followed the cabling that ran down the side of the lighthouse and into the water.

'I'm going in, mate,' I said, pointing to the water.

Dave took a deep breath. 'OK…'

'Listen, it's fine. I know you can't swim. Stay here, wait for Rita, find another way. I don't have time and the clues lead down there. There's no church, no cross, no natural way in up here. I'm going in.'

'OK, good luck…'

But I was already off, and into the Channel, the cold hit me like a gunshot. I took a deep breath and swam the several feet down towards the white light. There was a large gold number one on the side of the concrete slab in front of me; I was close.

I came back up for air; Dave had gone. I was on my own now. I took another breath and ploughed down into the water once more…searching…searching for something, anything… but I could find no clear access.

I came up and down once more, moving systematically around the concrete slabs and pillars that supported the Lighthouse and the Harbour Arm. In the distance, lower, I saw something glistening. I went down further into the gloom and the icy cold. There it was, the crimson cross… small, yet perfectly formed… the red rose glistening through the water.

I reached down to it, and it wouldn't move.

I pulled it again and nothing.

I was struggling for breath but wasn't sure I would make it back up in time, so I pulled the cross again, and it turned.

Once more and it turned again, a third time and the beacon faded to black and the power of the Channel sucked me inside a small opening that had appeared in the concrete.

Finally, my way inside.

62

I felt the wild power of the ocean as it breathed in slowly then spat me into the underbelly of the lighthouse.

There was a small, brick-built room that was (thanks to the opening), filling with water.

There was a further door in front of me that was metal and had a circular wheel to open it in the centre.

The soundtrack of the sea behind me powered me on, death by drowning was not a current option as I threw myself onto the wheel and used my whole body to wrench the door open. It was stiff but loosening.

Another wave of seafoam threw up on my back, as the little room began to fill up.

I turned the wheel again and again until finally it cranked to unlock and I pulled the door open. The ocean swelled, and its power spat me into a dark corridor.

I shut the door behind me and shook myself down. I was soaked through, but I still had my pistol. My phone was dead, unsurprisingly. I was either leaving here alive with my daughter or in a body bag; my phone was the least of my worries.

The corridor was lit dimly by candles along the

walls. I walked carefully, checking the rooms along the way as I went.

The same old story: shackles, chains, devices. That familiar cold, metallic smell through the faint glow of the eerie candlelight.

I continued silently down the corridor to the final room in the chamber. It was like a tomb, the cold, damp eeriness suffocating me.

Maddie was lying on a cold slab in the middle of the room.

Her eyes were closed, and she was peaceful. I went towards the table where my daughter was, breathing heavily, like an angel sleeping.

There was a sharp thud in my upper shoulder; a metallic dart.

I grabbed it and pulled it out, too late; another one caught me in my stomach. Modern darts release on impact, so whatever was in it, would be beginning to circulate in my system.

I turned for the cover of the wall outside and stood behind it, waiting for the next move.

'Come out, Charlie,' a soft purr echoed softly through the chamber, 'Come on.'

I looked beyond the door frame and back into the room. Green was standing over the stone table, like a doctor over her patient.

'Congratulations, Charlie. You found us. You found it all. Causing us a lot of trouble on the way.'

'It's my job, Jennifer. I catch murderers and killers,' I said dryly.

'If only you had just left this alone and stuck to the druggies and small-time gangsters of this dump you call home… you couldn't leave it though? You kept on coming.'

'It's all gone now, Jennifer, the whole thing. Gibson is dead, Wadham locked away, Pensborough's dead and Pieter, your boss facing trial…'

'Pieter's dead, Charlie. I've seen to that.'

I felt queasy. There was nausea in my stomach rising through my body. I felt weak; I could barely stand.

'Pieter..?' I tried, but couldn't finish the sentence.

'He's dead, Charlie. I killed him and Blewett. They are all gone… because as you need to learn, none of this matters, Charlie, it is all transient. What matters is the Order, the continuation of what has always been, you can't stop it.' Green said, pulling a long, gold blade from her jacket pocket.

'Jenny no… not her. You must kill me instead…' I pleaded with her.

'Commitment, Charlie…. sacrifice… my only child, Amy, I let that monster have her and kill her. Now you must know what it feels like to lose your most precious thing. You must sacrifice and understand how your petty interference cannot stop the Order!' Jenny's voice was raising; her knife hung precariously above my daughter's body.

'I understand, I get it, Jennifer. But, Maddie… she's seven!'

'She's the final piece, Charlie… you are going to watch her die. Ludibriums – we are merely all playthings, toys, irrelevant when we look at the bigger picture… pain too is transient.'

Jenny was pushing Maddie awake, jolting her body with shoves, raising her from whatever drug-induced slumber she was in.

I moved closer to the stone table. I was crawling now, my energy drained from whatever liquid was contained in the dart.

'Stay there, Charlie, enjoy the show from afar…' she purred at me once more.

I tried to stop myself from blacking out, but it was as if the shutters were closing every few seconds.

I summoned all of my strength and threw myself towards Green and her shiny knife. My arms tried to grab her, but it was impossible. I slid down her, unable to grip or grab. My hands numb. She shrugged me off and slashed the knife across my face.

I fell into darkness.

63

'A vodka and diet coke, Charlie?' the bartender said.
'Nah, I don't really drink anymore,' I said.
'OK, how about a mocktail, 'Up in the Clouds' I call it. It's a new one. You will like it… coconut and avocado…'
'Sounds interesting…yeah sure, knock one up.'
I scoped the room, and there he was, sitting at the bar on his own, flicking his gasper into an ashtray. He looked upset.
'Dad,' I said, but he didn't hear me.
'Dad!' I tried to push him to notice me, but my hand went right through him.
'Can you hear me, papa bear?' I said again. Dad was tapping his phone hard, and then it rang.
'Yeah, the boy. He wants to come over this weekend. Well, I told him. Yep. We can say we have gone away, just stay in for the weekend. Yeah, OK, see you later…ciao…'
'Oh yeah, nice one…' I looked down at myself. I was nine years old, I guessed. Little shorts and a t-shirt on. There it was that feeling again….
He turned around and saw me.
'What are you doing here?' he said.
'I don't bloody know, do I?' I returned.
'Watch your mouth…'
'Who was that on the phone…'

'Saint Peter.'
'Are you taking the mick Dad?'
'No, son. It's not your time. I bloody told you this how many times!?'

++++++++++++++++++++++++++++++++

Golden haze…candles flickering…that awesome feeling that you could stop fighting; that you could give up.
I had done all I could do.
Then, once again, like a flood, I would try and pick myself up, but it was no good.
Gunfire in the distance! Somewhere in the building, along the corridor, loud…echo… like a bass drum…. Bang! Bang! Bang!
I slid myself around to see if Green is there, she was gone, and so was Maddie.
I can hear shuffling towards the far side of the chamber. A door opens, light floods… I fall back on to the cold, hard floor again.
There is commotion all around me, feet running, chasing, there's a woman over me on the floor, checking my pulse, checking me over.
I feel the cold rush of a needle in my Arm and then a warm wave flooding my body, adrenaline; warm welcome adrenaline.
I was back in the room.
'Charlie, are you OK?' It was Rita, a welcome

face, her big Bavarian grin a welcome sight amidst this chaos and fear.

'Where's Maddie?'

'She's been taken, through that door. Dave and the others have gone after them,' she said. 'But Charlie, take it easy..!'

'Yeah right,' I was up and after them, my pistol still at my side.

I ran through the door which led down a series of maze-like corridors. I could hear commotion up ahead of me, and I sprinted through the tight, narrow spaces as quickly as I could to catch up.

Gunshots, two different types, it seemed that Green had an assailant with her, otherwise how would she be carrying Maddie and shooting at the same time?

I caught up with the chase just as we exited the underground corridors by the signal box; we were at the commencement of the Harbour redevelopment. The assailant kept shooting back at myself, Dave, Karl and Jimmy who were all in pursuit. They took a left towards the Burstin Hotel and down into the underground car park.

'Who's got a car?' I asked.

'The Dodge is where we left it, two hundred metres that way,' Dave reminded me.

'Mine is near, wait here,' Jimmy said, as he

sprinted up the road.

Dave got out his walkie-talkie.

'Tara, can you hear this? Rita? Anyone?' he called into it.

There was no response.

'If you can read me, Maddie Stone has been taken by Jennifer Green and an unknown assailant.'

There was the roar of a powerful engine, and a black Mercedes sprinted out of the underground car park and spun past us, around the one-way system.

'They are in a black Mercedes, number plate… nope…gone already…. Black Mercedes speeding through town… E-Class… tinted windows, you won't miss it…' Dave continued, hopefully.

Jimmy pulled up in the squad car, and the three of us got in.

'We are in pursuit of suspect Jennifer Green with one unknown in the car and…' Jimmy looked at me and swallowed, 'Maddie Stone. Detective Sergeant Stone's daughter.'

We raced through town, past the McDonalds then the Post Office and Radnor Park. The Mercedes was in the distance, but somehow Jimmy was keeping it in his sights, despite their head start. Folkestone became a cacophony of police sirens as the Force came to my aid.

The Mercedes swallowed up Cherry Tree Avenue, passed the restaurant and car wash on the left, and it glided onto the motorway, with terrifying ease. *We were going to lose them. Then what would happen to my little girl?*

The squad car gave good chase, but they were no match for a beast that size.

As predicted, the Mercedes eased away from the chasing pack and headed along the M20 and into the night. We tried to keep pace, but it was futile.

As the car moved further away, my heart sank. For all of the criminals we had brought to justice, if Maddie was hurt, or even worse, life just wouldn't be worth living.

Up ahead, the unfamiliar sight of brake lights pulsed in the distance. There was an almighty skid, as the car swerved and grey smoke from the tyres appeared around the vehicle. Then as we approached, we saw Tara's tank plough directly into the front of the black beast, grinding the car to an emphatic halt.

We stopped, and I sprinted to the Mercedes, grabbing my daughter from the backseat. I lay her on the tarmac, cuts seeped blood, she was bruised and damaged, but she was alive.

'Hospital, now!' I shouted to Jimmy, who was already getting back behind the driver's seat. 'Karl, go and see who is in that car, if Tara's there, get her to the hospital too!' I ordered. 'Jimmy, drive!'

He put the foot down, and the six or so minutes it should have taken to get to William Harvey, took about four. I rushed out at Accident and Emergency with Maddie, flashing my badge at the nurses, who were quick to attend.

They put her in a hospital bed with a ventilator and oxygen mask. I don't remember much, just being in floods of tears, watching her helpless, youthful frame being wheeled away by the nurses.

64

*'There's your cocktail, "Up in The Clouds,"' the
bartender said.*

*'Ah, thanks,' I realised I'd left before I had time to
drink it last time.*

*'What did I tell you? Don't serve him, or I'll box your
ears, sunshine!' Dad said.*

'Well…. He's here so often…'

*'I know. Listen, Charlie, what is going on? I'm getting
bored of this now. It's not time for you to be here!'*

*'Right, well… I don't choose to come here… and it's
just that… I miss you, Dad. Your ex-wife gave me
nothing to remind me of you,' I said.*

My body had transformed again; I was nine years old.

*'Well, I'm not being funny, Charlie, what did you
expect? You're like me, boy. You say it as it is and she
wasn't ready, really was she?'*

*'No, and I mean, there was your affair…you didn't put
him in the easiest situation did you… being honest?' A
voice said, a voice I recognised.*

My Dad's back was up.

I transformed again. I was back to my usual self.

*'I did what I thought was best,' he said, swigging from
his glass and hanging his head.*

'Oh yeah, we all do, don't we?' the voice said again.

*I came around the back of my father who, like me, was
a broad-shouldered man.*

'Oh wait… what?' I said, speechless.
'Hello, mate,' Dave said, exhaling deeply.
'What the heck are you doing here?' I said. '…And how do you two know each other?'
'We don't,' my Dad said interjecting. 'Listen, you made a right pig's ear of your first marriage, just like your old man did! But you've got a second chance, With that Toni... Terry….'
'Tara?' Dave interjected.
'Yes, with that Tara girl. Lovely, she is, Charlie. Anyway, you got a second chance. I never got mine with my new lady, did I?'
'No, Dad,' cancer, hospital, ICU, guilt… all swallowed him up before he got another chance.
'That's right. So rather than waste your time up here, get back down there, all right?'
'It's hard down there though, Dad…'
'I know, son. It is hard. But it's boring up here. And boring's worse. Finish the game, yeah? If not for you, for me. Listen, I love you, kiddo.'
Suddenly I felt like I was falling, falling far too hard, too fast… panic, sweat…
'Dave…! Dad…!'

'He's waking up,' I heard voices saying. My eyes did not want to comply.
'Charlie? Char..?' only one person calls me that,

my Mum. Boy, did I want to see her.

The light streamed in through the windows and was like piercing shards in my tired eyes, but I forced them open.

My Mum hugged me.

'Oh, my lad! I thought we had lost you this time!'

'Hi, Mum,' I got my bearings: I was in a hospital, definitely in Britain, odds on it was the William Harvey.

'Where is everybody? Where's Maddie?' I asked, beginning to panic, remembering what had happened to her with Jennifer Green.

'Ah, yeah, she is here… she's OK, but on a different ward,' Mum said.

'But she's OK?'

'Yes… a few scars, Char. Sleeping off the rest of it, but yes she's going to be fine.'

'Where's Tara?'

'Just at the café.'

I got up from my bed, undoing a few wires and taking off my oxygen mask.

'Charlie, stay in bed, she'll come to you,' Mum said.

'Mum, I love you, but when did I ever do as I was told, eh?'

Mum looked at me and smiled. She tried to remain a disciplinarian, but she also liked a rule-breaker, a peculiar dichotomy but one I had grown up with and understood now.

I felt dizzy raising myself from the bed, but I didn't care. As I got to the door of my room, there was Karl, Jimmy and Jackson all sitting outside.

They greeted me with smiles and hugs, although I was a little bit tender. I looked down the corridor and carrying two paper cups was my love, Tara. She saw me and smiled, dropping the drinks and running to hug me. Again, it was too hard and really hurt, but I didn't mind.

'Hello, stranger!' she said, pulling me in again. She smelled divine, a stark contrast to the sterility of the hospital.

The nurses came around the corner, possibly alerted by my mother.

'Mr. Stone, you must go back to your bed, you shouldn't be out…'

'Where's Maddie Stone please, nurse?' I asked.

'But, Mr Stone, there will be plenty of…'

'Where is she please?'

The nurse could tell that I wasn't going to relent.

'Ward C,' she thrust her thumb behind her, indicating the corridor.

'Come on, Charlie. I'll walk you down,' Tara said.

'Erm Tara, can we just talk to Charlie a

minute?' Jackson said in a sombre tone.

'Oh, yes, of course,' she said, as if remembering something from afar in her memory.

'Charlie, we have good and bad news. Good news is Jennifer Green died on impact at the crash site. So did her assailant, Arik Larsen, who was driving.' Thank god, I thought, relieved. It was finally over. Green was gone.

'Arik eh? I knew he had something to do with this!' I said eagerly.

'Yes, it looks like he has been in with the Green mob since the start.' Jackson said somberly.

'Hm. No wonder he was so evasive. What's the bad news, boss?' I asked.

Jackson sighed heavily.

'The bad news is that… Dave Woodward was hit with a bullet in the chase out of the harbour arm. He didn't realise, or if he did, he carried on to try and save Maddie. By the time he had got to the hospital in Jimmy's car, he had passed away.'

'What... no… not…'

'Charlie, I know it's a tragedy, but to die in the line of duty, trying to protect his best friend's daughter…' Jackson continued.

'Yeah but, I was in the car with him… I should have got him out…'

'Charlie, you did the right thing; saved your daughter. I got him out and took him in, but it was too late.' Jimmy said. 'If it was anyone's fault, it was mine, but frankly Charlie, it was nobody's fault. It was one of those things. As Jacko said, if he could have gone anyway, this would probably have been it,' Jimmy said.

I fell to the floor, my knees giving way. I was overwhelmed with sadness. My mentor, my friend, was gone. I sat in the corner, sobbing with my knees to my chest; like a lonely child. Jimmy sat next to me. He put his hand on my shoulder.

'It's all right, Charlie,' he said, comforting me. *Goodnight, my friend…*

I felt bruised and battered, physically and emotionally. I had dodged death again; I didn't know how I did it sometimes. I mean, the help of my friends obviously, but we had done it. Dave and I brought down these cruel, dark criminals. Their so-called Order would go with them. If they hadn't done so already, I would be getting Jackson to turn those chambers into gastropubs or community hubs, or something of hope.

Tara and I began to walk towards Ward C.

'Charlie, are you OK?' she said.

I was holding back tears, and I just didn't want to think about Dave. My emotions were all over the place, and I just wanted to see my daughter.

'I've been better.' She reached over and hugged

me. I leaned into her soft shoulder and breathed her in. *Comfort, home.*

I pulled myself together and remembered, I wasn't the only one who had been through a hard time.

'Are *you* OK? Were you driving your car when it hit the Mercedes?' I asked Tara.

She smiled, 'Yes, I was. I'm not going to lie. I could track where she was via the walkie-talkie Dave gave me. I don't think you could hear me, though. I kept talking into it, but no answer.'

'I see.'

'My Dad came back when I called him to say Maddie was missing. He helped get the radio online. As soon as Green escaped from the Arm, he knew she was motorway bound, so he suggested heading her off.'

'So, you went up to Junction Eleven and came back down?'

'Yes, and then tracked the chase on the police C.B. all the way! Look at me knowing the lingo!' Tara was delighted with herself. Another training day to tick off her induction to the Force.

'You do realise that Maddie was in the car, right?'

'Of course, but my Dad reckoned that it would be OK. We hit the car on the driver's side, and Green took a lot of the impact. He knows about this stuff with his work,' Tara said.

'Blimey, that is a bold, calculated guess! But jeez, did it pay off. Is your Dad OK?' I asked, really worried that he had sacrificed himself to save Maddie. I have had enough of sacrifice to last me a lifetime.

'He's here too! But he's going to pull through,' Tara smiled.

'Thank god!'

'I know, but it's over, Charlie. Finally. My Dad said when we decided to head off Green's car, "I'm sick of these people messing with my family!"' Tara said, mimicking her Dad's broad, Yorkshire accent.

'Wow… I didn't expect that, did you?' I was a little shocked. We always had the impression that he was never too keen on my relationship with Tara; funny how things changed.

65

'Ah! Here we are, Ward C,' Tara said.
I walked around the corner into the ward,
where there were six beds. I could feel Maddie's
aura pulling me towards her, and there it was,
her beautiful beaming smile. I ran to her and
gave her the biggest hug.
'Hi, Dad!' she said.
'Hey, Maddie! How are you feeling?' I asked,
holding her hands, not letting her go.
'Good. Much, much better.'
I looked her over, and apart from a few bruises,
she looked beautiful to me.
'I'm so sorry, sweetheart, this should never
have happened to you,' I said with tears welling
in my eyes. *Be a man son. You've got unfinished
business down there…*
'Yeah, all right, Dad,' I said.
Tara and Maddie both looked at me strangely; I
must have said it out loud.
'To be honest, Dad, I don't really remember
anything. One minute I was sick in bed at
home, next I was sick in hospital!' she said, full
of beans. I think she was trying to let me off
the hook a bit, god how I loved her kindness
and spirit.
'That's good, honey, that's good!'

'Dad, is it true you have caught all of those baddies now?' Maddie asked.

I looked at Tara, 'well yes, but I had a little help if I'm honest.'

'Your Dad has caught all of those guys now, Maddie. Just like he said he would.' Tara exclaimed.

I smiled.

'Well done, Dad!' Maddie said, giving me another big hug. 'I'm going home today, Mum's picking me up.'

'Awesome! Yeah, I think I'm going home today too, whether they want me to or not!' I said.

'Daddy, don't be naughty!'

'OK, darling…'

'If they want you to stay, you must stay… OK?' She continued.

'Sure thing.'

The air turned cold, and I turned to see that Jo had arrived. She looked at me with disdain as she grabbed Maddie's things together.

'Looks like I'm off Daddy,' Maddie said. 'I'll see you next week, though!' she said, giving me one final hug.

'Definitely!'

Jo eyeballed me.

'You think so do you? Put her in danger again and just think it's OK? Everything goes back to normal?'

'Yes Jo, it's in the court order. For the record, he *saved* her. Now sod off, we will see you for pick up next week,' Tara said, stepping aside and showing Jo the exit.

We all looked a little shocked, but Maddie and I had a little smile to each other before Jo took my daughter's arm and led her away.

'Bye, guys!' she called down the corridor. 'See you soon!'

I looked up at Tara.

'Come on, let's get out of here.'

66

It must have been the fiftieth time today I had climbed up from the pavement to the Luton van. I wasn't paying for a removal team at over five hundred pounds. We had done it before, and it wasn't worth it.

As I came to the end of the unloading, I was beginning to regret my decision.

Still, it was a great way to keep warm on a mid-January morning in England.

My pal, Bobby, was helping and he'd been awesome. I definitely owed him lunch after we had finished.

Tara came up to the van and tried to climb in; she was red-faced and sweaty, so I stopped her in her tracks.

'T, I know you want it done but just calm down, remember you need to take it easy,' I put my hand on her stomach, that was yet to enlarge, but would do soon. She smiled and reticently went back indoors.

We had finally had enough of the drama that Folkestone brought us. It wasn't the town itself; it was just for some reason crazy stuff just continued to happen there; we needed a change.

So, we decided to try something new;

Willesborough in Ashford. It was a family-friendly, suburb, and since the family would be increasing in numbers soon, it seemed like a sensible option.

'Right throw the rest of the stuff in Bob, we have a plane to catch!' I said, as we quickly dumped the rest of the stuff inside and locked up. I got the key's to Dave's Dodge that he had left me and got the others in the car.

Turning the engine was always fun, as the throaty growl of the Dodge roared into life.

'Come on then, let's eat!' I said.

Bobby lived in Folkestone, so we headed to the Hungry Horse and ate there. The food was cheap and cheerful, and the parking was easy. After lunch, we dropped Bobby at his house and then headed back towards the motorway. Tara was tired, the pregnancy taking it out of her on top of the move, so she closed her eyes and dozed for most of the journey.

I had a new Brian Fallon album, so I got lost in that and the mercurial power of Woody, our new car.

I paid for valet parking, and we took our hand luggage through the security into departures, stopping for a drink at the Wetherspoons on the way. It was strange, how sometimes this process can take forever and become painful, but today with bright hearts and minds, it was a breeze.

We touched down at Flughafen Airport around 10.30 pm. Rolf was there to meet us with a big, beaming grin.

'Charlie! Tara! Great to see you!' There were hugs and kisses all around, then we were whisked off to the KiezPiraten Hotel and then out on the tiles.

Rolf ordered three steins every round, but Tara didn't drink hers each time. Rolf didn't mind, so he and I just drank double.

'You not feeling good Tara? Probably the flight,' he said, and then regaled us with tales of away days with St. Pauli and the history of modern Hamburg.

At around two in the morning, we said our goodbyes and headed back to the hotel. Rolf said we would meet him at the gates of the Millerntor tomorrow at 1 pm.

For now, it was back to the hotel for a well-earned rest.

I slept until ten the next morning. Tara was still dozing so I got up, got changed and walked for a little while. After enjoying the sights of Hamburg, I found myself on familiar ground; outside the Pinneburg Church where I met Francesca Gruttel a couple of months ago.

The door to the church was slightly ajar, and I could hear soft organ music from inside the cavernous walls. The warm hum of the organ enticed me, so I peered in.

I always loved the feel and sentiment of the church, if not the practice, and when there was no service, I found it a soul-quenching place to be.

I took a deep breath and went over to the memorial candles, dropping the last three euros I had in the box.

I lit a candle for my Dad, my nan and through teary eyes, my best pal, Dave.

Rest up, buddy, I hope Dad takes care of you up there.

I wiped my eyes and left. It was time to continue this new chapter.

I rang Tara and said we would need to leave to meet Rolf in twenty minutes. I also grabbed us a sandwich each for the short walk to St. Pauli FC.

Rolf was not difficult to notice, with his sizeable purple mohawk, little circular sunglasses and brown St. Pauli top.

We waved from afar.

When we got to him, he had brought Rita Germann too, which was a lovely surprise.

There was a solemn silence between the two of us; I respected her and was sad that she couldn't get the life with Dave that she thought she would. I blamed myself. I felt guilty.

'Right, to the bar, let's get the party started!'

Rolf said, acknowledging pretty much every single fan on the way through to the main bar area.

The match was like nothing I had seen before. The atmosphere was raucous: people drinking and smoking marijuana in the stands, standing fans, proper singing and jumping and shouting, how football should be.

This was nothing like following football in England, certainly not the Premier League; this was far more liberating.

St. Pauli were playing Werder Bremen, and we won one-nil, much to the delight of the home crowd who hung around after the game talking to one another and the players.

We spent a few hours, drinking in my case and socialising in Tara's, with Rolf and Rita after the game. By 8 pm, things were beginning to get a little lively and given Tara's state; we decided to call it in for the evening; our flight home was early in the morning.

I said a fond farewell to Rolf and Rita. I had made some good friends here.

'Listen, Rita… I'm…' I started.

'Charlie, don't…It's OK,' she kissed me on the cheek and smiled. 'He loved you like a son. Honestly, it's OK.'

Thank you, Rita.

EPILOGUE

'The thing is I love the fact that she is there for me and doesn't mind me going out with…'

'…The boys? She doesn't mind because she is out with *her* girls and enjoying herself!'

'Leave it out, mate. you know she is loyal to me... isn't she?'

'Well, I don't know… you need to make it clear tonight though. if you want her to be with you, tell her how you feel.'

'Here, Jonno, come down here. It will be a bit quicker this way...'

'Whatever mate, I'm *freezing*…'

'My ex used to live up this way, that's her dad's garage…'

'What the hell?'

'Jesus…'

'Is that what I think it is...!? Call an ambulance!'

Carl went around the corner and got out the gold cross and wrapped it around his hands.

He took his phone out of his pocket and speed dialled the first number.

'Troy, hi… Yep, it's done… where we said… the alley… only two people…I'm with…Yeah… I've got the Cross. I'm going to leave it now. Yes, OK, Troy. Bye.'

Carl put the phone away and went back around the corner.

'I called the ambulance and the police. Listen lads, get out of here, I'll sort this honestly.'

'Nah mate, we aren't leaving you here,' one of the men said.

Another one of the men turned to the side and vomited violently at the disturbing sight of Bryan Rattle's dismembered body, fresh on the tarmac.

'Honestly, take him back… or down the club. Dave can sort him out. It's fine, I don't mind. I'll catch you up,' Carl said.

The boys conferred and decided it best to take their chundering pal to wash up.

'Call us if you need anything Carl, OK?'

'Don't worry, I'll be there in a bit,' Carl said.

'OK, mate.'

Carl watched his pals idle up towards the end of the alleyway and take a right. Carl waited for them to be entirely out of sight. He took out The crimson cross that was wrapped around his leather-gloved hand and hung it in the tree, above Bryan Battle's torso which he had placed there twenty minutes earlier.

He turned to recheck the alleyway before lighting a cigarette and walking off into the night.

++++++++++++++++++++++++++++++

67

I pulled the Dodge into one of two dedicated parking spaces we had at the back of the house.

T had been on Facebook searching for new cars, bigger and better than the tank; she was just waiting for the insurance money to come through.

I took the bags indoors, and we collapsed on our sofa, surrounded by boxes.

'Don't worry, I've got some time off babe. I will get all of this done.'

'As if! I will be organising the house thank you very much! You stick to fighting crime please, Detective!'

She got up and went to check the mail.

There were several circulars, a Domino's menu and a few bills addressed to 'The Occupier.'

Also, in the pile was a gilt-edged letter, handwritten and ornate in style.

Tara brought it through, and we opened it together.

'This is a very nice welcome card!' Tara said.

But we had received all the cards we were expecting: *My Mum, Tara's Mum, her Auntie and Grandma, they'd all arrived.*

Tara pulled out the letter, and we both read it:

Charlie,

I hope this letter finds you well.
A personal note from me just to say thank you. Like a diligent little lapdog, you have wiped out all of my challenges and difficulties in achieving my goals. I now am the leader of the Rosicrucian Order, and I cannot wait to get started.
Pieter and Jenny ran the Order into the ground with their antiquated and old-fashioned ideals: letters and secret meetings, how ridiculous! This is a new age! Dark Web, 5G, the age of social media; The Order is here. It's arrived. Thanks to you, Tara and your late friend Dave.
Oh, and yes, I appreciate the irony of sending this by letter, but I wanted something for you to remember me by. You won't hear from me again.
By eliminating my opposition so thoroughly, the Order is stronger now than ever. If you'd finished 'Original Sin' it would have explained all of this to you; but there we are, the modern age in all its glory. Time to run around like lunatics, eliminating 'the enemy,' no time to read and think and reflect on what you were actually doing. Bless you, Charlie Stone; my little puppet, my little fool.

Thanks again,

Troy Wood.

P.S. In six weeks, this whole world will be unrecognisable: panic, fear and death. Thanks in part to the Order and thanks also to you, for putting me here.

Tara turned on the T.V. and saw the news from China. I understood precisely what he meant. The Order went higher and deeper than we ever wanted to believe.

'Charlie, you promised this is done now. No going back, right? You promised me. A new start, yes?' Tara said with tears in her eyes.

'Of course, darling, I promise.'

THE END

ACKNOWLEDGEMENTS

The story for this book has been knocking about for a number of years, but it took a long time to get to the final version that you read here.

I remember planning the concept of 'Original Sin' initially with my wife, Tnaesha, on holiday in Egypt, 2017! I have to thank my wife immeasurably for her ideas and diligent editing. Without her, I could not have left my original publisher and done this myself.

I thank Edwina Twohig for reading and editing early drafts and for being a constant and endless support to my writing.

I wish to thank Kerry Barnes for her kindness and support throughout this process and giving me the belief to go out on my own.

I want to thank my daughter Skyla for believing in her Dad. I believe we learn more from kids than adults, due to their outlook on the world and her brightness and live, when doubt creeps in, is quite wonderful.

This book is dedicated to the memory of my friend Jim Woodward, and the character of Dave Marsh is loosely based on him. I thank Jim for only being in my life for a short time, but being a huge inspiration creatively.

R. I. P. Jimbo x

Don't forget to leave a review if you enjoyed this book! There are regular giveaways and prizes for those who are kind enough to do so:

https://www.amazon.co.uk/Crimson-Cross-Charlie-Stone-crime-ebook/dp/B089M2WN78/ref=sr_1_1?dchild=1&keywords=crimson+cross&qid=15963 67948&sr=8-1

If you enjoyed this book, check out Sunny Sands, the no.1 best seller by the same author:

https://www.amazon.co.uk/Sunny-Sands-Charlie-Stone-Crime-ebook/dp/B08BTRS449/ref=sr_1_2?dchild=1&keywords=sunny+sands&qid=1597854 291&sr=8-2